CHILD X

Also by Mick Lee

The Men Who Robbed The Great Train Robbers

CHILD
X

Mick Lee

Matador
9 Priory Business Park,
Wistow Road, Kibworth Beauchamp,
Leicestershire. LE8 0RX
Tel: 0116 279 2299
Email: books@troubador.co.uk
Web: www.troubador.co.uk/matador
Twitter: @matadorbooks

ISBN 978 1800460 270

British Library Cataloguing in Publication Data.
A catalogue record for this book is available from the British Library.

Printed and bound in the UK by TJ Books Limited, Padstow, Cornwall
Typeset in 11pt Adobe Garamond Pro by Troubador Publishing Ltd, Leicester, UK

Matador is an imprint of Troubador Publishing Ltd

1

Crawley, November 1999

Red Rum is to blame. For the sleepless nights, Ray's early divorce, the kids he and Steph never had, the bankruptcy, the probable heart attack he is hurtling headfirst towards.

That Grand National in 1973 was the first race Ray ever saw, the moment his life began. His old man confessed years later. Pretending to go to the bookies to collect his son's winnings, paying out of his own pocket. Watching the run-in together, Ray learnt a few new swear words as Red Rum staged a dramatic comeback, catching his dad's horse in the last stride.

The same excitement is still there when he watches the screens in the bookies. The only time he feels alive. In the GA meetings, they are told that gambling is a disease, that the best they can hope for is to be in remission. The orange book they dole out acts as a guide but doesn't mention the physical pain. Eastern European creditors don't care about your pleas, or your bad luck; they simply turn up with baseball bats and expect you to pay on time. A small town like Crawley offers no hiding place.

Ray's latest taxi fare, arranged by the Mirkovic brothers who own his debt, has that gangster look – trilby hat, overcoat, cigarette smoke. He leans in towards Ray's car window, smells of whisky and stale tobacco.

'I need you to find someone. Let's go for a walk.' The suggestion is a threat wrapped up in a cockney accent, the customer opening the battered Mondeo door with a forceful swing.

Ray pulls himself out of the car, remembering to lock it given where he has stopped, and falls alongside. They head away from the pickup point, The Downsman pub, which fronts a sad parade of shops. Local misery stretches out behind it, between the boarded-up chip shop and a launderette where drugs are openly dealt from the back room.

Another stranger flanks Ray, his eyes fixed on the road, scanning for traffic, dressed the same way as the trilby hat. Three sets of footsteps echo as they stride along the street, Ray working hard to keep up, and the only other sound piercing the early evening is the faint buzz of failing streetlights. Ray looks around at the tired terraces, curtains already drawn, sees no other pedestrians, has a sense that the world has been paused.

The Serbians don't work this way. Nothing they do is subtle or polite; they pull out their weapons and expect you to do as you are told. Immediately. Which you do, once you've learnt there is no word in whatever they speak for 'tomorrow'. Living a life surrounded by threat. Wondering each day if you will have enough for the next payment, and whether the dog in trap six will keep the pain at bay. Ray's fare resumes their conversation.

'You're a private investigator, right?'

'Yeah, I am. Most of the time.'

Ray is more of a taxi driver these days. The sleuthing clients have dried up, reputation waning, but if you want to keep up with the gambling, you need cash. He wonders how the stranger knows his other occupation. This might be a genuine request for his services, but if he is a friend of the Mirkovic boys, the work is unlikely to be subtle. Ray's breath catches, forcing out a cough, and the trilby hat turns around to stare at him, stopping. The dark eyes narrow, empty of concern.

'I want someone found. It's a job I think you're especially suited to undertake.' Trilby's forehead creases, letting the last word hang in the air. A slight incline of the head, demanding something in return.

'I'll do my best. Some people just go missing and stay missing.' The standard reply comes out at breathless speed, normally designed to reduce the levels of expectation. Failure might not be acceptable, judging by the audience. Ray searches for help in the gutter. Silence hangs between them, and Ray has an urge to fill it. 'It is my speciality.'

'Oh, I know you'll find this one.' The trilby resumes the walk, more leisurely now. Ray has always been an ambler, and it becomes easier to stay alongside.

He dares to study the side of the face under the hat. The hair is thinning and grey at the sides; menacing stubble adds to his charm. Ray would guess late fifties, unashamed of the scars he wears. The figure pulls his overcoat more tightly over his shoulders and catches Ray looking at him. Forced to turn away, Ray stares down the street. Still no pedestrians. The relaxed strides continue, that London accent freezing Ray's heart. 'My friend here has the details.'

The man to the left pulls a brown envelope out of the inside of his coat and passes it to Ray. The filthy hands and fingernails are difficult to ignore – a worker. Recently returned from Epping Forest, burying a dead man. Or torturing someone in a chair, dried blood an occupational hazard. Ray is out of his depth. If only he could carry off the confidence of Bogart, dealing with a Mister Big, on the trail of Eddie Mars. But that is some stretch when you are walking along a Crawley pavement surrounded by sad rows of houses long past their best. A place with the ambitions that came with the words, 'New Town', but in truth is starting to fray at the edges. The good times have gone, replaced by a tired acceptance of mediocrity.

'Don't open it yet,' Trilby demands. 'I want to tell you a story first.'

He stops abruptly and turns to face Ray. His frame blocks what feeble light there is from behind. Ray's shoes look tatty, compared to the shine opposite. His arms are fixed to his sides by sweat, no idea how to stand, or where to look. From somewhere Ray summons up a smidgen of bravado, mouth moving faster than common sense.

'I usually review a case before I decide whether to take it on.' A timid smile, looking up. Those eyes are at him again.

'You do missing persons, don't you? It says so on your card.' Trilby looks across at his sizeable friend. The hired muscle whips something dog-eared out of his pocket, tattily announcing all the tricks of a dubious trade, most of them borrowed or faked. The local shops are covered with them. There is no competition in this town for Ray's services, a pointless monopoly, but this doesn't guarantee keeping him busy. He might be able to string out the councillor and his lesbian wife for a while, but there is nothing new on the horizon. And the bookies are so warm and inviting during the day. Driving a taxi not only earns a bit of money, it also keeps him out of those dens of glowing comfort. Some of the time.

Ray nods weakly in answer to the question. 'Yeah, I do missing persons.'

'Good. Well, I need to tell a story, Raymond,' he repeats. 'It might be familiar.'

The figure picks up his stride again, and Ray is forced to increase the pace to catch up, dragging along the body of a man twenty years older. In contrast, Trilby has a steady gate, controlled voice, staring ahead as he imparts his tale.

'There was this bloke who had a bit of a habit. You know, he liked the horses, liked the casinos, that sort of thing.' Trilby pauses the speech slightly, as if he is thinking over what words to use. Leaves run along the street, their sound rattling in Ray's head. He pulls a thin jacket closer around him. The decaying smell of takeaway food reaches this far away from the local parade. Ray's legs wobble, and the nausea starts to rise inside.

'Well, it really gets out of hand. So, one day he needs more money. His life has gone down the shitter. Friends, family, wife, they all hate him, all because of this habit. And then he has to ask for money from someone other than his NatWest. You follow?'

Ray swallows something sharp, tries to concentrate on putting one foot in front of the other. This man knows him.

Apart from the third man, there is still no sign of life in any direction, a force field in place. The lights of the distant pub behind them are dimmed or completely out. Ray pushes on into the breeze, shivers.

'So, this bloke. Now he has nowhere to turn, to pay back the bank, don't he?'

Ray can only nod again. His soul sinks, because he knows where this is heading. The walking tempo picks up once more.

'And he turns to someone with less scruples than his bank, to get them off his back. And he now has a bigger debt, and he has to pay that back to his new lender, or he'll be in a different kind of trouble.'

The speaker's tread echoes along the pavement when he pauses the monologue. He turns right into a side street. More terraced houses, no glaring lights. This is Barrington Road. If he goes right again, a dead end.

'And this new lender, he, well…' Trilby snorts through his nose and shakes his head. 'He don't do business the right way. He don't think long-term. You do know what I mean, Raymond?' He turns suddenly, and places both his hands upon Ray's shoulders, tightening the threat.

This is the first person to use his full name since his old man, years ago. Back then it was usually followed by verbal abuse and a slap. Ray tenses, expecting the same. But the grip loosens, and Trilby pulls a cigarette case out of his pocket. Lights one with help from his minder. Nothing offered to the taxi driver. The spark glimmers in the gloom. Ray folds his arms across his chest against the cold, can barely hold himself upright. The tremors come from deep inside, from memories of Stefan Mirkovic and his psychotic brother, Marko.

The silence tears at Ray, who knows he should fill the void with noise, anything to blot out the reality of his situation. He can't see an end. Owes thousands of pounds, climbing by the week. Just paying the interest is breaking him. Forces him to work the cabs for those bastard brothers every day and into the nights. No choice but to run their shady courier jobs, the ones nobody else will touch because of either their morality or a desire to keep their limbs intact. He is desperate, and they know it.

'I said, you do know what I mean, don't you?' The voice repeats, as he pulls on his cigarette.

He may be slipping downhill, but Ray knows inside that all it takes is one big win and the debt will be gone. A decent stake on some outsider that nobody else sees coming, and he would be free of the Serbians and their dodgy packages, the human traffic, the whole debt. Free to live his life again. But he just can't seem to find a winner at the moment. Sometimes you simply have no luck. The Mirkovic brothers shape his life.

'Well, this businessman, he sells on this loan to me. You don't need to know why, or how come I know him. That's not relevant to our story. Still with me?'

Ray offers a small nod of the head, mumbles agreement.

'So now this person who used to owe money to him, he now owes money to me. Plus, the usual, you know, handling fees, admin, that sort of thing.' He gives what looks like a genuine smile for the first time, as he counts off the terms and conditions.

'And you owe what you owe,' he adds, with a low growl.

Ray sighs. They both know this man has got him by the balls. Someone usually does. How did he get into this bloody mess? Just a guy trying to get by, unable to help himself. He only needs to catch a break. Every gambler knows this feeling. It is just a matter of finding it and sticking to your guns when it comes in. He knows he can stop.

'Do you follow, Raymond?'

His mind clears, and the penny drops. 'I owe you, now.'

'Nice one, Magnum. You fucking get it.'

The playful punch to the arm catches Ray by surprise. The minder stands to attention, checking for a reaction. There was some force behind it, even for a simple jab. Ray's other arm unfolds to rub it, but something stops him. Focus on the money.

'How much do I owe you, then?'

He knows it is going to end up being more than the eleven grand in Serbian arrears. Give or take a few hundred.

'At the moment, all of it. But...' Trilby glares at his target, waves a bony finger in Ray's face. 'If you do something for me, find this person, nothing. The slate is wiped clean. You can start again.' Ray's jaw opens wide. 'Seriously. Doubtless you'll lose more money on your stupid habit, but that's your problem. People like you are born losers, that's not my fault.' The man pauses to cough into a handkerchief pulled from his coat. Smoking can't be good for you. 'I'm offering you a chance to start again, sunshine. No debts, after one simple job.'

It takes a while for the words to permeate. His brain finds certain things easy to process, like how to break and enter in the dead of night, or complex mathematical calculations. Picking a lock, or each way accumulators, both second nature. But working out what the trilby-wearer is offering takes a few seconds. He realises this man is his saviour. The envelope feels heavy in his hands. He tucks it into the waistband of his jeans at the back.

Images of Marko sharpening an instrument of pain with a wild scowl on his face return. The next instalment is due tomorrow, and Ray has nothing to give them. Got to double check. This might save him begging.

'Forgive me, but Stefan and his brother know this, do they? About the debt?'

'Of course. You won't get any more problems with them.'

'So, who do you want me to find?'

'It's in that envelope.' Trilby sighs deeply and points his index finger at Ray again. 'If you must know, this bloke you're going to find, he owes in a similar manner to you. That's all you need to know.'

Ray struggles to decipher the look on his face, a strange mixture of threat and disgust.

'You all right?' Trilby stares. The tone is still not one of concern. Ray nods slowly.

There is a question that he needs to ask his new client. He doesn't know what makes him brave enough, now a lifeline is being offered, but it is hardly fronting up. Just a simple enquiry.

'Who are you?'

The eyes narrow once more. 'It doesn't matter who I am. But I think you can work out what I am.'

This man is saving his life. Whoever he is, this is a way out. Ray exhales deeply and feels a stone lighter for it.

If there is a link between him and the missing person, this pulls him towards a gambler who owes a shedload of money, even more than his own debt. Hard to imagine that being possible, but someone else's stupidity might be his opportunity. Pity the poor bastard, owing so much.

Ray can handle finding people. Plenty of experience looking under the rocks and stones, sifting through the shit to find those who don't want to be found. Only once has a target stayed missing from a case, the father was such a bully he let her go. A private investigator with a heart.

'Don't piss about, though. I need him found by Christmas. Think of it as a little present for me. And you get your present, too. Understand?'

Ray nods, swallowing hard. 'I understand. No problem.'

This gives him six weeks. It sounds like forever for a simple job like this. Dusty, his hacker accomplice, will probably track this person down in an afternoon. Ray reaches behind him, feeling for the envelope tucked away, declining to open it in front of the trilby hat. Something makes him think this might be disrespectful. The potential reward is huge, so that is the focus.

This will be the best-paid job he has ever had, considering both the sheer amount of money owed, and the bones that will be broken if the brothers are not paid back. His attempts at raising the next payment amounted to driving fourteen hours a day for five days then throwing over a hundred quid at a three-legged donkey called European Charm at Lingfield. It went against all his principles, following the name rather than track and form. Ray rubs his right shoulder, the place Marko delivered the last reminder. The brothers are hardly operating at Bank of England rates. Gamblers on an unlucky streak can't be choosers.

'You only have to find him, let me know where he is. It's not fucking *Midnight Run*. We'll keep in touch, so don't fanny about. I want this sorted out,' Trilby continues. 'I'm taking a big hit doing this; you know that, don't you?'

'Sure, I get it.' Maybe it takes a gambler to find a gambler. Pity the poor fucker at the end of the rope. *At least it isn't me*, Ray thinks. *I'm the lucky one in this.*

The minder, all muscle and cheap cologne, makes Ray jump, tapping him on the shoulder, handing over a fatter envelope. Ray holds this out in front of him, staring at the dirty hands.

'Put it away. Expenses,' Trilby hisses. Ray needs cash to get started; the lack of it is why he is in this mess. That, and a few jockeys not doing their job properly.

'There's five hundred there, and I want it back. Think of it as an operational loan, no interest applied.'

A large blacked-out Volvo pulls up silently alongside. The driver winds down his window, nods in their direction. 'Mister H.'

The minder opens the rear nearside door. The face of his boss creases, staring at Ray, as if he is studying an irritating child. 'Don't forget the deadline. Christmas. You're supposed to be good at this. Prove it. Don't balls it up.'

The door closes, and the muscle joins his boss in the back. Ray is dismissed. As they pull away, two kids come charging around the corner from Wakehurst Drive, the first sign of human life in the past fifteen minutes.

Ray retraces their steps towards the parade of shops to where his Mondeo is parked, as some of the streetlights flicker back into life. His tread is livelier than before. The air feels cleaner, and the outline of the pub sharpens. The Mondeo is still in one piece.

The message is clear. There is a means of escape, an end to this bloody torment. If all he needs to do is find someone, he is on comfortable ground. As easy as picking an odds-on winner.

Ray ignores the car, feels the shape of the smaller envelope in his fingers, and heads for the friendliest Ladbrokes in town, next to the Southgate Indian takeaway. Time to make the most of his good fortune.

2

Milton Keynes, November 1999

Truth Time, within The Circle. Monday morning, 9:30 am.

The group are arranged in a ring of chairs. Their leader sits as one of them, rather than in the centre where he belongs. All other thirteen pairs of eyes are drawn to him, waiting for the decision. Once a month a chosen member becomes the centre of attention.

S's voice is soft and low. 'This time, the person we want to hear the truth from, is... Carl.'

Lydia breathes out slowly, thankful that eyes are not on her, continues to study S, rather than the chosen speaker who is to her right. She is the newest recruit, three months in, and their leader hinted it might be her turn. Lydia is there to observe. She counts four chairs between her and S, and notices there is no pointed finger, just upturned palms, non-aggression, an invitation to Carl to show himself.

The process is simple. Every member of the group will ask one question of the subject, who must answer truthfully. This way, there can be no secrets among them.

Ruth, sitting to Lydia's left, starts off, 'Carl, what brought you to Milton Keynes?'

Lydia catches S's eye, and she turns her body slightly to her right, to focus on Carl. A man who has been with them for a year, she has been told.

Carl pauses, eyes flitting around the room, then looks at S as he answers, 'It seemed a place of opportunity. Somewhere to start my life again.'

'What's your favourite colour?' This one brings a giggle from a couple of the group.

'Blue.'

Lydia sees Carl's leg twitch, his foot tapping at the carpet. He places his hands on his knees, presses down, as if to stop the shaking. She thinks through her own practised answers, in front of a mirror, rehearsed to the nth degree, ready in case it was her turn. Prepared for the ones designed to catch her off guard. Remembering how she was going to weave her fingers together in front of her, rest them on her legs, hide her own truth.

'Have your goals changed?' A different voice, male, Derek's, one of only three men in the group, across the room. Lydia has her eyes on Carl, like the rest of them, can't look up at S, in case she meets his gaze.

'I guess they will always keep changing. I'm on track now. I have literally dragged myself out of the gutter. Right now, I'm happy.' The accent is south-east, like the one she now uses, her east-coast drawl fallen away.

Lydia is ready for her turn when it comes, after everyone bar S has gone. 'What's your favourite drink? Alcoholic, I mean, not tea.' She has seen Carl timing his breaks to avoid the others, meticulously placing a bag in a mug, checking the seconds with his watch before it is removed. Measuring the amount of milk with a spoon. Always four helpings.

'I don't drink much, as you know.' There are a few nods around the room. 'Cider, if anything.'

And then the final question, his question, the most important one to get right. The examination that matters.

'Who are you, Carl? Who really are you?'

'I am Carl. You all know me by now.'

'Yes, but deep down, Carl. Who are you?' S presses, leaning forwards in the chair. Lydia pushes back into her own, stares at the floor. Carl's leg shakes again, despite the pressure being pushed through his hands.

'I was a drug addict. A hopeless case. I lived on the streets for nearly two years before I came here. I had nothing. Now I'm clean. Now at least I have something. I want to put my past behind me, look forward. It doesn't matter what I was before. It's the future that counts.'

S has saved them all. Every soul in the room has an individual story to tell, and they have opened their hearts to him. As a group they are stronger, have come together to build something. Lydia watches S, rather than Carl, now, sees how he maintains eye contact with the subject.

S nods and projects a thin smile. 'Thank you, Carl.' As their leader speaks, Lydia studies him, projecting his practised image. She has been watching closely. How he holds the rest enthralled. With the advice he provides, the comfort, and the way the eyes implore you not to look away.

She goes back to her rehearsal and how she had planned to respond. Would she really have turned the question back on S if it was her turn? The temptation would have been there. To put the focus on the man she has followed to this town. But Lydia needs to get closer, be certain, before his truth is revealed. To stay within the loving arms of The Circle for a while before she makes her move.

They are prepared for how the outside world views them. A cult. Deluded followers. But there is no blind faith in some higher being, no readiness to sacrifice their lives in a crazy massacre. They trust him. S is a facilitator, a life guide. Decisions are shared, and they grow together as a result. Business is booming, they are told. The Circle is a telemarketing agency; a shining example of how new commerce has been attracted to the bursting metropolis that is Milton Keynes. A living demonstration of how there is hope on the horizon going into a new millennium.

Lydia researched the history before she joined. S formed this group five years before, collecting displaced, needy souls, providing them a place to dock, to reassemble pieces into place, and breathe again. There is no reason to seek help from the outside, once you have felt the comfort of The Circle.

Lydia's backstory is a fabrication, carefully prepared to reveal no link between their pasts. She has benefitted from the extended grace you receive as a newcomer, before being subjected to Truth Time. The place where you come to terms with who you are, and who you want to be.

S stands and pulls the White Book from his jacket pocket. 'Our final words this morning,' he says. Silence extends, eyes and ears focused fully on him. S beams, looks at each of them in turn. He opens the pamphlet at a page, and gradually the group pull out their own copies. Lydia's has been under her chair. He takes them through the mantra, as they repeat it, clasping the booklet in redemption-hungry hands.

'Today I will improve myself. Today I will look forward. Today I have a vision for my future. And it is one of hope.'

The text inside provides guidance, particularly for when S is not with them. It acts as a reminder of how to conduct themselves. Most eyes are open as they deliver their words, but S's are closed. Lydia believes he does not need to look, to see who is committed. He can feel it. She raises her voice so it can be heard. The hands around the room then join, as he asks them to pray. They are as one, trusting in each other. Equal, in this shape, the same distance from the centre.

Ruth to her left feels clammy, Carl to the right has soft, smooth skin. This is the first time she has sat next to Carl in this room. The loner. She gives Carl's hand a small squeeze, which he returns after a short pause. Lydia resists the temptation to look at him, keeps her gaze across the ring. S is meant to be the focus.

To finish off the meeting, their supervisor, Janice, takes them through the week's schedule of work. Lydia has noted this is the only nod to hierarchy they have, apart from S, and Janice stutters as she reads out their instructions, a reluctant boss. Their task will involve outbound sales calls for two insurance companies, payment protection, a necessary fallback against future hardship. Janice hands around a printed sheet with the answers to potential customer challenges that might come their way. Lydia scans down the page. Most of it seems obvious. It makes sense to plan for the unexpected.

The service they provide is labelled 'outsourcing', S's term. Customer services overflow for some companies, sales for others. The clients seem to vary each week, as do the calls they make and take. There is a real business purpose to

The Circle, alongside the social one. But Lydia has her own mission to fulfil.

Back at her desk, as she plugs in her headset and brings up the first number on her screen, Lydia watches S close his office door. The static of the calling system fills her ears, and she stares at the barrier between her and the target. She needs to get nearer before she can expose him.

The dial tone rings out, a random number appears on her screen. There is anonymity as they choose false names for each conversation. Lydia is yet to use her sister's, fearing S will make a connection, wonders if he listens in to the calls. She urges herself to stay patient, knowing justice will come.

3

he was a rite pain in the arse he woodnt let me be
Obi what a pain so i just throught well get this you
and down he went danny it was like a movie you now
the ones you used to show me he hit the ground and
i ran so fast that was it. maybe she will take care
of me now and member that i am their in the flat
in my bed which is wear i am now our room. all your
stuff is still hear and ill keep it til you come home.
wish you was hear danny. if you were hear she woodnt
try to hit me with anything she wood just leave me
alone. she must look after me now and think about
me. this will make the bitch sit up and do her job at
last and member im even hear.

she can be a good mum again just like before all
she has to do is member that im hear and look after
me not much to ask is it danny its good i found a
place to hide out of school. you can go up the woods
were they take us for them mob runs. i member you

saying about them mob runs they are fucking awful
so i took some to smoke instead. i cant stand that
school its for jessies there just soft. teachers are
all on you case all the time and its a nitemare they
dont like you talking or having fun whats the point
danny. still i can hide if i want cause the hole class
is full of donkeys that barry briggs what a spanner.
i dont even go to maths any more its pointles and a
waste of time.

she gets worse yesterday she had a go at me for
not doing my home work you now that the first time
she ever even ask me about home work ever. the bitch
dont care like you did danny. i could kill her with my
bear hands you now that so could you danny how they
traind you maybe we should do it together maybe you
shud hav done it before you left. she would get drunk
like she does and we could make her drink herself to
deaf maybe that might work. is the army a better
place than hear it must be wish i was with you you
can take me away from this and her.

4

Crawley, November 1999

Leckie Harris.

His new client's name hits Ray as he writes out his first betting slip, barely ten minutes after the trilby hat stepped into that car. The focus is supposed to be on the race card at Catford. But his concentration has gone. An ancient piece of the town's murky history moves down through his body, making the hand pause. It is funny how you can try to block out the worst of your past.

When he was a security guard, what feels like a lifetime ago, there were stories about 'Bad Leckie'. Anybody who worked in security at Gatwick Airport, or Crawley industrial estate in the seventies, would have been asked to look the other way when told to by Leckie Harris. There was no choice, if you wanted to carry on working and walking.

By the time Ray began perfecting the skill of drinking coffee and staring at monitors at the same time, Leckie was a fading mythology. After Ray was fired for abandoning his post, he turned to the detective work, using the knowledge gleaned from the town's murkier side. Digging in corners people shy away from, unearthing truths, reaching into Crawley's underbelly. It was supposed to be a way of lifting himself out of the place. He is still there, paralysed on the stool, in this shop of horrors, clinging to hope.

The memories of the Bad Leckie backstory return, drawn up from old, whispered conversations in dirty portacabins and cluttered stockrooms. Brought up locally, one of the first generation parachuted out of their run-down south London estates into Crawley in the early fifties. Told this was a promised land, slum terraces replaced by comfortable semis and inside toilets. Streets paved with gold, and grass as far as you could see. The same promise brought Ray's old man there. Crawley represented a new frontier to conquer. Word was Leckie had moved on to prostitution, money laundering, and protection, before retiring to Spain in the eighties, when Ray joined the security racket.

And this raises questions that freeze his faithful writing hand above the betting slip. What is Leckie doing in this town again, handing out a lifeline? And why Ray? Surely, he could find a reputable investigator for the job. Someone capable of keeping money in their pocket. Or pay some henchmen to twist arms and smash bones. He is just a lowly sleuth, with a passing ability to track people down, and a talent for breaking and entering on the side. Ray can't imagine what else he has to offer. Then he remembers the final words of dismissal before his client stepped into the car.

'Don't balls it up.'

He might be the lucky one, working for this man rather than being tied to a chair and tortured, if the old stories are true. It doesn't matter how much of a nasty bastard Leckie is; this is a way out.

Ray exhales, tries to focus on the betting slip again. This is a world he is familiar with, knows how to play the game. In places like these, he is the master of what he surveys. He controls the outcome. Ray straightens his spine, grasps the tiny pen, shakes it to bring ink to the point, and writes out the bet.

His back is to the wall where they pin up the racing pages. There is no need to consult them. He will work on instinct. Ray studies what he has written. It says the wrong trap for the first race, his number one has morphed into a four. He knows the inside line is better at the start of the meeting. Ray looks around the shop, wondering if any of the regulars will see his mistake, notice the flawed logic. Just a few words and numbers on a small piece of paper, but a betrayal of everything he knows.

Ray screws up the slip, lets it sit on the table, the paper trying to remember its shape. He watches it reform, wondering if he could ever go back to the days before despair, before debt, before he threw his life away. To a place where a woman laughed at his jokes, cared how he was and what happened in his day, where there was a future. A place that is now a distant memory.

Smoke hangs close to the brown, stained ceiling, trapped like its human occupants in a world of faint hope. The racing commentary playing in the background reminds them there is the chance to win every few minutes. The opportunity to predict the future is always there.

Ray needs to focus elsewhere. Pulling out the larger envelope the minder gave him, there is only one item inside.

He shakes it to check there is nothing lurking, a bigger clue. Ray pulls out a photocopy of a birth certificate. There is no face to work with, just a name. Michael Keane, born in 1965.

His concentration is broken by one of the old lags from the shop, who walks past to study the form on the wall, tapping the pinned pages with a pen. Brenda behind the counter gives the man's back a hard stare. He stands just a couple of feet away, ignoring Ray. Nobody engages in here, even when they have a big tip-off. You keep those to yourself.

Ray returns the sheet to the envelope, files it away in his mind as something to tackle later. He looks around the shop at the other two punters. Both regulars, both smoking roll-ups and minding their own business, reading newspapers. Brenda goes back to counting money. Ray pulls out another betting slip from the pile on the table and starts again.

It takes him less than an hour to hand all the advance over the counter, fruitlessly scribbling nonsense. Dogs, horses, it makes no difference. Random mistakes he would laugh at if a novice were making them. His fingers ache. Maybe he thought he could recoup the whole Serbian debt with the cash advance, avoid the case. Fooling himself again.

The lifeline is still there, no harm in trying. If your luck is turning, why not make the most of it? Six weeks is an eternity for a missing persons case. He has a friend who can help him save time. Ray can go back to the cabs, and the errands for the Mirkovic brothers for a while. There is a glimpse now of the end of a desperate tunnel, that recently seemed so long and unreachable.

5

Milton Keynes, November 1999

When S taps Carl on the shoulder, walks past and beckons, he follows without thinking. He has no choice but to conform. S pushes open the door to Tiny Tim's vacant office. Envious eyes track Carl as he steps lightly across the open-plan space. Everybody wants precious face time. It shows how well they are healing, growing, when they receive individual attention.

Inside the room, S strides towards the desk and turns to Carl, showing perfect teeth.

'Close the door.'

Carl turns the handle and leans against the frame, looking back at their leader. Using the door to keep himself upright. Carl surveys the room, feels his cheeks start to glow. Pictures the beach he knows, a kite whirling in the sky, to help him breathe more slowly.

Carl knows what used to happen in the room. He shared a drink with Tiny Tim just before he disappeared. The first person to willingly leave the group, he was told.

Everything is shared. Air, coffee, biscuits, diseases, highs, and lows. But Tim had an office all to himself, the only person apart from S with any privacy. They all knew Tim was one of the early joiners, and worked separately, under S's direction. Carl's chat that night in The Ship Ashore pub revealed the reasons for the enforced isolation. Tim spied on them.

S clears his throat, a gesture that they all know means it is time to listen. Carl's attention is pulled away from the clutter on the desk, the paper hanging out of the waste basket, the lever arch files on the shelves with some facing inwards, some out. He itches to re-arrange the furniture but holds firm by the door.

'How are you today, Carl?'

S leans back on the desk, swings a leg casually, calmly pushing paper aside, so he can wriggle further onto the surface. There is no confrontation coming, only concern. The eyes shine, the hands make waves, a precursor to one of his sales pitches. Carl finds he has moved a couple of steps away from the door, to no man's land, leaning back on his heels.

'Carl?'

He hasn't answered, a response S will not be used to. There is a hold, that they readily accept. Carl can only think of one reason for S asking him in. To replace Tiny Tim.

'I'm good, thanks, Simon.' First name terms for one-to-one situations. The initial is only used in his absence.

'Excellent.' S pushes further back, dangles both feet. Carl is half a foot taller, wonders again how the women in the group find their leader attractive. Then focuses on those eyes, the way they pull you in.

'Carl, I'd like you to help us in a new role.'

And there it is. Someone to resume Tim's dubious job, dressed up as ordering replacement toilet rolls and copier paper when, according to Tim, he spent most of his time listening in to sales calls and reading emails. Carl remembers the stilted conversation they had, so many sentences starting with, 'I shouldn't be telling you this,' before going into detail about where the cameras and microphones were hidden and the electronic files he had access to. Carl never worked out why Tim decided to unburden the truth that night. Two days later, Tim was gone.

'What role?' Carl stares at the carpet, steps forward to pick up a discarded sweet wrapper, slips it in his pocket. Wonders if he has been careless. And if the others also keep secrets from S.

'I need your help, Carl. We need you to take over Tim's old job. In here.'

It is difficult to challenge; the group are used to doing as S bids. Carl questions whether he will ever feel the same way as the rest of them about S.

The smile returns. 'Carl. We are growing fast. But people grow, too. I want you to take this on. When life throws opportunities at you, Carl, you must take them.'

He appears confident Carl will accept. Carl stares back, rooted, thinking through all the conversations they have had in the past year, the clues he might have given that would suggest this is right for him. S sometimes inclines his head when he listens, as if data is carefully being stored.

'We need someone to look after the office, the facilities. This place is in danger of falling apart.' S half-laughs. 'I need you to keep things together. You're different from the rest of them.' Carl's breath catches, he stares at the back of the computer screen on the desk. 'You don't get too emotional. That's what we, as a group, need from someone in this role. We all need you in this role, Carl.'

Carl thinks through the recent history. A down-and-out lost to the world under a railway bridge whose life has largely passed him by. A man who is looking for a sense of purpose, hoping that The Circle might provide it. Searching for who he is.

'Why me?' As he asks this, Carl shivers, the cold of an unused room reaching inside. S doesn't blink. That smile is still there. S is good at this.

'I told you. You're different from the rest.' No impatience in the face. 'Somebody has to do it. Why not you?' The last three words added with a light-hearted touch.

Because he fears sticking his head up and being noticed, because there are eyes upon him, whispers, and questions.

'Carl. I had to do all this myself when we started. Then Tim took over, so I could focus on other things. You know I'm busy now, out there, growing the business. I can't bear to think I'll have to do it all over again.' S jumps off the desk and takes two steps towards Carl, who backs away half a pace. 'I need someone I can trust, to keep us safe. Someone all of us can trust. You could do it standing on your head.'

S opens his arms wide and moves further forward, so the two men are almost in reach. This isn't the offer of an embrace; bodily contact is not encouraged apart from holding hands at Truth Time. 'Just say you'll do it, Carl.'

Carl needs the invisibility of being one of the group, but knows disobedience won't be tolerated; not by him or the others. Carl's commitment cannot be doubted. S is eagerly followed. Declining would cause more of a ripple than accepting. They exist as one. He has been pushed into a corner, in the middle of this cold room.

'Okay, I'll do it.'

'Good.' S steps forward, close enough to shake, breaking the usual code. The hand feels dry, secure. Carl pulls away as soon as he can without making it look like rejection. A shiver returns.

Their leader glides to the door, leaning into the handle, glancing at his watch. 'I'll take you through the job tomorrow. Is that okay?'

Carl has a day to get used to the idea. 'Sure.'

'Good. Remember the words in the book. After acceptance comes advancement.'

Carl is left alone in what will become his fortress. There is a compulsion to act. Gathering together the sheets on the desk, he straightens them into a pile and examines them slowly. Nothing secret, just electricity and window cleaning bills, orders for boxes of paper. He picks up all the scattered pens, pencils and other stationery, and places them meticulously in a drawer, in the separate compartments of a tray. Breathes out, sees the wind blowing the same kite, and a child racing along the sands, a tenuous string in its hands. He might be better off in the room, rather than outside on the calls.

S seemed so confident he would agree to take the role. Carl must have given the correct answers at Truth Time. Along with the one-to-one sessions, satisfied him that Carl can be trusted to keep watch over the whole group. An ideal situation for him to be in, for the time being. Some will need to be monitored more closely than others. Especially the newcomer. His question for her Truth Time, when she comes under the spotlight, is ready.

'Lydia, are you looking for somebody?'

6

Crawley, November 1999

Stefan Mirkovic looks up from his desk when he hears his brother cough.

'He is here.'

Marko is a man of few words; his English is not what it should be for someone taking an opportunity in a new country. Stefan is more comfortable doing the talking for the pair of them. Marko has other skills, mostly of persuasion.

Stefan has heard the stories about his visitor, tall tales of the olden days, and doesn't care. What matters is money. And this man is offering it to him.

The printing shop in Tilgate provides cover for the less visible aspects of their business. A taxi firm in the shopfront next door provides a sheen of legitimacy. No rent to pay for either, given the hold they have over the landlord and his penchant for underage girls. The wheels of industry greased by whatever it takes.

The visitor removes his hat but doesn't offer a handshake as he approaches the desk. Marko fills the doorway space with his silent threat. Nobody of this man's rumoured stature would come alone. His bodyguards must be close by.

'Stefan, is it?'

'Yes. Mister Harris?'

'You know who I am.'

I know who you were, Stefan thinks to himself, does not allow a smile, knows that Crawley has changed beyond recognition from the old man's days. There are new chiefs in town, none of them local. His biggest worry is keeping the Moldovans and the Albanians at bay, not the ancient regime.

'Sit, please.' Stefan beckons to an empty chair across from him, but Leckie Harris stands his ground, plays with the brim of his hat, stares back. Said to have been a deadly opponent years ago. Sixty, maybe more, now, and looking every day of it. Not something for men like the Mirkovic brothers to worry about. A small town like this is nothing, compared to the ravages of a war-torn country. Where you could build your fortune with quick wits and a deep understanding of human nature. How everyone has a fear, and everyone has a price. And the knowledge that one change of political leadership and all you have built up can be lost. Forcing you to start again, somewhere new.

'You wanted to see me. I wish I knew why,' Stefan entreats, holding out his hands. Appearing to welcome an enemy, knowing that any who have come willingly this far into his empire cannot be trusted. Including the driver with the debt he sent to pick up the old man. 'He did turn up, didn't he?'

'Oh, yes, he did. I want to borrow him for a short while. He's going to be busy.'

Stefan knows people can be traded. He does it every day. The old man glares at Stefan, but it takes more to unnerve a soldier. He has commanded a unit, sent thousands on a march to their deaths in the snow, knows what it is like to control a city.

'How much?' Stefan asks. They both know this is the crucial question.

'How much does he owe you?'

Stefan opens a desk drawer, pulls out a piece of paper and jots down some numbers. None of them have anything to do with the debt; this is for show.

'Fifteen.'

'Really?' The visitor's eyebrows rise, and Stefan notices how dark they are compared to the thinning grey at his temples. Perhaps these English do care more for how they look than people say.

'Fifteen,' he repeats. The price could be anything; no way their debtor could question it, given the level of interest they charge. They receive the minimum every week and no more. Sometimes less, and that is when Marko goes to work. But there are bigger things to worry about than the English driver.

The visitor pulls out an envelope from inside his coat and removes two rolls of notes, places them carefully in a pocket, making a show of the fact he was expecting to pay more. Stefan bristles, rubs his temples. The man tosses what remains onto the desk.

'There's sixteen there. The debt is now mine.'

Stefan picks up the package, peers inside. There is no need to count it. Nobody does that these days.

'You think he can be trusted?' he asks Marko, in Serbian.

'I asked around. These days, yes,' Marko replies.

'Sure.' Back in English, for the old man. Stefan shrugs his shoulders, wonders whether he should have said a higher number. Still, it is a good piece of business. The gambler was never going to pay it all back.

'Why are you doing this?' Stefan is curious, no more.

The old man stares at him, frowns. The creases on his face intensify. Stefan has seen the look before, one of someone holding his ground. 'None of your business.'

The hat is placed carefully back on his head and the visitor turns towards the door. Marko steps aside, arms strongly folded. At the threshold, Harris turns and stares about the room, giving a slow shake of the head.

Stefan needs assurance; Ray is a nobody, but trusted couriers are hard to come by. 'He still drives for me as well?'

'He can, when time allows. When he's done a job for me, he's yours again. He just don't owe you any money now.'

Stefan ponders how easy it is to make a living in peacetime. No generals or politicians to interfere. Nobody stepping on his toes, looking for a cut. Straightforward transactions, flow of goods and people, an open society. So much simpler than before.

'The driver will be back for more, won't he?' Stefan asks Marko, again in Serbian.

'He can't help himself,' Marko agrees with a grin.

Leckie touches the brim of his trilby as he leaves, gives them his parting shot. 'I'd appreciate it if no harm comes to him. For the time being.' The visitor disappears, his soft footsteps echoing down the hallway.

'Depends how well he behaves,' Stefan whispers to himself, the old man forgotten, as he places the envelope in the safe behind him.

7

Front page of the *Crawley Observer*, 7TH MARCH 1978

LOCAL BOY CONVICTED OF MURDER
by Trish Watney

Martin Sullivan, thirteen, of Nash Road, Tilgate, was this week found guilty of the murder of a local boy, Philip Hughes, last September. Throughout the trial at Lewes Crown Court, the accused had been known as 'Child X', but Judge Patrick Coltart allowed the killer to be named after the verdict was reached. Martin Sullivan started as a pupil at the notorious local school, Thomas Bennett, a week before the murder. Now he will be under lock and key for the rest of his childhood, and some of his adult life.

Chief Superintendent Jon Sammells, of Sussex Police, speaking after the sentence was delivered outside the court, praised his officers on the case.

'I want to thank the whole team who worked so hard to bring this young person to justice. And also, to thank witnesses who came forward and did the right thing. This sort of bravery makes our job much easier. We think the people of Crawley, and of Sussex, will be satisfied with the speed and efficiency of the job we have done.'

Sammells would not be drawn into commenting on the boy who had been convicted. He stated that the length of the sentence was a matter for the court. Sullivan was still only twelve when the killing took place and will serve at least six years. However, he could remain in custody for the rest of his life, depending on his behaviour. Sullivan said nothing during his trial, refusing to apologise. He confessed while in custody but pleaded 'not guilty' at the trial. The sentence is scant consolation for the parents and friends of Philip Hughes. Judge Coltart would not reveal where Sullivan is being held, for the boy's safety.

Crawley residents are shocked that a child could carry out such a crime. Sullivan and Hughes had been involved in a fight, which resulted in a deadly fall. According to the Sussex Coroner, Edward Biggar, it would have taken Philip Hughes up to an hour to die from his head wounds. Sullivan made no attempt to call for an ambulance. The jury reached their decision in forty minutes.

The killer's mother, Sharon Sullivan, was in court for some of the proceedings. The whereabouts of the boy's father are unknown. The accused sat expressionless most of the time, flanked by social workers. Mrs Sullivan declined to make a statement after the trial, but had previously defended her son as 'not a bad boy'. In court, she was forced to admit that Martin Sullivan frequently played truant, although local social services were unaware of any specific problems. Sharon Sullivan has reportedly moved away from the area, for fear of reprisals.

A spokesman for the Hughes family said that nothing could bring their Philip back. The parents of the victim, Kevin and Delia Hughes, were in court every day, and clearly struggled with the details of his death when they were revealed. It is hard to see how any parent could forgive the actions of Martin Sullivan. There was an audible cry of 'justice' from the public gallery when the verdict was read out. This was then followed by shouts of protest when Judge Coltart revealed the sentence shortly afterwards. Six years can appear lenient when compared to the life that lay ahead of Philip Hughes.

How will our community react to the news that a killer has been raised and nurtured within? It is hoped that our residents can treat this awful tragedy with the same dignity displayed by the Hughes family. Airport expansion will bring more prosperity to the area. Can Crawley move on? Or will that old building site in Northgate where the death occurred mark the end of the innocence of our town?

8

Crawley, November 1999

'My name is Richard, and I am a compulsive gambler.'

Eight men greet the newbie with varying commitment. Ray wonders if Richard is his real name. When he started coming to GA, the temptation was to make one up, but he reasoned it was better to begin on an honest footing for once.

Richard is not required to unburden any of his secrets the first time. You can relax, listen, take in the sorrow that is shared around the room. A church hall in Pound Hill, as it has been every Wednesday night for the past five months for Ray. In the space of ninety minutes, the brethren outline the temptations and confess to where they have strayed. Ray wonders how much everyone tells the truth, given that they are all likely to be skilled liars. Borrowed money under false pretences, absented from work, or bailed out of time with children for some manufactured reason. It is part of the make-up. Deceive the rest of the world, but never yourself. God forbid they do that.

The collective mantra is mumbled, about taking life one day at a time. In turn they will be asked to show remorse, reflect on their shortcomings, accept the illness they have. Ray sits upright in his plastic chair, wants to talk first this week. He doesn't think he should tell the whole story, few people do, but he feels lighter, stretches his back muscles. He studies the men around him. Their shoulders slump and they look at their shoes, sipping at the tepid tea and coffee, waiting for Gordon to select the initial confessor. They are losers, but Ray is going to be a winner. He has a way out.

Ray raises his hand and Gordon nods in his direction. Gordon has lived their gambling lives and is used to bullying someone into speaking up first. The group leader leans back in his chair, slightly off-centre from the rest in the circle, pulls out a cigarette, taps it against the packet. There are signs saying 'No Smoking' on the wall, but these are ignored. Gamblers struggle to follow the rules.

'Hi, everyone. I feel better this week,' Ray says. 'I haven't won a thing, but that's because I've stopped.'

Most of the faces look up, eyes red from their own sorrow; a couple of them cough. They won't believe him, Ray wouldn't if anybody else said it, but he presses on.

'It's true. I haven't had a bet for six days.' Ray smiles, but only Gerry catches his eye, sitting to his left. Gerry grimaces, and Ray struggles to work out what his face is telling him. 'I haven't been into a bookies' in all that time. And I feel great.' The last line delivered with a small laugh.

'That's good news,' Gordon says, looking around the room, scanning for agreement. Ray senses their focus on him rather than the group leader. 'Remember what the book says. You are never cured; you are only ever in remission,' Gordon counsels.

They have all read it, heard it many times. Ray thinks none of them believe it.

Despite his words of caution, Gordon leads the praise. 'Well done, Ray. Six whole days?'

'Yeah.'

In truth, it wouldn't be six hours, but Ray feels he needs to make a statement. One about how it will soon be over. Now he has an escape route. He won't need this group any more. Or the quasi-religious words printed in their guiding booklet, deceiving them that there is a form of salvation, when all they really want to do, from deep in their bones, is have another bet.

'Can I ask,' Gordon presses, 'what made you stop?'

Ray looks at the posters on the wall, scattered images of drug addicts, smokers and single mums pushing prams. They need help more than him now. He has suffered from cruel luck for too long; jockeys not trying, footballers wasting their talent, good fortune has been overdue. Debt will no longer hold him back, impede his judgement. To bet with that fear is to lose before you start.

'My life is under control. I managed to pay off my debts.' Ray looks at Gerry, gives him a small nod.

'That doesn't mean…' Gordon starts.

'I know. But I have turned a corner. Six days it's been.'

Ray tucks his hands under his legs to hide the ink stains. Gerry may have already spotted them, knows the truth. That he spent half an hour that afternoon, frantically scribbling losses out on slips like a celebrity bustling their way past faceless fans, signing an endless stream of autographs. Everything he has earnt in the last week, gone.

Gordon addresses the room. 'Good luck to you, Ray. You know there is a place for you here if you need it.' The words echo in the stillness, and Ray sees a thin smile, struggling to disguise disbelief. 'Anybody else?'

Ray tunes out as they take their turns, studies the posters more closely. He already knows from the cab that he has a blind spot for motorcyclists. That cigarettes can kill him; these have already been sacrificed in return for betting cash. When Gerry goes through his own week of temptation and failure to rein in his desires, Ray zones back in. His seated neighbour has no choice but to be there. Gerry's probation terms demand it. An accountant who embezzled his company's money to fund his gambling, was desperate to be caught before he got in too deep. Happier now the world knows his filthy secret. They all have that feeling. The air is full of miserable stories.

When the session closes, Ray and Gerry walk their separate routes, and meet up as they always do in The Charcoal Burner. Gerry is unusually quiet. Ray fills the void with affirmation.

'I really am debt free.'

'You lucky bastard.' Gerry still owes the court, the banks, his employer. Enough to keep him down for years. 'How come?'

'Don't ask.' Which is precisely what Gerry does.

Ray sips at his drink to give him to time to think of the right words. How to say a guardian angel has dropped out of the sky to save him. That he has been given a simple task, and that is all there is to it. That despite a recent run of bad fortune in the betting shops, he is the luckiest man alive. And that he has done nothing about his task yet.

'I had a big winner.' He smiles, hopes Gerry falls for it.

'Nice one.' Gerry looks out of the window, and Ray follows his gaze. The rain lashes against the glass. Silence returns.

Ray wishes he was a better liar. Still has no money to pay his source. Knows Dusty won't raise a finger until the initial fee is on the table.

'The horses?' Gerry asks, not blinking at the rain outside.

Ray pauses. Gerry is devoted to the nags, would know if a big outsider had come in. He needs to think straight. 'No. It was the snooker. UK Championships.'

'Ah.' Gerry takes a drink and looks across the table. Ray searches his memory for the winner. There is nothing there. Not even the finalists. 'Tip off?' Gerry whispers. They are always looking for inside information.

'Nah. I just got lucky. You know how it is.'

'Just your big break,' Gerry sniggers, and returns his attention to the drops hitting the window.

Ray stares at the only GA member who doesn't seem to question his motives, or his gambling opinions. The joke hits him, but no laugh comes. Ray wonders if it matters if Gerry believes him. He will probably never see him again. He has no more need for GA. Not now he has a way out. Just needs to raise the first payment for Dusty's work, the initial search for Michael Keane, and move on. One simple task, keeping cash in his pocket, and he will be a free man. Sometimes the simplest jobs can be the toughest.

9

Milton Keynes, November 1999

S watches Lydia sit in the chair, absorbed by how her shoulders sink as she eases into the soft fabric. All the furniture in his room is selected for comfort, to place everyone at their ease. This is her turn for a personal session. Only the newest group members have these now, because once he has got to know them, the system can monitor their progress. But before that, he needs to make another assessment.

Lydia doesn't wear much make-up, has a model's cheekbones. He knows that she is the type of woman who doesn't need to accentuate her looks. She is inclined to tuck strands of her blonde hair behind her ear. Maybe it is that movement that prompts the feeling of familiarity that, so far, he has struggled to pinpoint. He has brought this session forward. There is a busy week ahead. Their future is in the balance, and soon his attention will need to be elsewhere.

She smiles, and her face brightens as he slides into his own chair, one with less give but with a deep memory. He has heard all their stories here, listened intently, advised, directed, bullied, all the things they need from a leader. Their lives were aimless before they arrived. He is providing focus to the people in this group, the same way he has done elsewhere.

'Are you ready for this?' he asks.

'Sure.'

Her lips part, and the tongue flicks out, just for a fraction of a second, but he notices it. Wonders if it is deliberate. There is something about this one. The way she looks at him in the office, in the group meetings, holding his gaze rather than averting, as so many of the others do at the start. He feels an attraction, although not a sexual one, one he can't quite pin down, and a sense that she is more open than most. Might grow to become accepting of his guidance.

'We need to go back to what you are looking for.'

Her head flinches up, then drops down to look at her lap, where her fingers are intertwined. He has noticed the hand placement before, wonders what it signifies. Always looking for non-verbal clues. Has learnt what they can signify.

'What do you want from this place?' he prompts again.

'I'm not sure.'

He looks away at the thin, metallic blinds that are drawn, ensuring the two of them have privacy. The others will recognise the session they are having, but don't need the details. He leans forward in his chair. Wants to reach out and touch her but knows he can't. There are appropriate ways to behave.

'You do want to stay here, don't you? To receive our help?' he asks.

'Yes. I need help,' she replies.

'Help for what?'

'To understand some things, get them clear in my mind.' Her fingers tighten in her lap. 'To understand past mistakes.'

'Mistakes?'

'Yeah. We've all made mistakes.' Her eyes narrow. He has her full attention now. 'I'm sure you have, too.'

'We're not here to talk about me,' he rebuts. 'We're here to talk about you.'

'Of course.'

Her cuticles turn from red to white; she is pressing her fingers so tight in that grip.

'Tell me about your mistakes,' he prompts, voice soft.

Lydia straightens her spine, shakes her head. 'I'm not sure where to start.'

'Try.' He offers the regular smile, the one that requests the truth.

'I was raped.' She stares directly at him as she utters this, fixes him, repeats the words.

'Being raped is not your mistake. What happened?' he asks. He has come across damaged women before. Knows they need to be treated carefully.

'It was my brother.'

He feels her eyes stare deep into his own. Forces out a neutral expression. 'Did you tell anyone?'

'Sure. My mum and dad; they didn't believe me. Jack was the golden boy. He'd never do anything wrong in their eyes. They said I was jealous.'

Her hands unclasp, and she studies her fingernails. He notices that they are bitten down.

'Jealous?'

'Hmm. He was about to go away to university, and that was the priority for them, getting him through that, and it was an inconvenient truth. The fact he raped his sister.'

'But it was true?'

'Sure.'

He runs a finger around the collar of his shirt, feels it stick to his neck. Increasingly convinced, as she speaks and as he watches her movements, that there is something familiar about her. He reaches into his past, wonders again if he has met her before. Nothing in the face, or even the name. But people use different names all the time, he knows this. The mannerisms claw at him. He cannot stop looking at her hands.

The silence sits there between them. Normally he is comfortable with this, when it happens in these sessions. Has no problem with letting them self-analyse. Has sat in the other chair, knows what it is like to turn trauma over and over in your mind. He looks at her face again. The eyes seem darker now, the lips drawn tightly.

'Secrets are hard to keep, aren't they?' she asks.

'Sometimes, yes.'

'I struggled to share mine. With anyone.'

'Who else have you told this to, apart from your family?' he asks.

Lydia scratches at a fingernail. 'Nobody. This is the first time I've told anyone, outside the family.'

'You're doing the right thing,' he replies, breathing more calmly. 'It's best to share.' His imagination is taking over. Seeing something when nothing is there. Lydia only turned up three months ago. Cannot know anything about where the group is heading next, or his past.

He relaxes a little, turns his palms upwards, opens up his body. The way he was coached. He can rely on the old methods, tease the truth out of her. 'Take me back to the day it happened. Share with me how it felt, that day.'

Lydia closes her eyes. He senses her recreating the scene. Has heard from women who have been assaulted, although not sexually.

'It was horrible. He raped me. That's all there is to it. My own brother.'

'How did you cope?' he asks, looking at her closely. The hands are interlocked again, back in her lap.

'I didn't. I thought about ending it all. Making the pain go away. The ache inside me. I left home. Had to get away. Couldn't stand it there any more.'

'How long ago was this?' he asks, voice as soft as he can.

'Eight years ago. I was very young. I still am very young.'

She pulls her hair back behind her ear again. There was a girl who used to do the same thing. Way back when. Before Milton Keynes. Before The Circle. How long ago was that now?

'I want to know if you can help me. If this place can help me. I still have those thoughts. The ones where I want to kill myself.'

'Do you feel like that now?' he asks without hesitation. 'Suicidal?'

'No. But it has tended to come and go, over the years. Have you known anyone kill themselves?'

He feels her eyes burning into him; her body leans forward in the chair, the intensity reaching out towards him. How to answer. She cannot know about what happened before.

'No, not personally, no.' He pauses, notices her lean back a little, and adds, 'thankfully.'

She nods slowly to herself, as if reaffirming something. More silence, as he studies her blunted nails scratching at her cheeks. He wonders why Lydia unsettles him, a rare feeling. Thinks of another woman who refused to conform. There was little he could do to prevent her leaving. Sometimes, they seem to be beyond repair.

'You've not felt suicidal since you came to join us?' he asks.

She shakes her head slowly. 'No. Things are different here.' Lydia raises herself up in the chair, almost defiantly, he thinks. 'You've not come across people who feel the way I do?'

'No.' An instant, honest response. Not in this place, anyway. She stares harder, creases her eyes up a little.

'But you think you can help me?'

'Everybody helps themselves. I merely provide a sounding board. What is it you want from The Circle?'

Lydia looks behind her at the closed door, then back to S. He wonders if she is still working out why she is there. Sometimes it can take them a while.

'Just...' She bites her lip. 'I want to know more about you. If you've ever felt the same?'

Conversations can only be one way. 'We're here to talk about you, not me.'

'But I want to know more. If you have any experiences I can draw on.'

The past must stay that way. This one is too much of a questioner. He needs to tread carefully, think through how to handle her. Cut the session short. And there are other, more pressing issues than Lydia.

'Look, can we continue this another time?' he asks, projecting the smile. He stands, gestures for her to rise. 'This is obviously difficult for you. What happened. And we really do need to talk about you, not me. Maybe we can discuss it next week? Same time? We are busy on those phones out there. We need to keep up the good work. People need our help.'

She slowly pulls herself out of the chair, retreats to the door as he backs away to his desk in the corner, perching on it, adopting the relaxed leg swing.

She leans on the door handle. 'So, can we do this again soon? I have lots to ask you,' she says in a calm voice.

'Of course. Has this been helpful, this little chat?' he asks.

Her reply comes in a low tone with no emotion, as she gives another nod of the head. 'Yeah, it has. You've told me a lot.'

10

Crawley, 7th JUNE 1977

The stakeout was underway. Bodie and Doyle, *The Professionals* in action. They were in Broadfield woods, having sneaked away from the jubilee festivities, bored with childish food and party hats, escaping drunken fathers singing on trestle tables, and clinging mothers. They sought the thrill of a secret cigarette, and a look at a girlie magazine they found the week before.

Bodie could still taste the shared acrid nicotine. He brought the cigarette, Doyle the lighter. Neither were too sure how to breathe when you took one in your mouth, and after some choking, they had stubbed it out, laughing at their attempts. Maybe nobody liked them, and it was all an adult lie, a Santa Claus myth for teenagers. Not that they had reached that age yet.

They were flat on their stomachs, close to their den, spying on two boys playing by the roundabout on the ring road. Bodie wished they had some binoculars, to look more closely, to gauge the expressions on their faces. They were no more than fifty yards away. Bodie could hear Doyle's steady breathing beside him, a near constant presence in his life, inseparable for four years since they started junior school. This was the one person who hung on his words, who shared an interest in football and detective programmes. *The Professionals* theme tune played in his head; all that was missing was a walkie-talkie linked directly to George Cowley.

'Who are they?' Bodie whispered, although it would have been impossible for the other boys to hear them.

'Dunno.' Doyle shook his head.

Neither of them looked familiar, certainly didn't go to their current school. Maybe they were from the neighbourhood on the other side of the dual carriageway. It was a day of mass celebration; adults were either in the pubs or at street parties. Bodie strained to hear what the boys were saying. One had his back to them, jeans, white T-shirt, trainers, so he focused on the other. He was dressed the same, but also wore a denim jacket, waved his arms about, then took up a karate pose, fists clenched. Started aiming kicks in the air. They had seen it on *Kung Fu*. He looked about their age, had a skinhead haircut. There weren't any in their school, but you only had to look at the walls at Broadfield parade to see what they thought about the world. The nearest boy was unmoved on the road verge. Bodie felt his breath shortening. They were four actors in a secret scene. He was comfortable doing the observing.

'I never seen 'em before.' Doyle broke the silence.

'Me neither,' Bodie agreed.

Doyle edged a little closer in the undergrowth, and Bodie was reassured. This was the excitement they dreamt about, television brought to life, intensified by the secrecy of where they were hiding. Bodie hoped no adults would come along to spoil the game.

An underpass swept beneath the boys they were watching, one that they would have to take when the summer was over, to reach the legendary Thomas Bennett secondary school. But that was forever away; there was a term to finish, plus the holidays to come. Bodie could feel his calves tighten and jiggled his position. The rustling sounded like it echoed around the woods, but the boys opposite didn't look at them.

Bodie felt Doyle grab his arm when he saw the one with the jacket step forward and kick the other in the stomach, dropping him to the floor. The figure retreated and looked up and down the road. Bodie followed his gaze, saw no traffic. It could have been the dead of night; everyone was busy celebrating. The second boy slowly got to his feet, leaning forward, and rested both his hands on his knees, eyes down. The skinhead took up a karate pose again, fists clenched in front of him, looked to say something.

'What's he doing?' Bodie asked, slightly louder than before.

'Shhh,' Doyle responded, letting go of his friend. 'Let's watch.'

Bodie felt his body sink into the ground, as if something was sucking him downwards. It had rained that morning, but a couple of yards into the woods the earth was dry.

As the skinhead charged forward his target made no attempt to defend himself. Falling backwards under the weight of another kick, he was now close to the edge. As he pressed his hands into the concrete to steady himself, Bodie

51

saw a trainer drive into the boy once more. Arms flailed, legs stumbled, and the figure fell backwards, disappearing.

'Shit,' Bodie heard himself utter, and looked across at his friend, who was staring at the roundabout.

'What?' Doyle whispered.

'Shit,' Bodie repeated.

Why didn't the boy fight back? A Russian agent would have done that, wouldn't have taken the punishment. Both boys knew what lay below, where he fell. Concrete.

'Did you hear anything?' Bodie asked, meaning 'did you hear a body hit the ground?' There was no traffic noise from the road.

'Nah.'

'Me neither.'

Maybe the boy had twisted as he fell, landed on the grass verge at the side of the path underneath. Bodie ached for him to reappear, run up the side of the bank, back up to the roundabout above, laughing at his friend. They waited. The world whistled in Bodie's ears. He glanced at Doyle, who looked transfixed, staring out at the top of the underpass. Bodie tried to imagine the mess. It was quite a distance to fall, about the same as falling off the roof of his house.

He focused on the empty space where the boy had been a few seconds earlier. Movement caught his eye. He saw the attacker walking down the cycle path on the opposite side of the dual carriageway, in the direction of Southgate. He was looking around, increasing his pace. No thought to what had happened to the friend he had been playing with. Escaping. They should shout out, challenge him. Emerge from their hiding place, sprint across the field and the main road, take down the assassin. This pair of agents lay still, eyes trained on their target as he made his way along the roadside path.

A green Triumph Herald crossed on the other side of the carriageway, followed by a white van, which sounded its horn. The boy looked away as they neared him, in the direction of the spies in the woods.

'Down,' Bodie whispered. Doyle sunk further. They were already well hidden. The attacker kept on walking, increasing his pace, eyes darting. Bodie knew an agent should be forming a description, to report back to control. The short hair made him memorable, a pale face. That was all he could take in. The boy was moving his head so erratically, looking around, it was difficult to focus, to create a composite for Cowley and his team. The figure clambered over a fence and disappeared into the trees on the other side of the dual carriageway.

Bodie felt himself exhale. Had he been holding his breath all this time? Doyle's cheeks were red.

'You saw that, right?' Bodie asked.

'Yeah.'

Bodie looked at his watch. They had been gone for nearly an hour, their pathetic attempts at smoking a first cigarette, reading a soggy copy of *Knave*, and finally the stakeout filling the time. He dragged Doyle up by the shoulders.

'C'mon, let's go. We've got to get back. They'll miss us.' Doyle nodded, stood alongside him. Bodie stared at his friend's dirty jeans. 'Shit. Look at you.'

Doyle brushed the dry mud off, and shrugged, before they headed into the heart of the woods, to join what they called the 'Big Path', where the dog walkers regularly patrolled, and you had to sidestep the mess they left behind.

No thought of going in the opposite direction, towards where a young boy's injured body might be lying. Instead they sought out the safety of the street party on Bodie's cul-de-sac. Doyle followed slightly behind him, eyes lost somewhere whenever Bodie looked back. They normally went everywhere side-by-side, Bodie on the left, Doyle the right, the dynamic terror-fighting duo.

They emerged from the woods onto the concrete path that ran behind a wall along the back of their estate.

Bodie turned to his friend. 'Christ.' He held him by the elbows and Doyle looked back at him, a strange expression on his face, one he couldn't make out. He looked to be wincing, as if he was the one lying on the concrete. 'We did see that, didn't we?'

'Yeah, we did. Should we tell anyone?' Doyle asked. It sounded like he was reluctant.

Bodie thought about what they had been doing in the woods beforehand. 'No way. No bloody way. I'd be killed if they knew we were smoking. You too.' Bodie's mother hated his father for his twenty-a-day habit. She would go mental. No mention between them of the magazine.

Bodie pulled a small, cracked pack of tic-tacs from his pocket, shaking and offering. 'Here.' They took two each and crunched away at the tiny sweets, Doyle struggling to swallow.

'So, we can't say anything, right?' Bodie suggested. The consequences of being in the woods, and what they were doing, overshadowed what they had seen. The boy that fell was probably running around already, wondering where his mate had gone.

'Nah,' Doyle confirmed. That was it, then. Nobody

would know where they had been. No good would come of it.

Bodie leant back against the end wall, savouring the remains of his minted sweets. They were still out of sight of the street party, although they could hear the festivities behind them, where his road backed onto the path. He thought about the guilty pleasure of the section of the afternoon they had spent together. He couldn't wish to be with anyone else. This was his best friend; they were inseparable. They were desperate to be put in the same class when they went up to secondary school.

Doyle leant in, and kissed Bodie, half on the mouth, half on his chin, and then stepped back. Doyle's eyes were moist, sadness across his face. Before Bodie could react, his friend walked around the end of the wall without looking back, to join the street party.

Bodie touched his lips, rubbing the bottom one where part of the kiss had landed. The taste was a mixture of nicotine and mint. It had been a surprisingly light touch, and he wondered if he had imagined it. His best friend, kissing him. He struggled to breathe, stared at the spot where his friend had been standing a few seconds before. Or was it minutes now? He touched his cheeks, feeling the heat. He wiped his lips with the back of his hand, realised he was shaking. There was no wetness, just shame. He had never even kissed a girl before. Then he realised it wasn't shame, it was fear. Fear of his best friend.

His feet refused to move. He would stay hidden. Doyle, the traitor, would be out there, at the party, waiting to embarrass him. Bodie's mind returned to the figure falling from the top of the underpass. He should do something.

But this had ruined everything. With fists clenched, he walked to the corner and peered around it. There was no agent, ready to pounce. He blinked in the weak sunshine, wondering if he could wipe out the past hour and what they had seen. Or even the last few minutes. He wasn't a poof. Neither was his best friend. How could anyone who ran that fast be a queer? It wasn't possible, not Doyle.

As Bodie walked into the close, cheers greeted him. He hesitated, before realising the attention was focused on four men standing on a long table, drinking beer. One of them was his father, unsurprisingly, who had been looking forward to the day for some time. Now he was enjoying it to the full. At least someone would have pleasant memories of the jubilee. Bodie worked his way around the edge of the crowd, along the pavement, seeking safety in his own house, his bedroom, his inner thoughts. A place where nobody would know what he had seen or done that day. A place where he would be safe from his fellow agent. That kiss had sealed the silence. Neither would be able to mention the attacker kicking out, or the boy falling from the top of the underpass, not after what Doyle had done. A day to lock away and forget.

11

Crawley, November 1999

Ray picks his way through the discarded pizza boxes, plastic cartons, and billowing shopping bags up the stairs to Dusty's level. A first-floor flat in Langley Green, in a block set back from Maiden Lane. The more respectable terraces on either side look on with distaste. The smell of rotting food hits him as he climbs, a reminder of home, above a Chinese restaurant. At least there are no syringes to avoid here.

Fifty years into the experiment, and this part of town is crumbling. Mini wastelands spreading their tentacles, grabbing at the nicer districts, pulling them under. Bacteria created by town planners with no understanding of human nature. Crawley is consuming itself. Ray sees it every night in the cab. But he cannot leave. This is his town; it owns him. Where else would he go? Where else would have him?

The neatness of the window box announces number eleven, an oasis of calm. Ray makes the arranged double knock, and two kids, who should be in bed at this hour, race past him on the landing, kicking rubbish around as they go, swearing like troopers, before charging down the concrete stairs.

He reaches out to rap on the reinforced door again, but it opens, and Dusty's head sticks out, looking left and right, then beckons his visitor inside. The host is dressed in shirt and tie, polished shoes. His normal get up for a prolonged session in a virtual world. Ray follows him directly into a living room, and a giant screen that is paused in a battle zone. They both make a left turn into the kitchen, where they usually talk. Dusty offers nothing to eat or drink. Cereal is the only foodstuff Ray has seen him consume.

'You need help, then?' Dusty asks.

'You expecting me?'

Dusty shrugs. Communication is normally through a PO box, because Dusty says the government is watching, and listening. He knows this because he is doing the same to them. Ray wonders whether Dusty has been monitoring him. Knows that he could, if he wanted to. Ray gave no warning about turning up. Thought it best to wait until he had some money in his pocket.

Ray surrenders to the inevitable. 'Yeah, I've got to find someone.'

'Usual rate, Ray. You know that.'

'I know,' Ray sighs.

'Sit down, brother.'

They assume the normal positions, either side of a large table with computer screens at one end, Dusty on a swivel chair, and Ray on a stool. Ray fidgets on his perch, looks down and plays with the height adjustment. It refuses to move.

Dusty has been a regular source of information for the

past three years. Lives and works alone, how he likes it. His forte is finding things that other people have hidden. Operates out there, in what Dusty refers to as the cloud, under the name 'Dagger'. Knows Ray needs his skills. Ray is a staunch technophobe, has no computer, doesn't even own a mobile phone.

'You got the payment?' Everything is cash in hand; Dusty has never offered credit.

Ray digs into a back pocket and pulls out two tenners, drops them on the table. 'This is the deposit.' Ray stares at the notes, saddened there isn't more to give.

'Who d'you want me to find?' Dusty sounds bored. The last job must have been an easy one, discovering money squirreled away in a secret bank account for a divorce case. There are no locked doors in his world.

'It's a bit different this time.' It would be novel to provide Dusty with a challenge. 'It goes back a few years.'

'Fifty for the trace, so I need the rest to hand it over.'

'Sure.'

Ray fiddles some more with the lever, wriggling on the stool, rubs his eyes. Catches his face in a computer screen reflection. He looks tired. He always looks tired.

'So?'

'I've got a birth certificate here. Name of Michael Keane. Born in 1965. I just want to find out where he is now.' Ray carefully places the photocopy on the table, ironing out the creases with his fingers. Folds his hands. Dusty leans forward and peers at it.

'Just this?' Dusty asks.

'Is that enough?' Ray asks. He has tracked people down with less.

Dusty shrugs, turns the paper around to face him, and studies it. 'No problem.'

'This is my biggest one yet. I have to find this Keane. And everything you can about him.' No point in divulging more. Ray knows that his predicament, or opportunity, however he might describe it, will make no difference to Dusty. A search is a search.

'So, looking at this, he's what, thirty-four now? Just like you,' Dusty says.

'Yeah, I know.'

Dusty pushes the paper away to his right, literally putting the task to one side for later. For when Ray has another thirty pounds. It could be a while. 'You get it when you give me the rest,' Dusty says, as if reading Ray's mind.

The hacker stands and heads for the living room, picking up the controls on the arm of the chair. Ray studies him from the doorway. He is an extraordinary resource, has not let him down before. All it takes is the money. Ray curses the last flourish at lunchtime, twenty quid on an odds-on favourite at Haydock Park, a jockey-trainer combination he couldn't resist. The bastard pulled up two fences from home.

The letters 'S-E-G-A' disappear from the screen, and a shadow walks down a dark corridor, lit by torches. It kicks down a door and shoots two figures before they can move. Dusty's eyes are focused, the pupils dilate. Speakers in the corners echo with gunfire.

Dusty talks above the noise. 'Come see me when you have the money. I'll find him.' Another blast sees off two more attackers, and he pulls himself more upright, scans the screen, flexing his fingers on the controls.

'I need you to do this for me, Dusty. This is important.' The second he has another thirty quid, Ray is returning. Dusty looks confident he can track down Keane.

'You said.' Dusty cracks off rapid fire into a wall, which crumbles in front of him.

The hacker's mind has moved on. The killer breathes out, knowing there are more deadly enemies in waiting. On the screen, Dusty morphs into a two-headed beast, as he weaves in and out of dark alleyways. Different identities, never his own. Nobody, especially the government, knows he exists, no electronic trail. Ideally suited to tracking down those who want to stay hidden.

Ray pulls the heavy front door closed behind him. He leans over the balcony, watching the leaves dance around the pavement, blown in the wind. They have no control over where they are heading. If he can just stay out of the shops, even for a couple of days, pocket his meagre share of the taxi takings instead of wasting it, he might be able to control his own path.

If.

12

Chapter 2, 'THE DETECTIVE', FROM *THE TOWN THAT FORGOT CHILD X*, BY TRISH WATNEY

Based on interviews with Detective Inspector Des Birkdale, July 1978

At the time of the Philip Hughes case, DI Birkdale had been a police officer for twenty-five years. Most of this was served in the Metropolitan Police, but from 1972 to 1978 he headed a team at Crawley and Gatwick CID, a new division created to tackle crime at the airport and its satellite town. According to his colleagues, Birkdale was a straightforward and honest detective, someone who led them with vigour and good humour, who prided himself on keeping the streets clean. In his career, Birkdale had been involved in over a dozen murder cases, but never one involving a child.

Birkdale refused to be interviewed prior to the trial, but the progress of the investigation could be monitored via other sources within Crawley CID. At first the discovery of the body of Philip Hughes was thought to be a tragic accident, was reported as such in this newspaper. Once an appeal went out in the *Crawley Observer*, a witness to murder was identified, who later testified in court. This man spoke of seeing someone kick Philip Hughes off the scaffolding on a building site in Northgate. This witness (Alan Gregory) is examined elsewhere in this book.

When he was finally prepared to speak, largely off the record, Birkdale was still clear in his mind that Martin Sullivan was guilty.

'He told me in his own words. It wasn't in front of other witnesses, but I know what I heard. He sat there, on the end of the bed in his cell, and cried his eyes out. I've seen some things in my time, some villains I wouldn't want to meet in the street. This was one of the toughest things I ever saw. He just cried. I think he hated his mother. Earlier, she just sat there in the interview room. There was plenty of others in there, the duty solicitor, the social worker, but she barely looked at him. She knew he did it. We all knew he did it. We had a witness saw him do it.'

The former head of Crawley CID also recalled the first time he saw Sullivan.

'We went to his house, after we got the positive identification from his teacher. The mother let us in, didn't seem to be all there. Then this kid walks in the front door, with his key – this was in school time, he was bunking off – he sees us (Birkdale and DC Jimmy Wood) and legs it. The innocent don't run.'

According to other sources at Crawley CID, Martin Sullivan was first interviewed for four hours over two periods in one day in late September. His solicitor and either his mother or social worker were present, in the main interview room at Crawley police station. In that time, Sullivan gave minimal answers to their questions, according to Birkdale.

'The solicitor, Merrick, he kept reminding the boy he didn't have to say anything. The kid looked scared. Scared of what he'd done, and the consequences. That's why he said nothing to start with. He kept looking at his mother, and she just sat there, smoking, never looking back. Like she knew he had done something terrible. Like he was evil. Merrick was interfering, but that's what they always do. And this kid stonewalled us. To start with.'

This apparently changed after being left alone in a cell for half the night.

'He had something to eat, a bit of sleep, we looked in on him regularly. Best cell we got. Then, late at night, one of my team comes running in, saying he wants to talk. To talk to me, on my own. We tried to find the social worker, but she had gone hours before. We called the solicitor, but no reply. So, I just went in there to talk to him, all calm and friendly. He was very chatty now. Didn't want his mum to know we were talking. And he just spilt it all, told me everything, right there, on the cell bed. It's all in the statement read out in court. He admitted it.'

When asked what he thought Sullivan's motivation was for killing another child, Birkdale was defensive.

'We didn't focus on that. Wasn't that important. He admitted he did it. He started talking about *Star Wars*, some character in it, how he and Philip Hughes argued about who would play who in their game. They had a fight and he deliberately kicked him off the scaffolding to his death. It was all there in court, in his words. I know some of you hacks think we make stuff up, but this is genuine. The boy admitted it. Saddened me, it did. That a kid could do such a thing. No remorse, that was the thing that really got me. He never said sorry, even when he confessed. Only sorry for himself, he was.'

The lack of any interest in why Child X killed is troubling. Why would the police not be interested in a motive? Not look further than the thought that this was a game that turned too violent? The prosecution didn't even cover this in court. And neither did the defence barrister.

Note: need to re-interview Birkdale to ask the following:
Who wrote up the confession? Does it still exist in the police files?
What is his view about the sentencing?

13

Crawley, November 1999

Driving a cab for over twenty hours without a break. Eating nothing but peanuts and crisps. Staring into the relentless night, thinking he is starting to lose sense of time. Essential for Ray, so that his hacker friend can continue his work.

He was close to having the rest of the fee in his hands. Took a decision any self-respecting gambler would, by backing a favourite. Stared at the racing pages for so long his eyes started to water. Carefully placed what he had on a sure-fire winner at Wincanton. The bastard jockey fell off at the last with the race in the bag. Back to square one; hence more of the night shift, day shift and any other bloody shift Stefan can put his way. Ray retains just ten per cent of the legitimate taxi fares but receives a flat five quid for every one of their more dubious drop offs.

The latest is a young woman who mumbles something in an Eastern European accent, and hands Ray a greasy slip of paper. Stefan has already told him where they are heading, so there is no need to read the address, and he drops it into the tray to his left for safety. She slips onto the back seat, extreme heels silenced, excuse for a skirt rustling and covering little, smelling like a chemical incident. The brothers have made it clear he is never to interfere with the cargo. She is made up to look twenty-five, probably as young as fifteen. They are in Bewbush, on Breezehurst Drive, where it curves away from The Dorsten, a pub to avoid at the best of times. An area of mean streets with soggy leaves cluttering the gutters, graffiti on the walls announcing casual racism. No sane person would walk there after dark, let alone wait for a taxi in a glass-shattered bus shelter.

Ray cannot judge. Some of the packages don't seem to do any harm. He simply transfers a product from one place to another. If it wasn't him, somebody else would get paid to be the courier. Obviously, he would rather be a legitimate private eye than a blind mule, but he still needs to get by, even if he has a lifeline. He will always be chasing the win that brings him back to the surface. There are occasional snatches of air, fuelling the invincible punter inside, offering hope. Leckie Harris might have thrown him a float, but he still needs to earn.

Her destination is in Gossops Green, no more than a couple of miles away. Rother Crescent curves its way in the shape of its name through the middle of the neighbourhood, covered in forlorn blocks of terraces at varying angles to the road. This target house is slightly different to those around it. Boarded up on the ground floor, shadows illuminated at an upstairs window. The dashboard tells Ray it has just gone midnight. A can clatters past and settles on a muddy patch of grass outside the house. The wasteland looks deserted, even though there must be life behind the doors.

His passenger totters out on high heels to do Lord knows what, probably to pay for her passage to this country. Morality is a complicated thing, and he prefers not to get too involved. It is best to focus on his own position; she is someone else's problem. The police must choose to ignore the trafficking, a well-known part of life in a town so close to an airport and the coast. He is just delivering a fare, if asked.

Asif on the radio reminds him that he has three quarters of an hour before the next scheduled collection, on the industrial estate, so Ray pulls away slowly. Rather than complete the loop, he retraces his route, takes a left onto Gossops Drive, heading north.

A lone woman stands on the corner where it meets Buckswood Drive, holding out her hand. She has no coat, just a short-sleeved top, tight leather trousers and ridiculous heels. It has started to sleet, and the sky threatens more on top of the icy cold, so he stops. It is strictly phone bookings for Ray; street pickups are only for the registered Hackney cabs. He pulls over to her side of the road, checking for police in his mirrors.

There must be a heart beating deep inside the loser somewhere. As he winds the window down, she steps up to the door, shivering. She looks as young as the girl he just dropped off. Another vulnerable woman, in a dodgy area.

'Creasys Drive, please,' is all she says, in a local accent.

Ray looks up and down the street. 'A fiver.'

Her reply is to slip into the back seat, shuffling across to the passenger side. Ray tries to smile reassuringly in the mirror. Decision made. This fare will be off the books, cash in hand.

He will have to double back to Broadfield, but can fit her in before the next collection, if he puts his foot down. She looks and sounds sober, which is unusual at this time of night. Her destination might be a little too close to the Lemon Tree pub, but the world he let a young girl walk into just now makes him feel he should redress the balance. He is still a part of this town. And if he sticks this fiver on a six-to-one shot, Dusty will have the rest of his fee, and he can get moving with Michael Keane. She says nothing more, the light from her mobile phone illuminating her face, as she studies it, pressing buttons.

'Seatbelt?'

'Oh, yeah,' she says, not looking up from her screen.

A blow catches him on the side of the head from his right. Before Ray can take in what has happened, he is struck again on the jaw. The window is still down, and as he looks across, a pair of hands reach in and grab him by the neck. The blood pulses in his temples, and he struggles to focus. Ray shoves his hands up to push the attacker away, and the grip slips. He lunges out of the window, and the assailant takes a step back. Then the true nature of the assault hits him. Reaching for the float, he paws at thin air. Looking across to his left, he sees that somebody has beaten him to it, from the passenger side. Two new thieving hands pull away. Ray swings his head from side to side, but there are no faces. There is also no girl in the back now; her seatbelt never made it across.

Distraction, and a good heart, have cost him. A cab driver's immediate response, when you have been scammed, is to give chase. Two men are already thirty yards ahead, running towards the local school. Beyond that is the Dower

Estate, not the roughest, but harsh enough. A place where they will be lost for good, if they make it that far. The one carrying the float looks back, wide-eyed, and shrieks at Ray. The words are lost in the thin night air. Ray focuses on pounding his legs towards them. What is he expected to do, just give up on the money? Desperate to get it back, within a few strides he pauses, realises he has left the hammer behind. It sits under the driver's seat for this very situation. Pursuit is now his only option.

Burning with anger, fucking furious they have the brass neck to rob him, and that this is happening again, Ray drives on, closing. Do they know who he works for these days? This flashes through his head, and out again. These toe rags wouldn't give a shit, and neither would Leckie Harris. That money belongs to the Mirkovic brothers. Not a wise move. But he also knows the onus is on him to retrieve it.

The thieves split up, and Ray hesitates, losing ground as one goes left, the other right at the end of the road, approaching a low wooden fence on the edge of the school grounds. His eyes are fixed on the one with the float, but he is the fastest, unimpeded by what he is carrying. Pain hits Ray's chest, then his thighs. He gasps for air but must keep going.

The two men both take the obstacle in one leap, the thief with the float throwing the metal box over ahead of him. It lands on the ground with a clang, and he stoops to retrieve it, starts running again. Ray stumbles at the fence, levering himself over by a metal post, doesn't have the bravado of their youth. Curses himself for his lack of fitness. Sport is for betting on, not taking part.

He sets off towards the one carrying nothing, then corrects himself in a few strides. Legs scream at him to stop, but the money is his responsibility. Probably only ninety quid in there, a fraction of it his. Money he could win back on a maiden hurdle with ease. But something pushes him on. Perhaps the face of Stefan, and his impatient brother. His target dashes across the school fields, dimly highlighted by the dull glare from the buildings. He isn't laughing now and keeps glancing back, faltering, weighed down at last by the takings.

Approaching a wire fence, where the school borders on the estate, the thief veers right to run parallel to it, searching for a way out. Ray corrects his angle of attack, closing in. His heart feels like it will burst out of his chest. He launches a dive, like a rugby full back, JPR Williams in full flight, targeting the legs. He catches a foot, just as the thief makes to squeeze through a gap in the fence. Ray pulls hard, and the man wriggles free, leaving him holding just a muddy trainer.

When he gets back to his feet, the robber and the float have vanished into the rabbit warren of the Dower. Ray slumps down, all the fight gone from his body, staring at the shoe. An expensive Reebok. Serve the fucker right. Maybe he should hand it to Marko as evidence, so he can go and play Cinderella on the estate.

He throws the trainer from the sitting position across the deserted playing field, and it turns in the air, laces spinning, before landing in the mud with a soft splat. He has failed again, more bad luck. Ray pulls his knees up to his chest, shivers in the cold night air. Shouts ring out from behind the fence, and footsteps echo as if they are heading up stairs, to safety.

Ray's car is in one piece when he returns to the street, a smidgen of fortune. Leaving doors wide open around there at night is not the best idea. There is also no meaningless destruction of wing mirrors, or keys scratched down the side, an advantage to having a beaten-up motor. What's the point in vandalising it when it already looks like a gang of joyriders have just dumped it? He curses his stupidity, chasing that extra fiver, knowing the dangers, but not locking the doors or moving away faster. Making their job easier, leaving the window down. He has been on the cabs long enough to know the odds were poor; she hit a soft spot.

He examines the facial damage in the driver's mirror, having wound up the window and locked the doors. Blood on his cheek and swelling to go with it. Now the adrenaline has been used up, breathing comes in short bursts, ribs feel like they are being crushed. Must be the rugby tackle. But it is the pride that hurts the most. He switches the radio on and tells Asif the news. His collection has been put back an hour; they will wait.

Reflected at Ray is a casualty of wrong place, wrong time. The victim of a town where desperation lurks at every turn. Michael Keane has gained a short reprieve. More hours behind the wheel, and he can make the money back. Throw in a decent priced winner, and that will be accelerated. He feels under the seat, finding the hammer is still there. But there is a gut-wrenching gap where the money was, and no sign of the woman who lured him into an obvious trap.

Looking back up at the mirror, the sobs begin. Real men don't cry. But how long is it since he was a man anyway?

Wiping away the tears, there is a moment of clarity. He is to blame for this. The debts, the immoral tasks he performs. The fact that he has no friends left from the old days, all either moved away or driven to shun him by their partners or wives, because of his habit. He must stop. Crying in a beaten-up old car is no way to react. A guardian angel has offered him an opportunity. He must grasp it and stop wasting his life.

Ray pulls away from the kerb and heads north to the next faceless collection, starting again as he has done so many times.

14

Milton Keynes, November 1999

He stirs his drink and studies the group members, busy chatting away into their headsets, soothing the complaints, pushing the policies. That tiny, nagging worry about whether anybody can tell, simply by looking at him, never goes away.

He is so overloaded with secrets, stories, and outright lies, the truth can become difficult to recognise. Trained to guard against revealing clues, projecting stories that force the old facts deep inside. What they say he did won't go away, but he can bury it deep enough not to be seen.

There is a fresh narrative now, one deeply embedded. The experts started the cycle of reinvention, reacting to campaigns, the name changes, teaching him how to hide. He smiles and nods at a couple of the group who head outside for a smoke.

The broader debates are still there, thanks to two kids from Liverpool and their crime, but the clamour for the head of Child X has disappeared. Interest has waned, he is hidden in the crowd now, fifteen years on from release. Accepted by society, appropriate boxes ticked. If not forgiven, certainly forgotten.

Even though he is several times removed from the original identity, he still needs to tread carefully. It can be tiring, always being on your guard, even though it has become second nature. Remembering the story, knowing that a false move could lead to that tap on the shoulder or the punch in the guts. Every new set of eyes has the potential to be a traitor of the past, someone who might recognise the face, the boy, the killer. That is why stillness is everything. But eventually someone will ask you the question. The final judgement said he was rehabilitated. Fit to participate in society. Penance served.

Lydia is a concern. She is an asker of questions. Probing away, picking at the corners, trying to see underneath. She is a danger. Newcomers must be watched carefully.

He looks across at her desk, sees her absorbed in a call, tapping at her keyboard, taking notes. Her head nods as she types, her lips moving silently from a distance, behind the tiny mic. Lydia looks up and stares through him, returns her concentration to the screen in front of her.

For years after his release there were so many changes. Probation workers and analysts, different names, all ensuring he stuck to the terms of his licence. He was educated, then liberated, through their therapy and training. Eventually the liaison officers cut him loose in the world, once he had proven his ability to stay in the shadows. Undertaken the social trials, held down a job, blended in. Society had washed its hands of that evil boy, years after the crime. He was free to mould himself into a new character.

When the smokers return, he turns his back, rinses his cup in the sink, dries and replaces it in the rack with the others. The wall in front of him contains various notices, birthday lists, the cleaning tasks they share, pinned up with coloured tacks. He smiles to himself, remembering the counters on his board of Risk, laid out at home, mid-game.

Time is one thing you have plenty of in detention. Time for yourself. Playing board games became his escape, somewhere you would follow the rules, obey the boundaries, take all the roles. Red is far ahead in his current game, although coming under increased attack from Green. The other four contenders are digging in, ready to defend themselves. He treats them all fairly; the roll of the dice dictates the outcome. Over the years, Blue has the most victories, Yellow the regular loser. He notices that most of the pins on the board in front of him are also blue.

Games of Risk can stretch out for weeks at a time, which was part of the appeal, once he had accrued enough credits for a set of his own. The edges of his box are held together with Sellotape now, but there is no need to upgrade; it has survived with him, moving every time. It provides both comfort and a reminder of how far he has travelled.

Back then, any personal item was a target for abuse or destruction. If someone found a way inside your room, they would go for your weakness. One kid scrawled 'psycho' all over his first Monopoly set in black marker. The lad was moved on soon after, but this was another wake-up call, to keep his details secret, stick to the arson story, respond to the nickname of 'Firebug'. Reveal nothing personal. An infamous past merely attracted the attention of the unhinged, those desperate to climb the ranks, gain notoriety. If you were careful, and avoided the television room, close contact was limited to mealtimes. He sat next to warders whenever he could. His room became a sanctuary, and games his means of escape.

As he turns back towards the open plan, he catches Lydia's eye again, offers her another smile. Drops the connection when he reaches his door, returning to another room where he can control the environment, ready to play his part in taking the group forwards, outwards, and preserving their safety.

15

Crawley, November 1999

Approaching his office door, Ray pauses. There are small, patterned clumps of mud on the floor outside from the soles of boots. Boots of men who bury people in the woods.

Looking through the frosted glass, there are no human outlines, and the room is so small there are no corners to hide in. Ray needs two hands to turn the key, to stop himself from shaking. Nobody jumps him. It doesn't seem like there have been any intruders. Ray looks back outside to the marks on the floor. A strange business.

He breathes in and has another sharp reminder about the cab attack. Coughing brings more pain, so Ray closes his door carefully and sinks into his best chair, the one for visitors. It doesn't swing, but at least the arms still work.

This tiny place offers an escape from the world, behind a door with no name, above West Green parade. This is one of the better-appointed neighbourhoods in town, meaning no more than two of the shops at street level have had their windows smashed this year. Visitors are rare, but if you are a gumshoe, you need a meeting point where the glamorous blondes come to cry about their cheating husbands, the hoods come to threaten you, and the lunatics come to piss in your waste paper bin. In his six years as a private investigator, Ray has only experienced one of those three. It was days before the smell went away.

The metal chest of drawers is jammed shut, no key. The microwave on top acts as the real filing system. Ray runs a finger over the dust on the microwave's door, tuts to himself. His desk is clear, apart from an ancient answering machine, orange light unblinking. There is no need for clutter, to allow his office to descend into a cliché. Ray comes here to do his thinking. His rented studio flat is only slightly larger than the room, sits above a Chinese takeaway in Furnace Green, and is not conducive to solving mysteries, or tracking down missing persons. Private investigators don't tend to work through the complexities of a case with the smell of chow mein invading their every thought.

A poster of Sam Spade frowns down, an icon Ray has latched on to. It is there for the clients, to lend an air of credence. He can't help thinking that Bogart disapproves of how this career has panned out and avoids eye contact. Ray fell into the private detection game, but remembers time as a kid following imaginary assassins, spies, and gangsters, lurking in the shadows. Is constantly surprised that he has taken up this shady way of life.

Maybe he hasn't shown enough ambition. Few people seem to know he is there, despite the business cards dotted around local newsagents. This is a sleepwalking town, with only one sleepy private eye.

Footsteps echo on the concrete landing, and then there

is a rustle as the source shuffles to a stop. A large figure looms at the door, rattles the handle, then turns it, opening inwards. There is a way out, through the window, down the fire escape, but Ray has been seen. He jumps up and moves to the safety of the other side of the desk, leaning against the back of his chair, to hold himself steady. A river of sweat runs down his backbone. There is nothing worth stealing.

As the door swings fully open, Ray recognises the suit who accompanied him and Leckie Harris on their walk.

'Raymond?'

He nods eagerly.

'I have something for you from Mister Harris.' The visitor looks around the office, shaking his head, knowing Ray isn't going anywhere.

The bulking figure steps forward and blocks out the light from the landing. Ray hopes he hasn't come for the expenses. Only two quid left in his pocket, another dry afternoon in the bookies, chasing his tail, throwing bad money after bad. Four hundred and ninety-eight short, then.

His visitor just stands there, arms folded. 'Mister Harris was wondering how you were doing?' The face creases, lips narrow. Maybe Leckie employs him because he matches up to the stereotype. The hands are clean this time. No burying bodies today, at least not yet.

'Oh, good, good. Nearly there.'

'Really?' Bushy eyebrows rise momentarily, and a thin smile emerges.

'Yeah. We are narrowing things down nicely.'

'Well, don't forget. Mister Harris wants to find him by Christmas Day.' No picking up on the use of the word, 'we'. The smile has gone.

'I know.' The focus on the task is returning to Ray, although he is still rooted to his position behind the chair.

'He has a message for you. Something else for you to do. Not too difficult, he says.' *Here we go, the big fuck-off catch*, Ray thinks. Clients do this, change the brief. He sighs and wipes his hands on the back of his chair. The minder looks at the poster behind Ray, inclining his head, then stares back at him. 'You need to give him the history of our missing person as well. What he's been up to for the past twenty years.'

'Twenty years?' Ray's voice rises to an embarrassingly high pitch.

'Yeah, twenty years. Mister Harris was very insistent.'

Ray focuses on breathing in and out. Dusty should be able to help there as well. And when he can't reach into the murky corners with his fingers and keyboard, Ray can do the legwork. As a combination, it tends to be effective. If only there was more missing persons work like it around. Just one ongoing case, apart from Keane – a messy divorce.

The figure leans forward and places something wrapped in a brown paper bag onto the desk. Unfortunately for Ray, it isn't more money. 'Here. Look after this. Mister Harris wants you to keep it on at all times. So he can keep in touch with you.'

Ray unwraps it and finds a mobile phone. He has never bothered with them. Not after all the scare stories Dusty has given him, about people listening in. Then there is the cost. It would also have been something else the Mirkovic brothers could damage, or destroy, in lieu of debts. Ray stares at it, runs his fingers over the protruding buttons. They are oddly smooth to the touch. The screen lights up, and he places it face down on the desk. Dusty said they could be used to track where you are, something like that.

'Yeah, he wants you to keep it with you. So he can be informed immediately when you find our man. There's a charger too. Keep it on.' The instruction is terse and to the point.

'I will.'

'Nobody knows you've got it, or where it came from.' Leckie's man looks up suddenly, as if he has just realised there are more important things to do than hassle a private investigator.

'Right. Mind how you go,' he says, as he walks to the door. 'Remember, keep Mister Harris posted.'

The door shakes as he closes it, and Ray fears for the glass. As the footsteps fade down the stairs, Ray looks out of the window down to the shopping parade below. He catches sight of the man, walking towards a black Audi in the car park. The front door opens, and he climbs inside without looking back.

Ray breathes out at last. Still not ready to face his fears. How did he end up in this job, in this life? When he left school, work was easy to find in Crawley. Careers advisors were redundant. 'Take the bus to Gatwick, son,' they might as well have said. 'Stand there, put your hand out, and start on Monday.'

Everyone was hiring, and the first place he looked was security. It was a tough profession in the eighties. You had to stay alert in front of those screens. Anything could disappear from a warehouse at night. The real rules of the job quickly became clear, which was to know precisely when to look the other way. Learning how to go missing when asked. By the time Ray started in the trade, security was run by the Greeks and the Turks, rather than the local villains.

He was eventually fired from one of the cushiest numbers in the whole airport. An offer came that was too good to refuse, given the growing debts. These were Brighton Cypriots who had done their homework, knew he had a soft underbelly. No choice but to be somewhere else for a couple of hours, when he should have been guarding cargo. Except the idiots got caught, and questions were asked about how they knew the security man would be missing when they struck. There aren't many places to go if you are a failed security guard, so Ray took up with the investigation business. Six years, and still barely a private eye pot to piss in.

He must deserve more than this. Perhaps the visit from Leckie Harris is fate giving him a hand. An escape route from purgatory at last.

Ray weighs the mobile phone in his palm, wonders at modern technology. Maybe he should be embracing the new world, the coming millennium. Buy a computer when the debts are cleared. Sort out his paperwork. He opens the microwave door and peers inside. No bills, in fact nothing other than the GA orange book.

The corners are worn, victims of repeated consultation when he joined Gamblers Anonymous. The small pamphlet is given to everyone in their first week. Now he has seen how the group works, it has been ignored. There are some unsettling religious statements inside, and only one aspect ever seemed to be of any value.

The twenty questions on the inside cover draw Ray's attention. They were encouraged to revisit them regularly. Given that Leckie Harris is turning his life upside down, offering a way out, he answers them out loud to an empty office.

Q: Do you lose time from work due to gambling?

A: Rarely. I can easily fit gambling around the work patterns. I drive a lot at night, when the betting shops are closed. There's always time to slip into a bookies'. And lots of them in this town.

Q: Is gambling making your home life unhappy?

A: It's already ruined. Steph left me years ago, after one more 'last chance' to get myself sorted out. I let her down countless times.

Q: Is gambling affecting your reputation?

A: Not much reputation to protect. I don't think anyone knows I gamble, apart from the bastards I used to owe money to. Cabbies are the lowest form of life; everyone treats you like shit.

Q: Have you ever felt remorse after gambling?

A: Regularly. Every time I lose.

Q: Do you ever gamble to get money with which to pay debts or to otherwise solve financial difficulties?

A: Life is a financial difficulty. I'm in this mess because of the debts and have the debts because I'm in a mess.

Q: Does gambling cause a decrease in your ambition or efficiency?

A: I've no ambition and have always been inefficient. There was that cushy security job once, but I blew that.

Q: After losing, do you feel you must return as soon as possible and win back your losses?

A: Yes. You can't lose forever; your luck has to change. Even a monkey can pick a winner every now and again.

Q: After a win do you have a strong urge to return and win more?

A: Yes, of course. Make the most of it.

Q: Do you often gamble until your last pound is gone?

A: Until the last penny.

Q: Do you ever borrow to finance your gambling?

A: You have to. Only some banks lose patience and force you to look elsewhere.

Q: Have you ever sold anything to finance gambling?

A: My soul? Seriously, a few LPs, but I have never had much to sell. When I was younger, I did get five hundred quid for my car, and the proceeds lasted one afternoon at Plumpton races.

Q: Are you reluctant to use gambling money for normal expenditures?

A: I'd prefer to reinvest winnings on racing. I did go without eating for three days earlier this year. Two quid on trap four or a sandwich? The former usually wins (or doesn't).

Q: Does gambling make you careless of the welfare of your family?

A: I couldn't give a toss what happens to Steph now. I might drive past her house sometimes, to see if that moron in his Vectra is there, but that's just idle curiosity. Mum was all right, last time I visited.

Q: Do you gamble longer than you planned?

A: Only if I'm either winning, or a big win is just around the corner. Or come to think of it, if I'm losing too.

Q: Do you ever gamble to escape worry or trouble?

A: It's an escape from absolutely everything. The only time I feel truly alive.

Q: Have you ever committed, or considered committing, an illegal act to finance gambling?

A: I commit enough crimes as a private eye and cabbie. Watching a favourite fall at the last never made me break and enter or bug somebody's office. Gambling never directly forced me to traffic prostitutes or drugs.

Q: Does gambling cause you to have difficulty in sleeping?

A: Yes. I have to work nights on top of the day job. Sleep has been a stranger lately.

Q: Do arguments, disappointments, or frustrations create an urge within you to gamble?

A: A need to gamble makes me want to gamble. All the frustration and disappointment comes from losing. Or not winning enough when I do win.

Q: Do you have an urge to celebrate any good fortune by a few hours' gambling?

A: When the good fortune is related to a good win, yes.

Q: Have you ever considered self-destruction as a result of your gambling?

A: If this means killing myself, then no. If it means increasing my debts with Serbian thugs with no qualms about breaking my kneecaps, then yes.

The book says that most compulsive gamblers answer 'yes' to at least eight of these questions. Ray thinks he might be over the limit. In truth, the answer to many of them is, 'it depends'. You could substitute something else for gambling, and it would be just as appropriate for many people. Sexual desire. Booze. Drugs. At least betting is socially acceptable. If anybody were to ask Ray, he would simply point at how everyone joins in with the Grand National.

The temptations are everywhere. Newspapers, television, sport, all of it dragging you in. Gambling machines in the shops, shouting at you, press this, nudge that, lights declaring love. Three cubicles for placing your bets for every one that delivers a payout. They all study the odds; they should know. But there is so much fun to be had. High streets are littered with bookmakers; society condones what they do.

Ray can't find anything from this set of questions to change the way he is, or his situation. It is what it is. Gamblers spend their whole lives lying to themselves. Ray has years of practice, starting as a kid making racing predictions, looking up results the next day in his old man's *Daily Mirror*, deceiving himself he was picking winners.

He screws up the orange booklet, and tosses it into the waste basket, where it settles, scrunched and defeated.

16

god not run as fast not ever. you member when we
used to sprint cross the field of desmond anderson
and how fast you wood run it was like that only
faster you would chase me i wood dodge and weve
and zig zag and i know you pretended to chase me
and you could catch me danny if you wanted to. this
time i ran so fast could feel the wind in my ears
and it wistled so loud it stopped the shaking and
the exitement was running though me so hard it felt
great danny. we was fighting and i didnt want them
to catch me he woodnt let me be Obi so i showed him
danny he been at me all day the spanner just on me
all day so i showed him and down he went and i just
ran and he didnt move he must be dead.

she dont care no more since you went danny no
matter what i do i might as well be invisibal. so long
as im in bed when she gets back from the pub thats
all that she cares about. maybe i can come and join

you danny maybe i can come and join up like you did maybe thats the best thing to do. will they take young recrutes? let me now if they do. you new who i was you new what i was up to. you cared. she dont give a damn she dont even want her son any more she not missing you danny i can tell you that she couldnt give a fuck about us any more.

she is got to notise me now. yesterday i came in she was on the sette with a mans hand in her fanny dont know his name and she just shouted at me just his hand in her fanny and didnt care. so i ran off to the park and thats where i saw the boy from today the boy that fell. why did she do this danny you wood know. the bitch just does it to embrass me get me to hate her well it working danny. so today i made sure she notised me she cant forget me now she has to think about me.

dad wood put her in her place like he used to he wood dont forget me danny im not forgeting you. you shoud tell me whats happening in the army.

17

Milton Keynes, November 1999

The birthday party has been reduced to two people. Thirteen began the evening, in a Harvester pub, a humble setting for humble people. Celebrating birthdays is an important element within The Circle. Not biological ones, but anniversaries of when they joined the group. This night belongs to Carl Marsh, one year old, and he and Lydia are the final members left after a large number disappeared when he was in the toilet.

Lydia chinks her shot glass at Carl's, which sits on the table. He knows he has had enough, is in hazardous waters. If he sticks to the cider, he can control himself. An important factor. But half an hour earlier Lydia moved them onto something new. She is something new. A woman who seems to be interested in him.

'Come on, Carl. Don't lag behind.'

He brings the glass to his lips, the smell making his stomach lurch. Knows a couple more of these, and he will be on the floor, or kneeling over the toilet. He sips, lips tingling. Lydia laughs, a hand across her mouth, wobbles on her stool opposite.

'In one, Carl, come on.'

He knocks it back, feels the burn in his throat, swallows hard. He chokes, laughs, and she joins him, bending over opposite. She looks up and he shivers. Carl wonders how she copes. He needs to act, to stop her ordering more.

Lydia is the newcomer, but there is something different about her. She asks questions of everyone, always probing, digging. Particularly interested in S, something he had put down to physical attraction, a phase he now suspects many of the women in the group have gone through. A desire to get closer to the man who leads them through their lives. It is no surprise that most of those who stay in the group are female.

Not that Carl has a reference point for normality when it comes to women. Personal relationships are discouraged in The Circle, but since he took up the new role, Lydia has given him more attention, made eye contact, bumped into him in the kitchen area when she can. Carl now waits until she starts a sales call before making a drink, so he can avoid her. But here, in the pub, under lacklustre lighting, there is no escape.

Her foot rubs his under the table, a fleeting touch moving up to the ankle. Carl pulls his feet back beneath him. Looks across the pub at a couple with their hands linked, lips almost touching. Wonders if that is what love feels like. If that is how it is displayed.

Lydia stares at him, forehead creased, a serious expression. 'Carl, I need to ask you something.'

'Go on.' Carl plays with his shot glass, turns it upside down, watches a trickle of clear liquid run down, is suddenly thankful that talking will mean less drinking.

'Your new job. What do you do?'

'I order the stationery.' No need to provide more.

'Really?' She snorts, hand over her nose. 'Yeah, right.'

'Just office management.'

'Come off it. Really, what do you do?'

What is it with her and all the questions? Carl thinks to himself. Out loud, though, he plays along. 'You really want to know?'

'Yeah. I want to know what you do in that room all day. Most of the day, anyway. You on the internet? Looking at something you shouldn't?'

'No.'

Carl struggles to work out exactly how Tiny Tim filled his days. Has started to mix his new role with periods back on the phones, out in the open plan, to maintain his sanity. No challenge from S to this, as their leader has been missing all week.

Carl has read all the files, listened in to calls. Read the boring emails that go back and forth. Knows Ruth is having an affair with a woman who works for National Rail. Cannot see the point of his role.

Lydia pokes his nose with a finger. 'Come on, tell me. Do you spy on him? On Simon?'

'No.'

'But you do on us?'

Carl rubs his lips with an unsteady hand, tastes the alcohol again.

'Yep.'

She doesn't appear shocked. 'Why not spy on him?'

Her question is a surprise. 'Why would I?'

Carl has wondered why there are cameras everywhere,

apart from S's office. Was intrigued to find there is nothing on the system regarding their leader, not even a personnel file. If it wasn't for swipe cards, and the occasional piece of video footage of him entering and leaving the building, you wouldn't know S was there.

'He's one of us. Same distance from the centre, and all that,' she says, her foot reaching out under the table, stroking his leg below the knee again.

Carl shrugs. Lydia is the first person he has heard question S aloud.

'What do you see in him?' Carl asks. He wishes he knew what the appeal was. Is confident that his own fake support is believed, a year in. Looking into her face, suddenly has a suspicion that Lydia might be hiding her thoughts too. The newbie who doesn't quite belong there.

'Not what you see,' she replies, eyes darker.

'I don't see anything.'

'No, you wouldn't, since you're spying on us and not him.'

Carl looks at her more closely, as she gazes off towards the bar. Lydia fiddles with her hair, twists it in her fingers.

'Don't you think there's more to him than meets the eye?' she asks. Carl swallows, tastes the alcohol again. Lydia presses on. 'That there might be more to Simon Paterson than he lets on.' Looking back at him now.

'How did you know his surname?'

Lydia folds her arms across her chest. 'I just do.'

Carl studies her, thinks about the stray foot that has been playing with his leg. Has no reference points for this. Returns to the techniques they gave him, pictures the gulls swooping in the sky.

'Why do you think there's more to him?' Carl asks, understanding that his own doubts have been there for some time. That there might be something lurking behind that need for followers. They all unburden their souls to S, but he struggles to see what the others get in return. And the man they follow so faithfully has been absent all week, and Carl has had nobody to discuss this with, until now. Realises that this was why he took the new role. The need to get closer, to understand what their leader is doing.

Lydia leans forward into the space between them, stroking his arm gently. 'I know something about his past. What he used to be. Let me get you another drink.'

18

Crawley, December 1999

The BMW saloon picks its way among the potholes down the track towards the Nissen huts. The fog gently shifts and swirls like a slow-moving ghost in Tilgate Woods. Ray dims his own lights, following safely from a distance. The councillor's wife told him her husband would be working late. His secretary is in the front with him. A strange place to finish off the paperwork.

Ray watched them two days earlier, discreetly, from a corner in The Plough, over in Rusper, a village a few miles out of town. Hands touching across the table, the delicate stroking of a palm, thinking they were unseen. The pub was half-empty, barely a glance around in case they were being observed. His own disguise, an itchy fake beard and glasses. Ray is astonished at the arrogance of a man unable to spot his tail, despite them having met before.

This is his only other live case apart from Keane, and it is about to end, if he can catch them at it. Role reversal now, as Peter Bevan initially asked Ray to follow his wife, Kathleen.

Suspecting there was another man. Would probably have a heart attack if he knew she was a lesbian. And here Bevan is, fooling around with his secretary, nearly twenty years younger. God knows what she sees in him. Ray has been several rows back from the councillor and this woman on a ghost train at Horsham fair, even listened outside a hotel door in Copthorne. And Bevan seems to have no idea the private detective he hired has enough photographs to incriminate him many times over. All Kathleen wants is a final piece of hard evidence, she says, with no hint of irony. Forty quid when Ray delivers it. Ray needs the money to meet up with Dusty, discover where this Keane is.

The second half of the case started after Kathleen Bevan caught Ray following her, doubling back to confront him at a bus stop, after she spent a couple of hours at another woman's flat. Initial outrage on her part, before Ray explained the situation. Kathleen turned things to her advantage. He has met Eunice now; they seem a nice couple. Ray is working the same assignment from both ends. Except he doesn't think the councillor is going to be happy with the results. All he has passed that way is that his wife is not sleeping with another man. Sometimes you need to pick sides, and Ray opted for hers. She pays promptly, and her husband shows a great reluctance to cough up.

The councillor's car comes to a stop outside the battered old huts. Ray parks a hundred yards behind, killing his lights. People think private investigation is a glamorous job, but they forget the time spent eating stale food in cars, the desperate attempts to stay warm and hidden, the skill of simply watching and waiting. He wipes the pasty crumbs off his fingers on the steering wheel, wondering how much longer he can take the tedium of such a lowly occupation. Knowing that the rewards are so small. Until the Keane case. Tries to focus on the vehicle ahead. After ten minutes, Ray is certain they are not going to drive further into the woods.

The fog lifts, half a moon shining down, pale and insignificant, barely making an impact through the trees. He pulls his coat around him, carrying the equipment over his shoulder, slowly picking a path in the trees along the edge of the track towards them. Two figures in the front seats. Their car radio plays a soft ballad. They won't hear him approach.

Ray crouches down at the rear of the car. It rocks a little, the music inside pauses then begins again. He thinks he hears a groan, but it could be the wildlife. The camcorder is lifted above his head, and the red recording light shines back at its operator. The viewfinder helps him focus. They could be anyone from this angle, just the work of a peeping tom, of no use to Kathleen Bevan.

He shuffles round the car on his haunches until he is level with the passenger door, then moves back a few feet. No need to get too close. Ray lifts the camcorder again, so he can focus in on both the driver and passenger. On his screen, Peter Bevan's face appears from side on, contorted, eyes closed, facing the front. He scans down a fraction, and blonde hair bobs gently up and down in the recording. The dirty bastard. Ray holds his breath. Getting both in the same shot is the aim. After a few seconds, his calves start to ache, then pain shoots down the right leg, forcing him to stretch and stand. He pushes his foot into the ground, the camcorder briefly pointing at the sky, then back across at the courting couple. Peter Bevan's eyes meet those of his hired detective, face freezing in horror. The top of the blonde head is still.

The cramp slows Ray down as he jogs painfully back to the Mondeo. He should be getting fitter with all this recent exercise. Ray is surprised that nobody gives chase or jumps out of the BMW and swears at the pervert filming them in the woods. Nobody seems to care that a career is about to be ruined. Ray leans against the car, panting, scrambling for his keys. So much for planning a fast getaway. He finds them in a back pocket and throws the camcorder into the passenger seat. Looking back, they are locked in an embrace. The BMW is illuminated by its internal lights, two people clinging to their part of a wreckage he has just contributed to.

Just before he pulls out onto the dual carriageway of the A23, Ray stops to flick his internal light on and pull his coat off. He studies the face in the mirror. It reflects a man slowly shaking his head, wondering what he is doing, and why he is reduced to skulking about at night to stay afloat. Why he is still compelled to courier packages that bring short-lived joy and long-term misery. Why he is not brave enough to simply run.

Kathleen and Eunice are waiting at Eunice's flat, across town. They will have everything they need, and in return he will receive the rest of Dusty's fee. So long as he drives to Langley Green directly, avoiding the local parades, as well as the high street, and the glorious temptation they contain, he will soon be down to the last suspect. One foolish man who has wronged Leckie Harris, who stands between him and freedom.

19

Worth Church, near Crawley, February 1980

This is a different type of van, he can tell.

No more blacked-out windows; he can see the sky through them, high up through the bars. But at least there is real light, and nobody banging on the outside, or frantic swearing.

This is the first time he has been allowed out of a secure home for nearly two years. They encouraged every one of them to stay in touch with their mothers, but after the guilty verdict, he heard nothing. Within a few weeks she had left Crawley. They found her dead on a filthy mattress, needles in her veins and empty bottles on the floor. And there the bitch is, on a bright, blustery day, in a box being lowered into the ground, sympathised with, cared for. He is now the only Sullivan left.

He is loaned a pair of sunglasses when they arrive. Mud clings to the bottom of his best trousers as they walk across the churchyard. The demon boy offering blank looks of neither sadness nor shame to anybody who tries to make eye contact outside the church, hidden behind borrowed dark frames.

There are no handcuffs. He could outrun the lazy guards, charge off into the bushes at the side of cemetery. There would be a short-lived sense of freedom, a fugitive for only a few minutes. But no escaping the truth they need him to accept. He has already worked out that slipping into the background is the way forward. Starting to understand how to play their game.

He sits in the second row of the church, flanked by two warders. Men he knows not to trust, who can take away a privilege on a whim. There will be no escape today. A handful of faces sit behind him, separated from the killer; he notices the occasional accusing finger when he looks round, stares hard at them. They cannot see what is inside.

The music echoes around the church, from the ancient ceiling and walls, the oldest things he has ever seen; his neck aches from looking up to see how high it reaches. This is his first time inside a place of worship. A man dressed in black and white robes stands and addresses those gathered.

'We are here today to remember Sharon Sullivan.'

She was their favourite topic of conversation in the sessions that followed the trial. The talk switched from Philip Hughes to her. No mention of John Ellis, the boy they knew nothing about. He wonders if Ellis is buried here. Nobody cares what happened to him. That bitch became the focus of attention in those airy rooms, bordered by plaques and textbooks. What did the two of them talk about? How often did she cuddle him? Did they argue? Did she beat him? The bruises on his back and legs had faded by the time they asked these questions. Nothing he could give them would help; they knew he was guilty. Danny had always been her favourite for abuse, and with him gone, he became the next target. There was no love left for the remaining son. He could blame his brother for abandoning him, but the IRA blasted those thoughts away. He can still picture the deep frown on the face of the woman who told him about Danny's death. Watching for his reaction. He kept the tears for his pillow.

The words from the pulpit fade away as he looks at his scuffed shoes. He scrapes them against the back of the pew in front. One of the warders taps him on the arm, a warning to stop.

When he tunes back in, he recognises only lies. Painting her favourably, talk of the difficulties of being a single mother, how God has saved her from her torment. Meaning him, the killer, escorted and pinned to his seat, freezing in an ill-fitting donated coat. She has been absolved of all blame.

When he is guided into the daylight again, and marched to a graveside, none of the congregation follow, apart from a woman he vaguely remembers from the first time he was at the police station. Julia something, social services. She nods in his direction but says nothing. She wasn't much help before. Women never are. Only one person was interested in what he had to say. He remembers the frantic scribbling in a notebook, and the smile that spread across the policeman's face as he told him about the fight. A fight that sounded so different when they read his words out in court.

As he is loaded back in the van, a distant camera flash catches his eye. One shout of 'little bastard.' They never understood the truth; nobody asked why. He realises the focus will be exclusively on him now. The bitch has been forgotten. He needs to provide the answers they want, if he is ever going to be free.

20

Crawley, December 1999

Dusty rocks on his swivel chair, sipping coffee. This time Ray is offered one, and he takes the opportunity to refuse.

'This Michael Keane, he's been busy. You have the payment?' Dusty asks.

Ray turns his back and withdraws the notes from the inside of his boxers. Recent experience has taught him to keep things hidden. Dusty doesn't react to the source of the cash, counts the notes, folds them and carefully places them inside his back pocket. He is wearing a black and white piano tie, over a crisp, white shirt. Ray wonders if fashion passed Dusty by.

'Go on, then.' Ray hopes this won't take long.

Dusty sighs gently, looks at Ray, who assumes he is pondering how much to tell. He has held information back before, in lieu of payment. No reason to now.

'There'll be a bit of work for you to do, to finish the job off, but we're close.'

Ray struggles to hide his disappointment, frowns, shuffles on the wobbly stool. If only the geek would get the bloody thing fixed.

Dusty places a thin buff folder on the kitchen table, pulled from a cutlery drawer. He removes several pieces of paper, carefully placing them face down in a pile. 'Michael Keane. Here he is.' He turns the top sheet over. 'Remember this,' Dusty says, jabbing his bony finger at the sheet, 'his birth certificate. Michael Keane, born on the 24th of May 1965.' There is a wide smile on his face, but Ray can't imagine why. Exactly what he handed over. It says he was born in Swindon.

'Right.' Ray fiddles with a lever, can't make the stool move up, so leans forward.

'And here,' Dusty says, turning over another sheet, checking it first, 'here is his death certificate. At the age of four.'

Ray stares at the paper in front of him and the hand-written words on a sepia background. Frowns. It is dated July 1969, again in Swindon.

'So, I'm tracking down a dead kid?'

'No, you're not.' Dusty smiles patiently. 'This dead kid, he comes back to life.' He stretches out his hands, turns over more sheets.

'Michael Keane dies at the age of four. Then another Michael Keane, one I can't find anywhere else for years, shows up. Bank accounts, driving licence, before they had photographs, but all using that same date of birth.'

Dusty fans out photocopies of documents with Keane's name on them. The name of a dead boy.

'Wait. I don't get it. Are these the same person?'

'Yes and no. It's the same identity, same name, same date of birth, but the original Michael Keane died. It's a new person, using the dead child's identity.' He leans back. 'It happens.'

'So, somebody took over his life?' Ray asks.

'Yeah. The life of the dead kid, anyway.'

'Fine. But where is he?' That, after all, is the nub of it. Ray has a job to do. Doesn't need these complications. Leckie Harris wouldn't be interested. 'Where is he now? Just tell me, no more sheets.'

Dusty nods and looks down at the table. 'Well nothing happens really. I can follow him, jobs, bank accounts, driving licence; it's all there.' He jabs a finger at the sheets on the table. 'Then, thing is, in 1993, Michael Keane, this new Michael Keane, disappears. Completely.'

'Dead?' Ray asks. That would be a neat ending, something he can take back to Leckie Harris, case solved, manhunt over.

'No. The trail stops. There is no death certificate. He never left the country, there was no passport issued to Michael Keane.'

Dusty slips his hand into the folder, then withdraws it, leaning forward across the table, halving the distance between them. 'This new Keane exists between 1984 and 1993. Then…' he rocks back and hesitates, appearing to select his words carefully. 'Then, he empties his bank account and disappears. On the nineteenth of October 1993.'

'Yes, but where is he now?'

'Well, I think they did the same thing again.'

'They? Who's they?' Ray feels his cheeks glow, his heart race. Is Dusty winding him up? Inducing the stress? The dope on Dusty's breath fills the space between them as he inches closer.

'It took me a little time to find it.' The hacker studies the table top. 'I found another person who comes out of nowhere, using another dead child's identity. At the same time that Keane disappears. The very same week.'

'What?'

'They repeated the trick. A dead child brought back to life, just like Keane.' Ray feels like he is shrinking. Dusty continues with the history lesson.

'Just when Keane disappears, someone else turns up.' He turns over another sheet of paper, one Ray didn't notice being pulled out of the folder. 'Say hello to Neil Duggan.' A copy of a passport page this time.

Ray stares at the face. There is something strangely familiar about it, but he can't work out what it is. Or maybe he just wants it to be familiar.

'This Duggan is reborn when Keane disappears.' Dusty rocks back in his chair, with a satisfied grin. 'It has to be the same man.'

'Couldn't you find a picture of Keane? So we can check if they are the same?'

'No, there was nothing. No picture record of Keane anywhere. He had one of the old driving licences, before you needed them.'

'He changed his identity,' Ray says, thoughts drifting to a world where people hide or disappear. It sounds attractive. He looks up to see Dusty studying him, wondering what he might be holding back. Perhaps there was somebody else looking for Keane, years ago, forcing him to move on and change identity. Maybe Leckie has searched for him before.

Dusty places all the pieces of paper in a neat pile and pushes them forward on the table. They shake in Ray's hands as he picks them up. This is the man he is looking for. Now called Duggan. The face stares back at him, a man

Leckie Harris wants to find. And here Ray is, about to sign a death warrant. Wondering how much you would need to owe a man like Leckie for it to be fatal.

'Witness protection?' Ray asks.

'Possibly. Why do you say that?' Dusty's turn to look puzzled.

'Just…' Ray wonders how much he should reveal about his client and looks at the spotless kitchen worktop behind Dusty. At the geek's quiet, pure life. 'Let's say it might make sense, given who's looking for Michael Keane. Or Neil Duggan.'

'Witness protection,' Dusty repeats. 'Guess so.'

Then the point of the quest returns. 'So, where is this Duggan now?' Ray focuses on the face again. The face of a dead man, one way or another.

'Well. This Duggan has gone missing.'

Ray deflates, air pushed out of a cushion. Blinks slowly, tries to focus. 'He's done it again?'

How could you live like that? Being hunted, in constant fear of a tap on the shoulder, or a bullet through the brain. It is hard enough living just the one life. Dusty gets up and makes himself another coffee, not offering one to his client this time. The clink of spoon against mug echoes around the spartan kitchen. Ray runs his tongue over his teeth, conscious he hasn't brushed them in a while.

'Yeah,' Dusty says, after a long pause. 'I've got three possible identities he could be now. Three people who fit the way he's been reinventing himself. About the right age, new identities coming back from the dead, or starting up again.'

'Three?' Ray asks, his voice rising. There is still work to be done.

'They fit best. I could narrow it down a bit, but you know…'

Dusty leaves a pause, and Ray knows what this means. More money. 'I'm skint.'

'I figured.' Dusty pulls another folder out of the drawer, drops it on the table. 'You can do the rest. There are some details here you can use, addresses and so on.'

'Thanks,' Ray mutters. 'I mean it, Dusty.'

Ray will have to do the legwork. He is a gumshoe after all. He pulls the file closer and flicks through the pages. Three sheets, one per suspect. Reading, Portsmouth and Milton Keynes. All in easy reach. If he is going to condemn a man, he needs to be certain, look him in the eye. If the subject crossed Leckie, he must have known the consequences. Hiding in witness protection to save himself from a vengeful criminal. This Keane, whatever he is now, must face up to his past, admit the mistakes, the wrong turns taken, his relationship with telling the truth. Just the way Ray needs to.

One more thought hits Ray. 'The history. I asked for that as well.' The additional instructions from the minder.

'More money, Ray. You need to pay.'

Dusty turns his back, moves to his armchair in the main living space. The screen in front of him erupts with gunfire, as a figure dodges in and out of the doorway of a wild west saloon bar, eluding oblivion.

'There's nothing more you can give me? No previous name?' Ray calls across the space, between a blaze of bullets.

'Money, Ray, you know it.'

The reason he is in this mess. Ray's judgement has faded. It has become a struggle to keep anything in his pocket. Every parade in the town has a bookies' now. They know his weakness. He is preyed upon at every turn. None of the shops offer him credit, yet all are happy to take his cash. Jockeys, trainers, horses are in on it too. Nobody can be trusted.

Ray gathers up the folders on the kitchen table and studies the screen avenger, consumed by his quest. To rid some town of the baddies. The living room echoes to more gunfire as a gathering of gold prospectors is scattered. Ray keeps one eye fixed on the figure in the armchair as he creeps up to the cutlery drawer. Peering inside, he spots another folder. One Dusty omitted to share, given the lack of funds at Ray's disposal. 'Keane' is scrawled on the cover. Without checking the contents, he slips it silently underneath the rest of the information in his hands.

He will need to act like a real sleuth now, go forwards and backwards from Michael Keane. To whatever he was and has become. Rely on his own wits rather than the freakish skills of someone like Dusty. Three weeks should be plenty of time to track down the grass, eliminate two men. Fortunately for Ray, money is no longer a requirement for finding whoever Keane was, and is now.

21

Chapter 4, 'THE MOTHER', FROM
THE TOWN THAT FORGOT CHILD X,
BY TRISH WATNEY

Based on interviews with Sharon Sullivan, mother of Martin Sullivan, October 1977 and February 1978

Sharon Sullivan lived with her son, Martin, on the second (top) floor of a block of flats on Shackleton Road, in Tilgate. The first time I met her was in her local pub, when she was drunk. This was immediately after her son had been taken into police custody. At this point the public did not know the name of the boy who had been arrested, but inside sources in Crawley CID had revealed his identity to me. On the *Crawley Observer* we were reminded that the accused's name could not appear in print – yet. At this point in time, Sharon seemed to have no interest in telling her side of the story.

When I met her a few days later, she was more open. Martin was still being questioned by the police and was being held in a detention centre (later revealed to be Shire House in Horsham). She had been drinking again but let me into her flat. Sharon seemed to be afraid of her neighbours sticking their noses into her business – complaining that they were talking about her. The initial reluctance she showed to give an interview was ironic if you consider she sold her story to the *Daily Mirror* after the trial.

The walls of her flat were very thin – you could hear neighbours opening and closing doors. Sharon seemed paranoid about them knowing that her son had been arrested. She mentioned the subject of a fee more than once during our conversation. Clearly Sharon was struggling to make ends meet, was surviving on her dole money alone.

The family background is worth noting. Sharon's original partner, the boy's father, was an Irish labourer called James (Jimmy) Sullivan. They had two sons, Martin the youngest. Jimmy served five years in prison between the birth of their two boys. He finally left the family home in 1971, when Martin was six, shortly before beginning a longer sentence for armed robbery. He is still in Pentonville prison. Sharon Sullivan said that she never told her sons the reasons for his absence, just that their father had abandoned them.

Martin's older brother, Danny, left home at sixteen in June 1975, more than two years before the death of Philip Hughes. He joined the army and was stationed in Northern Ireland at the time of the murder. Danny Sullivan was killed by an IRA bomb in South Armagh in March 1978, two weeks after the trial. The relationship between the two brothers was not mentioned in court; in fact, Danny wasn't referenced at all. Enquiries with Danny Sullivan's military unit have unearthed nothing.

Sharon drank steadily from a bottle of vodka when I spoke to her in her flat.

'He's a good lad,' she said. 'He wouldn't hurt anyone. They made this whole thing up. I don't know where they got it all from.' Her account of the interviewing of her son is in stark contrast to that of the police. DI Birkdale described her as passive and unengaged. She maintains she was fighting for Martin all the time. As a reporter covering the trial, I noted that Sharon Sullivan only attended for three of the nine days, and was absent when the jury delivered their verdict.

There is one piece of evidence that was missing from the trial. Martin Sullivan kept a form of diary, hidden in a schoolbook, in the weeks leading up to the death of Philip Hughes. He continued to write in this until he was taken in for questioning. This diary reads like Martin Sullivan writing to his older brother, somewhere he thought his mother wouldn't look.

Sharon Sullivan was not aware of the diary. It reveals a boy struggling to handle an abusive relationship with his mother. He writes of beatings, verbal assault, intimidation and neglect. In court, Sharon said that her son was happy at home, that they had a good relationship. 'We did a lot together. We shopped. We watched telly. He's my son.'

Off the record, the local police said they found no evidence that would give them any indication of the mental state of Martin Sullivan at the time of the murder. They claimed to have searched the boy's bedroom, but this reporter found the diary hidden in a pile of magazines, on a subsequent visit to Sharon Sullivan after the trial. What would the jury have made of his thoughts if they were made available? We may never know. The police had no interest in reading the diaries when told that they existed.

22

Milton Keynes, December 1999

He hears the familiar noise of the front door open and close, and arranges himself in the kitchen area, leaning against the work surface, mug in hand, prepared. Wonders why Carl has decided to look for him on a Saturday, a time when he is the only person who ever visits the office. Only Carl, from the security logs, would know he is there.

The surprise is genuine when he sees Lydia striding towards him. He should challenge her but waits for her to speak.

'I thought I'd find you here,' she says, voice raised. Lydia looks around the open-plan area, as if checking for other members of the group. They are alone.

'Why did you think I'd be here?' he asks.

'Carl told me.'

The loner, the one S is still wondering about, and what he sees in the group, other than an opportunity to start his life again. The men are always the most difficult to work out. S thinks he should have pushed harder in the last Truth Time.

Needs to have another one-to-one, in case Carl has stumbled across something he shouldn't. But Lydia, although she has been evasive, and asks a lot of strange questions, is harmless.

'Why him? Are you two an item?' he asks, suddenly wondering if they are working together. Couples are not allowed. Small internal alliances only break the larger bond of the group.

Lydia shakes her head. 'Carl? No, he's not my type.'

'Oh, and what is your type?' He flashes his trademark smile. S has been able to control women before. Not by force, but simply by showing them the way forward. Yet, in five years with this new group, he is yet to find one that truly captivates him. Not like the previous place, when things ended abruptly. But this Lydia is different to the others. There is a spark, a curiosity that appeals.

'I don't have a type.' She flicks the switch on the kettle. 'You want another?'

He holds his mug out towards her, to show it is half full. 'No, I'm good.'

Lydia busies herself extracting coffee from a jar in the cupboard. He watches her move, again questioning what it is about her that is familiar. Her top stretches across her back, outlining the contours. He pulls his eyes away in time, as she looks around.

'Sure?'

'Sure. I'm trying to cut down.' One of those platitudes you throw out, to be civil, to fit in.

Lydia swings around, places a mug carefully on the edge of the sink.

'Why are you here, Lydia? We don't work weekends.'

'You're here.'

'I'm often here. Carl told you that.'

'I need to ask you something.'

'Go on.'

He is usually the one doing the asking, making demands, shaping the vulnerable.

She lets out a long sigh. 'I know about your past. About what happened before,' she says.

He swallows, feels his cheeks flush, forces himself to stare at her. Needs to see deep inside.

'Why did you move on? From the previous place? The one in Worcester?' she asks, leaning back into the sink.

'I don't know what you mean.' He hadn't expected to go through the denials again, but here he is.

'You do. The last place, what did you call it, The Foundation? Were there others before that?'

S shakes his head, digs his fingers into his arm. Feels like he is sitting on a carousel ride, the room spinning past him repeatedly.

'I…'

'I know, Simon. Or whatever you're really called. You used to have a different name. Steven it was last time. Do you always use an S? Have there been other names, before that?'

He closes his eyes; wishes she would vanish. He has not been confronted this directly before. There have been questions, but he has always been able to counter them, pull the inquisitor in, wrap them up in his safety blanket. S wonders how long Lydia has known. Probably before she joined the group. This might explain why she is there.

'That rape story you gave me, is that true?' he asks.

'Does it matter?

'So, you've been lying to me, to the whole group.'

'I only mentioned rape to you. To see how you'd react.'

S studies her. Her head is turned slightly to the side, as if she is listening for distant noises. Or others, coming to help her, to track him down. Her body is still, breathing slowly, as if she is trying not to look scared, that she will not run.

'I know.' Lydia tucks a strand of hair behind her ear. He searches the memories again, wondering what it is about the movement that disturbs him. 'Do you remember a girl called Lena Talbot?' she asks.

The name swirls around in his head; he holds on to the worktop to steady himself. Lena. She showed so much promise. Could have done so much with her life. Why did she do something so stupid? Is this what Lydia is searching for? Revenge? It was hardly his fault the girl was deranged.

'No.'

There is a fire in her eyes now, staring wildly, mouth thin and drawn sharp.

'Don't deny it. Lena Talbot. You must remember her. She was in The Foundation. Your Foundation. A place just like this one. Somewhere she was supposed to feel safe. Then she killed herself. Because of you.'

He is intrigued by the fact she does not raise her voice. Her teeth clench, he can hear her panting as she delivers what he thinks must have been a well-rehearsed speech.

'How do you know Lena?'

'So, you knew her? That she was in the last version of this made-up crap you came up with. The reason you reinvented yourself, changed your name. And forgot about her.'

'Who are you?'

'I'm her sister.'

'Her…' He falters, and then nods his head, the pieces falling into place. Lena had mentioned a sister, Cora. He looks at her hands, the bitten fingernails. She isn't doing that thing now, the clasping thing, but now he remembers. Lena had similar habits.

'What did you do to her?' Lydia's voice is still calm. He is struck by the jagged shapes of her clenched teeth.

'I didn't do anything to her. She left us. She…'

Lena was an enigma. One minute, willing to do anything he asked of her, like some followers had done in the past, the next, flying at him in a jealous rage. Eating herself up over attention he gave to others.

He tries to find the right words, ones that will calm her down. 'She gave up on all of us.'

'She would never do that. Not Lena. What did you do to her?'

Lydia pulls a bread knife from behind her back. Points it in his direction. He can hear her breathing, a wheezing sound through her mouth, sees the knife waving about in front of her. He backs away towards the corner of the kitchen, realises he is trapped. By a crazy woman, desperate to avenge something he had nothing to do with. For once he might have to fight back.

'What did you do to her?' she repeats, emphasising every syllable, grasping the knife in two hands. Lydia takes a step forward, then another. He focuses on the blade, watching intently for any quick movements.

'We can talk about this.'

'What's to talk about? You as good as killed Lena.'

'I didn't… there was…' He creeps towards her, hands pleading his case. 'You've got to believe me, Lydia.' Keep using the name she has given him, even though he knows it to be a lie. 'You must know what she was like. She was jealous, I did nothing to encourage her.' Then, what he hopes is the clincher. 'She wasn't well.'

'No.' Lydia shouts for the first time. S understands the need to act quickly. Looks to his left and she follows his eyeline, then steps forward and grabs the knife, wrestling it from her. Points it at her chest, then drops it to the floor, kicks it away, spinning into a corner. Breathes out. Holds her, the way he once did with Lena, when she would go into one of her rages, and he needed to bring her out of it. Lydia hangs like a rag doll in his arms.

'I promise you; it wasn't my fault. Lena was ill.'

Lydia looks up at him, then tries to wriggle free. He pins her arms behind her back, whispers in her ear.

'We can forget all about this. You should move on. Leave me alone. You're wrong.'

Lydia pulls one arm free but makes no attempt to escape. He remembers an embrace with Lena, on a doorstep, one she initiated, that he enjoyed, before backing away from. Controlling them, taking them on a journey with him, that is enough. There has never been a need for intimate contact, despite what some of them have hoped for. With Lena, he had to think of the group, pushed her away. She was looking for more than he could give her. And she threw herself in front of an express train. When you deal with the weak, things can go wrong. Sometimes they just didn't know what they wanted.

'You used Lena. You destroyed her,' Lydia says, voice cracking.

He can smell the perfume, a mixture of jasmine and citrus. The same one as Lena.

'She was a mess. Damaged,' he protests.

Lydia turns her face sideways with an expression he struggles to make out. Then he sees the anger in her eyes, realises the danger. Twists her wrist, a defensive move he has used before. Presses her back into the work surface, pinning her so she cannot attack his groin. He is defending himself, defending the group, its history. And the secrets.

The metallic thunk echoes around the kitchen and the dizziness hits. He pulls a hand up to the side of his head, touches something wet. The noise repeats, his head goes numb, and he falls into a whirlpool of black, sucking him in. His legs give way, and he sinks to the floor.

23

Crawley, December 1999

The summons has come.

Ray leans against the wall in the cab office, staring at Asif, waiting. The despatcher ignores him, shuffles pieces of paper on his desk, relays messages to the other drivers. Ray understands none of the languages he uses. There are no incoming taxi fares, as far as he can tell.

Marko Mirkovic opens the adjoining door to the print shop and stands aside. Ray's temples throb. His damp hands are rooted in his pockets.

'This way,' Marko whispers, pointing through the door. 'In back. Package for you.'

The physical threats have gone, but the marginal civility that has replaced them is sometimes scarier. The not knowing what might happen next. In the violence vacuum, Ray is still treated like a foolish errand runner.

Instead of following him through the door, Marko heads outside via the cab office, leaving Ray to find his way to Stefan. He passes through a room containing two men hunched over a desk, studying passports of various hues. He cannot get involved.

'Come in, Ray. Sit down.' Stefan's voice booms through the doorway from an office at the rear.

Ray was expecting a murderous reception, but Stefan is alone. Ray keeps his hands in his pockets. Sits where he is bid, on a plastic chair. He wonders how many people have been tied to it before. Searches the room for rope, twine, anything that might be used to interrogate him. The walls are bare, no blood splatters.

Stefan tosses a thick envelope on the desk in front of him. 'For you.'

Ray doubts it will be a payment. Too heavy.

'What's that? Where to?'

'A delivery.' Stefan ignores the specifics of the question. 'Address on there.'

This is normal. Packages to deliver. But Stefan has never given him one directly before. Not in here. A room he has only entered once, with a hood on his head, when the debt climbed above ten grand. He left with threats ringing in his ears, bruises across his back, and a damp patch.

Ray stands as he reaches out to pick it up. The contents slip from one end of the envelope to the other.

'Sit down.'

Ray falls back into the chair, feeling the plastic dig into his thighs. The room smells of blood, persuasion, and confessions. He has a new benefactor, but the brothers have maintained their hold. He still needs to work.

The driving came about by chance, two years earlier. He heard on the GA grapevine about someone losing their car keys in a poker game, so a local minicab firm was a driver short. Ray needed the extra source of cash. Stefan and Marko weren't interested in references. Just wanted to know how far he would go to make a living. Far enough, it seemed.

'I hear you were robbed. We were robbed,' Stefan snarls.

'Yeah.'

'Unfortunate.'

'Yeah.'

'Twice in three months. Doubly unfortunate.'

Ray thinks back to the end of the summer. A drug-addled teenager tried it on, snatching a parcel that he had stupidly left on the passenger seat. The reason he now keeps the hammer in reach, and all packages out of sight. The Serbians tracked the thief down to a flat in Northgate and removed three fingers.

'You've got to earn the money back.' Stefan announces this, as if it is part of an everyday business deal. They both know this is how the game works. 'Money that goes missing has to be replaced.'

'I know. It wasn't my fault.'

Stefan holds up a hand, shows he isn't prepared to listen to excuses. 'No matter. It has to be replaced.'

Ray sinks deeper, looks around, expecting hands to tether him, the forgers to come in and reveal another skill that helps the Mirkovic empire. Or Marko to reappear and exercise one of his pleasures. But he and Stefan are still alone.

'I'll make it back. Just give me the jobs.' Ray rubs his eyes, can't remember the last time he slept for more than four hours at a time. His dreams usually involve horses leading races and suddenly stopping, or even going backwards. He just needs to catch a break.

'You will get plenty of jobs.' Stefan breaks him out of his sinking thoughts. 'Starting with this. Address on there. Go.'

With a fiver a time for the courier work, Ray knows he can replace the missing money from the cab attack in an instant. Stick one payment on an outsider, and he will be on the level.

Ray walks back through the rear of the shop and finds the link to the cab office closed. He exits onto the Tilgate parade through the front door of 'Axiom Printing' and walks around to the rear of the shops where his Mondeo is parked. Force of habit, placing it out of sight. The stench from the back of the units reaches out to him: decaying food, discarded waste, gathered against the walls. Ray takes short breaths, his eyes water.

The wind whips around the courtyard, and he pulls his jacket around him, fumbling for his key. As he places it in the lock, the menacing figure of Marko catches his eye, smoking and leaning against the wall in an oasis of cleared rubbish, by the rear exit of the print shop. Ray needs two hands to open the car door, to combat the shaking.

'Don't let police catch you,' Marko shouts over.

Ray pulls away from the car door and stares at Marko. The brother strolls over, a hunter easing his way towards his prey. Ray feels stuck on the pavement, an immovable object in Marko's path.

'Look,' Marko says, pointing to the smashed rear light on the Mondeo. 'You might get in trouble.'

Ray stares at the broken glass on the tarmac, the result of an unseen accident, realises what Marko has been doing while he was inside with Stefan. Knows the brothers are determined not to let him go.

'You did this,' Ray says, as loudly as he dares.

'Be more careful,' Marko mutters, and turns to walk away, flicking his cigarette into the gutter. It fizzes and points an accusing finger. Ray leans into his car, and reaches under the seat, checks the hammer is still in place. Feels the cool metal against his fingers, his mind turning to the treasonous thought of smashing Marko's head in, before sanity grabs a hold. Then, to Leckie Harris, and their arrangement.

He still can't work out why Leckie has chosen a gambler to track down his mark, unless he has the same vice. Ray won't have time to pity the poor bastard when he is caught, has no choice. Witness protection means nothing. Ray knows it will be him or Keane tied to a chair, pleading for his life. And, at this moment, Ray has the advantage of knowing the situation, that only one of them can go free.

2 4

Milton Keynes, December 1999

Two pairs of hands push the body forward, tipping it over the concrete barrier. It twists slowly, like a dead-weight diver, dropping onto the dual carriageway below.

Lydia watches the corpse fall. Scans for traffic either side of where it lands. The only sound is the faint echo of the thump when it hits. Returning her gaze to the body, it has arranged itself in an L shape, as if it has been placed there. Lying on its side, in the recovery position.

She looks across at Carl. Remembers how he turned away when the body overbalanced, declining to watch it drop. Carl is passive now, eyes closed, hands out in front of him, holding on to the barrier above the bridge. Lydia looks up and down the road that runs over the dual carriageway. Her car is parked twenty yards away, in a lay-by. She hitches her shoulders up, releasing the tension built up from the pair of them carrying S first to the car and then from that to the bridge, just a mile from the office.

'Carl?' she implores.

He appears to be ignoring her. Lydia looks down again at the road below. A car passes on the other side, oblivious to the dead body that will eventually stop the traffic in the other direction. It is past midnight.

'Carl. We need to move.'

'Hmm?'

Carl's eyes open. The whites stand out in the half moonlight. Unblinking. Something has changed since they tipped the dead body over. Until then, Carl was the one doing the thinking. Suggested where to take the body to make it look like a suicide. Typed out the note, using S's computer. Cleaned up the blood, mopped the office kitchen floor with bleach, retrieved a couple of sacks to truss the body up in, to take out to the car via the delivery bay at the side of the office. Suggested they wait until the world was asleep before moving it. All this while she shook, turning over the death in her head, the metallic clunk of a kettle hitting S, his grip loosening, a repeat of the noise when she must have hit him again, harder she thinks, before he slipped to the floor. He lay there, lifeless, clocks stopped, blood leaking from his skull. And Lydia simply stared at their leader, the charlatan she came there to expose, who fooled the others, and wondered whether she should have struck out as soon as she knew it was him, avoided the dalliance and the months of waiting. Not wasted time trying to understand why he had made Lena throw herself under the Bristol to Birmingham express six years before.

Lena. Her elder sister. Who left home and moved to Worcester, finding comfort in The Foundation, a place where, according to her letters, needy souls came to rest and discover faith in a leader who showed them how to live and love. A smaller group, since disbanded, replaced by the one she herself joined. Lena found more than faith in an icon. Judging by her letters, was ready to do anything for him. Worshipped him. Lydia didn't discover what Simon, or Steven Harding as he was known then, had done to make her throw herself under a train. Broke her heart probably. Jealousy, he mentioned. But what did he ever say that was true?

'Carl. We got to move.'

Lydia reaches out, finds that he is shaking. He is still staring wide-eyed into the distance. This loner who responded immediately to her desperate phone call, who was calm and composed while she panicked. Lydia was prepared to face the consequences of what she did, when she saw the body on the floor. But then some form of self-preservation must have kicked in. Knew she had to talk to somebody. Instinctively knew Carl was the one who would help.

She pulls his hands out in front of him, folds them over in her own. Carl seems to come out of a trance, drags her in for a hug. Lydia squeezes tight in response. He needs comfort as much as she does. She will not be alone in dealing with this. But they are standing on a bridge above a dead body. Someone will discover it soon. Their roles from earlier have been reversed. Now Lydia is the one doing the thinking, taking the decisions.

'Come on.'

Lydia pulls Carl by the hand, leads him to her car. There are no lights on the bridge, there has been no traffic, unlikely they have been spotted. The turn of her key kicks the Astra into life. As she pulls out into the deserted street, she studies her accomplice. His eyes are closed, legs twitching up and down in the passenger seat, hands waving in front of him as if he is conducting a small orchestra. He starts humming to himself, a low tuneless noise, in time to the movements. This continues all the way to his flat as she steers carefully, sticking to the speed limit, not wanting to draw attention. Carl seemed confident they could pass the death off as a suicide. As far as she could tell, had instantly decided this was the way forward. Maybe she won't have to pay the price for revenge.

As she pulls up outside Carl's flat, a couple of miles from the bridge, a thin smile creeps onto her face.

'Rest in peace, Lena,' she whispers to herself.

25

danny. sounds like there at it again. shes got that
jim or something in there. the one with the big nose.
shutting my ears this time. pissed both of them. they
had a good ecxuse today. everone busy i didnt even
look back once you would have been impressed danny.
you love cowboys it were just like them. i cant tell her
anything about it. she wont understand any of it. its
her fault. she hardly even knows im here any more.
not since you went. im nothing now. its you and me
danny and nobody else.

   i didnt look when he went down. doing it like a soldier
wood. or a kung fu master. a kick and down he went
not even any noise. he had it coming the wanker. calling
me stupid like that. shut him up. nobody calls me stupid
not now. he shoodnt have had a go shood have let me
play the game and done the kung fu thing.

   you wood have liked it. one karate kick. he had it
coming we was just playing a game though you see it

on telly when one keeps getting up he probly in hospital now he probly laughing about it with his mates they telling him dont be stupid dont call him stupid you learn your lesson.

there shagging im sure i can here them now. the noise they make youd think she wood know it was obvious. i might as well not be here god. going to hide under the sheets now and get some sleep. another day of tomorow wile they all celebrate the queen. she will be in the pub all day again. all day its open anyway with him with the big nose. think will go and have a look tomorow what a mess he made where he landed see if there was any blood that would be cool will go and look wile shes in the pub danny.

2 6

Crawley, December 1999

Sandra Murray is Ray's first office visitor in nearly two weeks. The loneliness doesn't worry him. Ray can get all the friendship he needs in the betting shops. The managers welcome him with a smile and a knowing nod, confident he will lose. Most of the time. Other punters are different, probably view him as a curse.

Sandra sits opposite, dressed in a dark trouser suit, coat over her lap, no make-up. Puffy face, tired and listless eyes, she sniffs as she drops the news on him.

'Paul's dead.'

Ray stares back, wondering what to say. Thinking, *Why has she come all the way here to tell me?* When he hasn't seen her or her son for over twenty years. The son she took away, thinking he needed to be fixed.

'Sorry, Mrs Murray. What happened?'

'Call me Sandra. You never did, did you? Back then.' Ray wonders how she can remember that long ago. She looks up and her eyes show the sadness. 'Suicide, they said.'

'Suicide?'

'Mmm. Hanged himself with his Marks and Spencer tie. The only one he had.'

Ray looks around his desk for tissues, something to provide comfort. He has no words. He opens the top drawer, finds just broken pencils, Post-it notes. Nothing to soothe a woman who has lost her son.

Sandra tugs a hankie from her coat pocket, dabs under her eyes. 'I thought I should tell you in person. You were such good friends once. It took me a while to find you,' she adds. 'They've only just given me his body. We can have the funeral now. It's a week on Friday.'

Ray sneaks a look at his watch, as if it would tell him if he were free. Knows there is nothing in his diary, apart from a future appointment with a man who used to be called Keane.

'Where?'

'Brighton. Near where he lives. Lived.' Sandra corrects herself, pulls herself up in the chair. 'I live there too, Brighton. He moved to be near me, when they let him out.'

'Out?'

'Of prison.'

Ray sinks into the fake leather of his chair, wonders what became of his boyhood friend. Paul Murray, his sidekick, the fellow agent who worked on cases with him around the estate, and in the woods, before they were teenagers. When their existence was lived out through television, when there was no other reference point for adventure. He wants to ask how Paul ended up in prison but can't find the words.

'Sorry to hear that.'

'He wasn't in prison for long. It was all a mistake. You knew Paul. He was a good boy.'

Through his own mother, Ray heard the idea was to move before they started at the next school, remove Paul from the influences, the stress. Meaning Ray. Never to use the underpass together, on their way to the new school. A walk Ray had to take every day, passing that spot each time, facing the shame alone.

'We lost touch.' All Ray can offer her. They were just kids. How were they to know what would happen?

'Yes, you did.' Her voice sounds stronger, as if she is challenging him. He thinks back to the unanswered letters he kept in his bedside drawer. Scared to let the world see them. Scared to admit what he was doing, shutting his friend away.

'Can I come? Next Friday?'

'Of course.' Her eyes still accuse. She will never know the truth.

'I'll be there.' Ray intends to keep his word.

'It starts at two o'clock. Preston crematorium.' Sandra pulls a small letter out of her handbag. 'And I found this. In his things.' She reaches out towards him, hand shaking. 'The reason I came here today. It's for you.'

Ray leans across the desk to take it from her, places it carefully down in front of him.

'To Ray Mercer,' it says, in sloping handwriting. It doesn't look like the scrawl he remembers from over twenty years ago.

'Thanks. I'll…' He fixes on the envelope and doesn't notice Sandra Murray has risen until he hears the familiar squeak of the door handle.

'See you next week.'

He listens to her footsteps echo down the stairwell,

disappearing from his life again. Ray retrieves a pencil out of the drawer to slit the letter open.

There is one sheet inside, folded neatly. He places the paper flat against the desk, fearing it will escape. The edges feel like they will cut into his fingertips. Ray realises he has been holding his breath, and as the words reach out to him, he slowly exhales.

Dear Ray,

My mum, bless her, she seems to think I'm still that unspoilt little kid she used to know. Her little boy. Blind to who I've always been. And she lives just up the road, in the same town now. Surely, she can't be that blind? It is Brighton. But I think I can talk to you, Ray. You know, you understand.

I think I still love you, Ray. There, I've said it. I've not been able to forget about you. I still wonder what I was doing when we were kids. I've come to terms with it. You will never love me back, not the way I wanted you to. All I ever wanted was to be close to you. That was enough for me, just to see you every day. Then I went and blew it. I've done some bad things since then and paid for them. Don't blame yourself for how I turned out.

We went out that day to play our game, and we came back different. I can't believe nobody worked out what really happened, what we saw. Passed off as a suicide, when we knew better. Nobody seemed to care. I read about when that boy did it again, in the paper. Don't feel guilty, Ray. I don't feel guilty. Without that day, I probably wouldn't have worked out who I truly am. I would have gone to Thomas Bennett and got into a right mess, not understanding how I felt. Think mum did the right thing, taking me away.

Please write back this time. I wish you'd written back, even once. I just want to know how you are. One way or another, I will find a way to get this to you.

Take care.

Your oldest friend,
Paul

Ray folds up the note, carefully slipping it back into the envelope. They don't sound like the words of a man in turmoil, about to commit suicide. Ray wonders if Paul came to terms with his sexuality, living in a place like Brighton. There is no address on the sheet of paper, no means for him to reply. That is, if Paul intended to send it. Maybe he was just thinking out loud.

Would Ray have written back if he received it? When his mother passed on the letters when he was young, probably three or four a year to start with, he did nothing. Eventually they stopped, and he was relieved. Paul was a queer. Lied to him about what he was. They should have supported each other, faced up to what they saw, but Ray always blamed Paul for their inaction. Without the kiss, they might have spoken out, even gone to look for the fallen boy at the underpass. Prevented the nightmare that followed. Ray kept ignoring his best friend, punishing him for the betrayal, for leaving Crawley so suddenly. Blocked him out, afraid of being tainted by the madness. You steered away from poofs back then, repeated the jokes, helping you to fit in. Paul would be there in his head, but he still made the wisecracks in class. You just did when you were twelve. Now there is nobody he can talk to.

The pair of them allowed Child X to have a secret trial run before he killed Philip Hughes. Two innocent kids, not knowing the consequences of their inaction. Burying the scene in front of them. Sandra Murray lost her son that afternoon, the same way Ray did. She probably thought Paul's withdrawal was driven by homosexuality. She needed to exorcise him. But Ray has always known there was a different reason for Paul turning his back. Sees those flailing arms as the boy fell. Cannot believe they simply went back to the street party, rather than raising the alarm. Never spoke about what they saw, and how they should have reacted.

Ray fishes out a lighter and an ash tray from the deep bottom drawer, and watches the flame catch the envelope and its contents. Then he adds the orange book to the pile. That will also be of no help to him now. It is too late to change what happened, what they could have prevented. Opportunity is smiling, and he needs to grasp it. Dusty has reduced the runners to three. All he needs to do is eliminate two, then close in.

Ray ponders what it would be like to have no debts, be free of money worries. It feels like a distant memory. The places he could travel to, the delights he could witness. The bets he could lay. Time to focus on Michael Keane, rather than those two boys who saw something horrific and did nothing.

27

**Transcript from session between Doctor
Geoffrey Toshack and Michael Keane,
Murrayfields Secure Home, Tunbridge Wells,
October 1983**

Toshack: Tell me about what happened with Philip Hughes.

Keane: I've gone through this loads of times.

Toshack: You know I have to report back to the parole board.

Keane: They don't like me.

Toshack: Why do you say that?

Keane: I can tell. They stare at me and they've already made up their mind beforehand.

Toshack: The people on the board do change. I think they might be different this time. People change too, just like you.

Keane: You think I got a chance?

Toshack: Do you deserve one?

Keane: You're good. You never answer my questions, do you?

Toshack:	Does that worry you?
Keane:	There you go again.
Toshack:	Indulge me. Take me back to that day. One of the things they are looking for is what we refer to as consistent recall.
Keane:	What, like I'm not making it up, changing the story all the time?
Toshack:	Something like that. Go on.
Keane:	He was winding me up all day. Saying I was scared, he dared me to go up the scaffolding on the building site with him. I never told anyone that before.
Toshack:	Why not?
Keane:	Dunno. Just didn't.
Toshack:	You didn't think it would help you? To tell someone that detail?
Keane:	Nobody has believed anything I've said. Until you.
Toshack:	What were you feeling that afternoon?
Keane:	Just annoyed; he was bugging me.
Toshack:	Do you regret what happened?
Keane:	Of course I do. That kid died. It was my fault. You can tell them that. We had a fight and he fell off. It was sort of an accident, but nobody believed me. So, I know I've got to take the blame.
Toshack:	Should you be taking the blame?
Keane:	Yeah. I killed someone; that's bad. Not evil, like they kept saying, but still bad.
Toshack:	Do you know right from wrong?
Keane:	Yeah.

Toshack: How do you tell right from wrong?

Keane: Society says. I studied this. It was in one of those exams you suggested. I did well, didn't I?

Toshack: You did very well. Those results will help you, when it comes to the parole board. Tell me what society says about killing. Without referring to any of those textbooks. What you think instead.

Keane: Killing somebody is a crime; that's why I'm in here. Might be here for the rest of my life. Well not here, but a prison.

Toshack: Do you expect to go to prison?

Keane: What, when I'm too old for this place? Probably. I don't want to go to prison.

Toshack: Why not?

Keane: Because they'll kill me in there. They'll find out who I am, what I did. They won't understand why I did it. You need to tell them prison is a bad idea.

Toshack: Don't you think going to prison is the right punishment for what you did?

Keane: If you're an adult, yeah. But I was just a kid. I didn't know anything.

Toshack: Did you know right from wrong when you killed that boy?

Keane: I don't know what I knew. I know it's wrong now. I was just a kid.

Toshack: Did you do it for the attention? Killing that boy?

Keane: No.

Toshack: Some time ago, you told me it was your mother's fault. You blamed her.

Keane: I didn't know what I was saying. I was mixed up. Angry. She abandoned me, course I blamed her. You've got to tell them different now. I was responsible. I'm sorry about it. It was a long time ago.

Toshack: Are you sorry?

Keane: Yeah, really sorry.

Toshack: What does being sorry mean?

Keane: Like I wish it never happened. Like I wouldn't do it again. It was a mistake. We all make mistakes.

Toshack: Don't you think you should be punished for your mistake?

Keane: I have been. Every day. In here.

Toshack: And has that punishment been enough?

Keane: Don't think that's my decision, is it? It's down to you.

Toshack: You'll need an answer for that. When you're in front of the parole board, they'll want to know. All I do is recommend; the board makes the decision.

Keane: Just tell them how sorry I am.

Toshack: Let's talk about something else. What makes you angry?

Keane: Other kids.

Toshack: Give me a for instance.

Keane: It doesn't happen as much as it used to. When I was first in here, they used to steal my things, get my privileges taken away. Get too close, try to wind me up.

Toshack: Like Philip Hughes did.

Keane: Worse than that. There's proper nutters in here, you know? Kids who'll bite you and stab you if they can get their hands on a knife; worse, probably. That's why I keep away from them all.

Toshack: You've not formed any friendships in here?

Keane: No point. I keep myself to myself. They move on, change all the time.

Toshack: Do you get stressed?

Keane: Sometimes.

Toshack: Tell me about the last time you were stressed.

Keane: They shut me out of my room. Searched it. I know what it was. Someone grassed me up, telling them I had something hidden in my room, so they would search it, turn it upside down. He's gone now, but it wound me up. They found nothing. I follow the rules.

Toshack: Do you think it's important to follow the rules?

Keane: I do now. I understand you need rules. Society needs them to function. I've paid for my mistakes. I'm well behaved. Some of them in here, you know what they're like. And I'm not like them. Do you think I'm dangerous?

Toshack: That's one of the things I'm trying to establish.

Keane: I have an exemplary behaviour record. That's the word, isn't it, exemplary?

Toshack: It's a good word. Back to times of stress. Are you still doing that thing I suggested?

Keane: What, imagining I'm on a beach? Yeah, I do that to stay calm.

Toshack: Is it the beach you told me about before? Where you went with your mum and your brother?

Keane: Margate? Nah, it's a nice one. One that I like.

Toshack: Let's talk about your mum again.

Keane: Don't you have any new questions?

Toshack: Don't get defensive.

Keane: Sorry, but you always ask about her. She's dead.
            I blamed her years ago. That was wrong. I'm to
            blame. Does that cover all the mum questions?

Toshack: Okay, we'll move on. Have you had any more
            dreams?

Keane: Nothing new. Just the one about falling and
            never landing.

Toshack: Where does this take place? This recurring
            dream?

Keane: Loads of different places. It's never the same.

Toshack: Never a building site?

Keane: No, never.

Toshack: Something else. Do you want to be released?

Keane: I don't think that's up to me. Here's okay, I'm still
            locked up, but… I have my own room, my own
            space; I can control things. My environment.

Toshack: Is that important to you?

Keane: Yeah. I don't like people touching my stuff.

Toshack: Have you started a diary yet? We talked about
            this before; it might be a good idea to get your
            thoughts down on paper.

Keane: No.

Toshack: Are you going to?

Keane: Will it help my chances of being released?

Toshack: It might help you get your thoughts in order.
            Did you keep one before?

Keane: No.

Toshack: Well, something for you to think about. One
            more thing. Let's talk hypothetically now. If you
            were released in the future, whenever that is,
            what do you think you would do?

Keane:	Lead a normal life. Obey the rules.
Toshack:	And tell me what normal means?
Keane:	Just normal. I suppose this place has been normal for the past five years.
Toshack:	That's very astute.
Keane:	A good word, I'll use that one.
Toshack:	How would you feel, out there, fending for yourself?
Keane:	I dunno. Scared, maybe.
Toshack:	Scared? Of what?
Keane:	Everyone. You'd be scared, if you were me.
Toshack:	Don't you want to be a part of society?
Keane:	I'm not sure if society wants me to be a part of it.
Toshack:	Okay, final question before we wrap up today. What do you think I should tell the parole board?
Keane:	You've never asked me that before.
Toshack:	No. It's not been relevant before.
Keane:	Just don't send me to adult prison.

28

Crawley, December 1999

The crunching ceases as Ray's boots settle on the soft matting. 'Don't attract attention', he was told on the phone. 'Come alone.' Like there is anyone who cares what happens to him. Two mothers, pulling their children along, watch him enter through the gate from the street, hurrying with their journey, muttering to each other. The playground is empty, and Ray is early.

He settles down to wait on the bench, studying the primeval carved markings with his fingers, expressions of juvenile love, ignoring the additional demand that 'wogs go home'. There is rusty paint on the climbing frame opposite. The swings sag, motionless, tired. Town planners, eager to bring people together by creating spaces for communal living, have failed. Not knowing that what they built has set the town residents against each other, sold on a dream they cannot realise. Escape will not be easy.

This encounter might go away, if he closes his eyes. Two birds are at war, chirping their argument, standing out from the steady drone overhead. He isolates them, wondering if they are simply a message being played for his benefit. Two antagonists, in conflict, approaching an ending.

Leckie chose this place. Ray shudders, imagines the retired gangster watching him, relishing the fact that he cannot feel his toes, that those women suspect he is a pervert, that Leckie has a hold over him. He stamps his feet on the matting, then stands, wondering how much to reveal. He has three names, with locations, but knows that when his finger points, it will probably be a death sentence. Movement might help him concentrate. He empties his pockets of sweet wrappers, dropping them in a litter bin, then pauses by a slide. The early morning sun blinds the view of the top, rising so the slide appears endless, and a puddle sits flatly at its base, reflecting a drab loser. *This town is stagnant, slowly dying*, he thinks, taking him with it.

A cough makes Ray turn around. Leckie is standing on the centre of the roundabout, an apparition from nowhere. Beneath the trilby hat, his breath forms controlled, perfect circles in the cold air. Leckie beckons Ray over.

'Morning, Raymond.'

As Ray approaches, Leckie steps back to allow room to climb onto the roundabout. When Ray gets his balance, Leckie sets it rotating with a skip of his foot. Ray grabs at one of the rails, before falling onto the wooden boards, leaning his back against the metal, short of breath.

'I said, morning.'

'Good morning, Mister Harris.'

'Is it? You tell me.' His voice is calm, monotone. Non-committal.

Leckie increases the pace with another push, the scuff of his foot echoing across the playground.

He stares down at Ray. 'Go on, then. Where is he?'

Ray raises himself up with the horizontal rail, trying to reach his client's height. The playground spins quickly, forcing Ray to look down, searching for something to focus on. Leckie's shoes shine.

'I'm nearly there.'

'Nearly?'

'Yeah, nearly. Down to four men.' The lie hangs above them, forming shapes in the thin air. Ray reckons it is better to surprise him with good news later, buy himself a little time, under-promise and over-deliver. He needs more certainty before he pulls the trigger on his victim. Something to stir him into action. Distracted by visitors from his distant past, words scribbled in an unfamiliar hand, from a lost friend. And mixed fortunes on the horses, despite sticking to favourites.

The roundabout judders, then slows, Leckie pushing backwards with his foot on the ground, braking. When they stop, Leckie leans in, softly takes Ray's chin in his hand, then squeezes, forcing his tobacco breath into Ray's face.

'Four? I thought you was looking for one man, not four. They told me you was good at this. Don't piss me about, sunshine. Time is nearly up.'

Ray shakes his head slowly, and the grip tightens even more.

'I want to know who he is, where he is, and who he was. I'm not normally an impatient man. Remember, I've bailed you out of the shit. Remember that.' Leckie pauses, glares at his hired detective, a look on his face Ray struggles to read. 'You're not getting any grief off those brothers, are you?'

'No.'

Ray looks down at the wooden boards, spots an outline shape that reminds him of a mushroom cloud. A sign of impending disaster. He can't look Leckie in the eye.

'If they give you any trouble, you tell me. You should be free to work for me.'

Ray nods, but the movement makes his head feel like the roundabout is spinning again, even though it has stopped. If it wasn't for Leckie, Marko would have rearranged his kneecaps by now. But a part of him still wonders if this is just a stay of execution. A new tormentor, in front of him, holding him in his grasp.

Leckie releases his grip, and Ray stumbles sideways, falling face-first onto the boards. They taste of floor polish and dried blood.

'Go on, then. Enlighten me. Tell me where he might be.'

The question of how much to tell, when the deadline is three weeks away. There are innocent men out there, who have changed their identity in an unfortunate alignment with Keane and Duggan. Ray needs certainty before he hands someone over to a man like Leckie Harris. He sits on the roundabout base, not wanting to stand, conscious Leckie might send it spinning at any moment. He can avoid confrontation down there.

'Wouldn't you rather wait until I know who it is for certain?' Ray's voice feels like a squeak.

'Maybe.' Leckie spits on the floor of the roundabout in front of him. 'I just want to know you ain't pissing me about, sunshine. You been at this a while. I got a lot invested in you.'

'You'll have your man in time for Christmas Day,' Ray promises.

'Good. See to it. And don't forget I want to know what he's been up to. That's important.'

'How far back do you want me to go?' Ray asks the brave question, still not looking up.

'As far back as time. Since before he was born, if you have to. Fuck, do I have to spell this out for you? Don't forget what I'm doing for you.'

'No, no, I won't.'

Ray shakes his head. Realises he must cut a pathetic figure, slumped on the roundabout in front of a man like Leckie. There were tales years ago about the beatings he delivered, the bodies he rearranged, the teeth and other body parts that went missing. Ray assumes he has men to do that for him now but is sure Leckie wouldn't be averse to handing out something that might come out of the Mirkovic handbook, if provoked.

Leckie sighs, and Ray looks up at him. 'Well, actually, Christmas Day is a day for family. So, let's make it Boxing Day.' Then he curls his lip. 'I'm being generous.'

'Thanks. Boxing Day. No problem.'

Boxing Day means Kempton Park. The King George Chase. Ray has not missed it in fifteen years. He will aim to exceed his client's expectations, deliver the man he is looking for early so he can relax, enjoy the day with no debt and a clean slate for the horses.

'Don't forget, I need the expenses paid back. In full. Same time.'

That might still prove to be the trickiest part. The original money has come and gone, despite a recent good streak, and Ray is still scrabbling to keep everything he earns in his pocket. Will need to come up with more winners before Christmas. Wonders whether, if he has his man, Leckie might give him a little more time to pay it back. Five hundred quid won't mean much to a man like Leckie Harris.

Ray's silence prompts Leckie to offer a reminder. 'In full. All of it.'

'In full,' Ray repeats. More hours in the cab, then, and a couple of good selections, to provide the necessary payment.

'Right. My boys will be staying in touch. You still got that phone?'

Ray reaches inside his jacket pocket and realises in the hurry to get there early he has left it beside the bed.

'You have still got it, for fuck's sake?' Leckie hisses.

'Yeah. Just not with me right now.'

Leckie frowns, curses under his breath. 'Don't screw this up, Raymond. Keep that thing with you, like you were told.'

'Sure. I will.' Ray's voice sounds an octave higher than normal. The blood pulses in his ears. His fingers and toes are numb.

'We'll meet Boxing Day, ten o'clock, here. Got it?'

Ray nods and mumbles a weak, 'Yeah.'

Leckie leans against one of the metal rails, then drives his foot off the floor again, to start the roundabout in motion. Ray closes his eyes and sits there, hoping this will bring stability. He is unable to move, can feel the world spinning around him, accelerating. Ray has no idea how many turns they have taken before the weight on the boards lessens, and something lands on the matting nearby. Leckie must have jumped off. After a few seconds, Ray looks up to see the figure in the trilby hat striding over to one of his men, who greets him at the gate, the sight of this moving in and out of his vision as he tumbles round and round. There is no looking back at the foolish errand boy who needs to save his own neck by handing over what is bound to be a dead man.

Ray closes his eyes again as the roundabout slows. He will wait for it to stop before getting off. There is an exterior force dictating when his agony will end, nothing he can do about it. The urge will never go away; he knows he has been deluding himself. All those sessions in cold church halls have done nothing except expose him to other men with a similar problem. None of them can escape from the hold that the thrill of a bet brings. None of them have a genuine way out.

After Boxing Day, Ray will just be starting with a fresh debt, one laden with guilt, about what Paul and he didn't do, how they could have saved a life. And of a man he will be sending to death, a grass who should have known better than to betray Leckie Harris. He will still be an accomplice. Ray won't owe any money, but he won't be free either. As he steps off the roundabout, he wonders if Dusty could create him a new life, one with a fresh slate.

29

Milton Keynes, December 1999

Rising from his sofa, somewhere he has not slept before, Carl calls out her name, but there is no response, only the empty echo of a small flat. A reminder of how comfortably alone he has become. But for one night, she broke in, found her way inside, the first person ever to cross the threshold. None of his neighbours could describe him as noisy. Carl doesn't think any of them could describe him at all. He rents one of the top floor flats in a three-storey block on Fishermead, a sad-looking estate near the city centre. Nobody seems to live in this part of Milton Keynes by choice.

Residents refer to Milton Keynes as the 'city', even though it is still officially classified as a town. Getting ahead of its status. The local newspapers and radio tell him this is an up-and-coming place. There used to be a railway industry nearby, since swallowed up by the greedy tentacles of the new town. Nothing is manufactured any more. The focus is on what is termed 'service delivery'. It feels like a Mecca for middlemen. Perfect for somewhere to hide. The Circle is a prime example. Although he cannot see it continuing any more, after what Lydia did.

Carl finds his shorts on the floor. His clothes are always tidied away, an unshakable habit. Until the previous night. Lydia has upset the balance. Apart from the bedroom, there is only a bathroom and the living room, which has a small kitchenette adjoined, to search. No sign of the siren. But he senses her presence in the corners, under cushions, behind pictures on the walls. A feeling of invasion haunts every step as he pads around.

Two wine glasses are moved to the dishwasher. When there is a minimal amount of space, efficiency is necessary. He breathes in deeply, and the smell hits. Smoke. Images form, alien scenes of bodies writhing, kissing, fumbling, laughing. Her cigarette end sticks out of the top of a can of Coke in the kitchenette. He has exposed himself. Allowing a woman into his space for the first time. There has been sex before, but never anywhere that could be called home. Another picture hits him. Of Lydia leaving, coat over her shoulder, with a smile rather than the usual face of pity. Certainly not one of worry, after what she did.

And then other images of the night before hit. S lying on the office kitchen floor, blood forming in the grouting. Scrubbing with bleach. A body falling to the concrete below. Echoes ringing around his head, forcing him to look away as it dropped.

He pours a long glass of water and takes two aspirin. His scalp itches, he scratches, feels the throbbing pain. They had a drink together, not to celebrate a death, but perhaps the relief at finding a way through it. Normally Carl is so careful. Checks in place, ensuring nobody gets close, forgotten for one night. Wondering if deep inside he has decided to live life at last, rather than stay in hiding. Seeing the fear on Lydia's face, the blood solidified on the floor, pushing him to act. To help another human being, for the first time in his life.

His body clock has let him down. Six is his regular waking point every morning, ingrained by institutions with a desire to instil discipline. But not today. Carl studies the second hand on the wall, watching it hesitate at each faltering step, dragging out a Sunday. A day that marks the fact that he is not as safe as he thought he was. Going through fragments of conversations from the night before, after they returned to his flat, and what he might have let out when they moved the body and cleaned up. The lies are so deep, over half a lifetime of practice, ensuring nothing escapes. Doesn't recall her face showing shock, or horror. He must have kept his own truth inside.

He took the lead, before they disposed of the body, while she stood in horror at what she had done. Empathy, he remembers they called it, in the therapy sessions. Needing to understand what it felt like to be other people. A prerequisite for his release. He showed it to them, for their assessments, and now he realises at last what it feels like.

The liaison officers guided him in how to sink into the background. Don't reveal anything from your past, apart from the storyline you have been given. Don't return to where you used to live. Keep away from everyone you used to know. Only open up to your appointed helper. He has cast himself adrift of the officials by now, with an extra change of identity. Confident they are not watching. But still wary, in case he is recognised.

He pulls their freshly washed clothes out of the machine. Recalls she left wearing a pair of his joggers and a T-shirt. He wipes around the sink, another act of certainty. Removing anything that could link them to a dead body. Lydia suggested the clothes came off, to be safe, then reached for him on the sofa, and he surrendered. A different submission to when the blows would rain in from that bitch and her men. Panic, followed by excitement, when he saw Lydia's slender body. The act prompted by what they had both just gone through. *United in fear*, Carl thinks.

Lydia didn't seem to want to talk about what she had done, just hold on to another human being. And Carl was the one she reached out to. Remembering the hysteria in her voice when she called, the repetition of 'I've killed him.' Startled by the fact that he knew precisely how to respond. Resisting the temptation to stay in the shadows, overcoming the training they instilled in him, a fear that kept him frozen out of life, for longer than the original sentence, even the licence period. That boy may be forgotten, but he has always been paying for what they said he did. Now recognising a sense of relief as he cycled over to the office to help her, knowing that S, who had been probing into his own history, was gone.

He suspects the reality of his past would be too unspeakable to share with her, even after what they just went through. Even if it meant stopping the lies. And lies become the truth eventually. There hasn't been anyone close enough he could trust not to scream and run, to resist telling the press and the lynch mobs where that child is.

A full search of the flat provides no more scares. Bookshelves with titles sorted alphabetically. CDs in the stacker, similarly arranged. Everything in its place, undisturbed. Without order, you cannot keep control. Cannot ensure nobody has been reaching inside, pulling at the truth. This way you will not be punished.

There is one more place to check. The heavy clunk of the combination lock on the battered suitcase reassures him, and Carl breathes out. No way she could have reached inside this place. The reminder of an ordinary life.

The items shuffle around, asking to be picked up, to be loved the way a boy once did. A *Planet of the Apes* sticker album, half a model Spitfire, a jumble of Top Trumps cards, three pieces from a Buckaroo set. Other childish odds and ends retrieved for him when he was finally placed at Murrayfields, with a new name, hoping they would help him settle. The mementos rattle, but he ignores them, is comforted by the fact they are intact. Reminders of that young boy, and a possible other path. But also of the stone he crawled out from under. He closes the case firmly and replaces it under the bed.

Reassurance comes from his oldest friend, the radio. He has heard the firm click of the switch thousands of times, and the words will drown out the tick of the faltering clock. This far out of London the reception for *LBC* can be temperamental, but phone-in voices are calming. Carl runs a hand over the familiar top of the radio set, and a calming sense of solitude returns. Television was a shared experience in the homes, when it wasn't being trashed by some maniac, angry at not seeing his mother or being denied a fix. Radio was a personal privilege. This first set has stayed with him, wherever he went, whoever he was, still works provided you are happy with medium wave.

Carl pulls out the battered Risk box from a drawer in the coffee table, and carefully selects the cards for each player, allocating them starting points on the map. A new game for a new beginning. Concentration and discipline take over as he moves pieces around the globe, deciding fate, rolling the dice. Reverting to the safety of this other world, manipulating his subjects and accomplices in warfare. Putting the shutters back up to protect against invaders. The past will be safe, lost in the manoeuvres and coloured combat.

30

Sevenoaks, December 1999

Alone with a psychiatrist, long overdue.

'Raymond, is it?'

'Ray is fine.'

'Good, Ray it is.'

Doctor Geoffrey Toshack sits opposite, gently stroking his short, grey beard with his index finger. Ray looks around the consulting room, at the certificates, the family photographs, the metal filing cabinet. In truth, he is searching for where the archives are likely to be, but there is no harm in appearing interested in other things. Toshack's private practice sits on the first floor of a Victorian building in the middle of Sevenoaks, above one of the many estate agents that haunt the high street. A street that feels like it is from a different universe to Crawley.

They are opposite each other, on comfortable chairs. Toshack doesn't have a couch. A small, round table sits between them, a convenient barrier.

'Right, Ray.' Toshack leans forward, rubbing his hands

together, expensive-looking checked shirt a surprising detail to Ray. No white coat. 'What do you want to talk about?'

Being a patient would involve paying money, which Ray doesn't have. No recent winners, not even when he backed a string of favourites. He even tried something new, offered on the screens in his local Ladbrokes, Irish racing. Ray is convinced that is fixed too.

The playground meeting has focused his attention on digging into Keane's past, as well as where he is now. There will be enough time to narrow his target down to one man in hiding. One of the sheets in Dusty's stolen folder was the final release recommendation for Michael Keane from Oak Dene Detention Centre, in 1984. It was penned by this Toshack, a juvenile psychologist who also worked at a Murrayfields Secure Home, where Keane was previously locked up for five years. The man who would have advised if Keane was ready to be released.

Breaking into the archive in a damp basement at Murrayfields taught Ray nothing. Two hours sifting through boxes of index cards and folders, torch in his teeth, sweating and wondering what his life has come to, and no sign of a Michael Keane. Or any other name that he recognised from Dusty's list of identities. If anybody knows who Keane originally was, this Toshack is the man.

'To be honest, doctor, I want to ask you about something.'

'Firstly, you don't need to call me doctor. I'm Geoffrey. And secondly, you can ask about anything.' Toshack smiles, but Ray detects something behind it. A master of disguise, someone used to digging into your innermost secrets. Ray shivers.

'What I mean is, I'm not looking for any therapy sessions. Not paid-for sessions.'

'Oh.' Toshack looks down at his pad and scribbles a few words, before looking up. Ray imagines this includes, 'time-waster'. 'Do explain,' he says, still sounding patient.

'What I mean is, I'm researching something, and I hope you can help me.'

'I thought when you booked it was to see me. Professionally.' More writing on the pad. Maybe 'untrustworthy' this time.

'Mister Callahan at Murrayfields gave me your name.' A lie; it was the receptionist. Callahan is the head of the unit, but a middle-aged lady with a badge that told Ray she was Helen said Toshack was the only staff member with over fifteen years' service.

'Did he?'

'Yes.' Ray holds his hands up, then pulls a notebook out of his jacket pocket. Now they are evenly matched. 'I'm a journalist. Writing an article on the treatment of the young. The young with issues. And how it compares to say, fifteen, twenty years ago. That sort of thing.'

'Sorry, you…' Toshack breaks off, and puts his paper and pad down beside him.

'I didn't mean to mislead you, Doctor Toshack. Geoffrey.' Ray places a fake business card, 'Ray Mercer, Freelance Journalist', on the table. Toshack gives it a fleeting look but declines to pick it up.

'I don't talk to the press about my patients. You should know that I can't talk about them. Past or present.'

'Oh, I know.' There are ink stains on the doctor's hands. Ray wonders why this is distracting him. Needs to focus on what Bogart would do. He would be forthright. He would quickly get to the heart of the matter.

'Geoffrey.' Ray forces a smile. 'I'm writing an article on young offenders, and how they are treated today. And comparing it to the past. I appreciate that I can't use anything specific. I just want to talk generally about how they are evaluated, assessed, you know, and how this used to be done.'

Toshack nods and leans back in his chair. 'I really don't think I should.' Ray folds his arms across his chest. Believes this man can see straight through him, knows he is a chancer, on a fishing expedition, ready to throw one surname at him, to see if he reacts.

'You used to work on the assessment of young offenders, didn't you?'

'I did in the past, yes. But I don't any more.' Toshack mirrors Ray, folds his arms.

'And how long ago did that stop?'

'Is that relevant?'

'Not really, sorry, I'm just trying to get an understanding of your background.'

Toshack stares, dark eyes scouring Ray's face for clues. 'Have you not researched my background?'

'Yes, I have. That's why I want to ask you about this subject.' Ray tries a little flattery. 'You are an expert.'

'I'm not sure what you're after, Ray.' Toshack bends forwards and picks up the card, taps at it with a finger, then stands. 'I don't think I can help you. Sorry.'

Ray should sit tight and blag it. 'That's a pity. I've spoken to a few ex-offenders. Some of them had stories to tell.'

'Oh, did they?'

Ray rises, so the doctor is no longer looking down at him.

'Yes. Some had respect for their analysts, some hated them.' Ray offers a smile.

Toshack tuts. 'Well, they are hardly best placed to evaluate the help we give them. That's our job.'

'I'm just gathering information from all sides. Including the police.'

Toshack retreats to sit behind his desk. 'They wouldn't have much idea. Anyway, it was the probationary service I gave information to, on offenders. Not the police. You should know that.'

The doctor taps on his keyboard, looks at some notes in front of him. It might not matter. Five minutes outside the office and an inspection of this room have provided Ray with Plan B. Plan A was a million-to-one shot. Toshack would never react if he threw out the words 'Michael Keane'. A large filing cabinet nestles against one wall, a key sitting in the top. Large folders on his shelves, and more on the floor behind him. Toshack might have a computer system, but there is a paper backup.

Ray has the mental map he needs. Now to leave without raising too much suspicion.

'Sorry, Geoffrey. I'm just trying to write a truthful article.'

'This article, where will it appear? A medical journal?'

'No. It's for the Sunday supplements. I'm freelance, but a couple of them are already interested.'

'Are they.' Not a question. 'I thought these things got commissioned before they were written, or researched.'

'Not this one.'

'Why are you so interested in young criminals?'

Ray walks towards the desk, stopping a stride away.

One last flutter. 'Okay. The truth is that someone came forward to me who was a young offender, who wasn't happy with how they were assessed, you know, before they were released.' Ray clears his throat. 'Someone at Murrayfields.'

Toshack looks up, hands paused over the keys, but doesn't appear threatened.

'Really? That doesn't surprise me. Like I said, they're not experts.'

'I suppose not.' Ray places his hands on the edge of the desk. 'Hence talking to someone like you, Geoffrey.'

Toshack starts typing, then pauses again to look up, mentally dismissing his visitor.

'Well, sorry, Ray, you're wasting your time. I can't talk about specifics. Or generalities. It's unprofessional. I still do some work for Murrayfields, as you seem to know, even if most of my time is spent here, with private patients. I can't say anything.'

Ray slips the notebook back in his pocket. Shows a suitably contrite face. Holds his hands up in submission.

'Sorry, Geoffrey. You can't blame me for trying. I've got to earn a living.'

'Well, I suppose so.' There is a flash of a short-lived smile. 'Good luck with your article. You sure you don't need my help in any other way? For any personal treatment? For professional help?'

'No, thanks.'

'Well, goodbye then.' Toshack waves a thin hand in Ray's direction, and the non-patient carefully counts his steps out towards the waiting room, where he makes a short detour, before heading down the narrow stairs to street level.

31

Chapter 5, 'THE WITNESS AND THE 999 CALL', FROM *THE TOWN THAT FORGOT CHILD X*, BY TRISH WATNEY

Based on an interview with the eyewitness to the murder, Alan Gregory, April 1978

The case against Martin Sullivan hinged on two things. His confession at the police station and the eyewitness account of a man who saw him kick Philip Hughes off the scaffolding at the development in Northgate, Crawley. Alan Gregory testified on oath in court to this effect. He was barely cross-examined about what he saw, or even why he was standing at the perimeter of the building site, with a vantage point over the fence. Nobody thought to question him properly.

This was convenient for the prosecution. Alan Gregory had no criminal record. He was twenty-two years old, smartly dressed when he gave his evidence. But the police knew something wasn't quite right about Alan Gregory, which was why they were happy they had a confession as well.

Local detectives were aware of Gregory prior to the killing. Inside information from Crawley CID reveals they suspected he was interfering with boys as young as ten, in local parks, and had been doing so for a couple of years. No case had been brought against him, although according to an anonymous source, there was one incident which nearly came to trial. In that instance, the parents of the boy interfered with decided to drop the charges.

On paper, and during the trial, Gregory appeared to be an upstanding citizen, who just happened to witness a murder. To the police, he had the classic profile of what they call a 'nonce', a child molester. From these same internal sources at the local CID, it is clear they were tempted to dismiss his description of one boy killing another and pin the death on Gregory. However, they discovered Gregory suffered from vertigo, so would have been unlikely to climb up to the top of the scaffolding.

I met Gregory after the trial, where he worked as an assistant at Tilgate golf course. He maintained the mowers and other equipment for the council who manage it. This was the only job he had been able to hold down for more than six months. Our appeal in the *Crawley Observer* led to him being identified by three separate passers-by as being on Barnfield Road in Northgate that evening. Gregory later admitted under questioning that he had placed the 999 call which led the police to find the body. According to sources in Crawley CID, they immediately knew who it was once his description was provided.

Gregory insisted that he was out walking when his attention was drawn to the sounds of two boys shouting on a building site on Green Lane. He watched them for about fifteen minutes. The police found two cigarette ends that matched the brand Gregory used outside the fence. There was no evidence he had strayed onto the building site. Gregory repeated what he said in court, that he saw a boy matching the description of Sullivan kick another boy off the scaffolding on the building site. He estimated he was about forty yards away at the time. There was no challenge over his ability to identify Sullivan in court. The police used the description of the boy Gregory provided to track down Sullivan in local schools. He also confirmed the identity of the killer at the station, with the help of a police officer. He could not recall his name, but my sources later identified him as DS Charlie Brennan.

'The man (Brennan) asked me to sit near the desk at the entrance to the police station and watch a group who came in. He said to tell him when I saw the boy who had kicked the other one off the top of the scaffolding. To tell them who the killer was, he said. Said I had to do this, or they might start thinking it was me what killed him. Only one boy came into the police station, and it was him. I had seen him in the playground at West Green before.'

Gregory was reluctant to talk about his initial police interview with Birkdale and Brennan. All Gregory would reveal was that, 'they were annoyed I didn't come forward when the appeal went out in the paper. But they don't understand what it's like being me. I'm trying to be better, to change who I am. They still think I'm a bad person. They would rather it was me in the dock than that boy. They would have liked that.'

When interviewed, Birkdale had nothing to say about his star witness, other than that, 'he did what was asked of him. He told us what he saw.' Gregory probably read the situation correctly. Birkdale and his team would rather Gregory was found guilty. They had to settle for second best when they got Martin Sullivan.

32

Sevenoaks, December 1999

The window opens slowly in Ray's patient hands. It has been a few months since he climbed up a fire escape and wormed his way through such a small space into a building at night. He left the toilet window just an inch open about eight hours earlier, having checked it would move up far enough to allow him to enter. Knowing he was the last appointment of the day gave Ray some confidence it would remain untouched.

There is a small squeak as his foot pivots on the floor, and Ray holds his breath. The place should be deserted, and he transfers the torch from mouth to gloved hand. Creeping into the waiting area, the layout is familiar. Three plastic chairs sit against a wall, in stark contrast to the comfort of the office. The doctor's door is locked, as expected, and the usual tools come out of Ray's back pocket. He would struggle to open a safe these days, but standard Chubbs are easy once you know how. Despite the lazy image that is portrayed of security personnel, back in his day, training included more than just learning how to watch monitors and drink coffee at the same time. They were shown how burglars operated, including a couple of hours on how to prevent breaking and entering. Sharing the tricks of the trade. Useful skills for gamekeepers to become poachers.

Anything resembling proper security and he would have struggled, but the earlier visit showed Ray how little this was a concern for the doctor. After following Toshack to a rather nice detached house on the edge of town, Ray slotted in a four-hour shift for the brothers over in Crawley, then back to watch his target turn his light out at midnight. Best of all, not one step inside a bookies' during that time, despite having a tenner from the shift in his wallet. He kept the focus, knowing what lay ahead of him. There is hope for Ray yet.

The torch goes back between his teeth, as the lock slides smoothly, then he pushes the door gently open. Ray feels his temples pulsing. Another creak, like a warning system, but no alarm. The room layout is unchanged, although the desk has been cleared. The computer is off but is of no interest. A key still dangles from the top drawer of the filing cabinet.

Ray wonders how much Toshack saw through his story. A man adept at analysing if people are lying to him, establishing whether they are fit to rejoin society. The assessments he weighed might have swayed decisions. According to what he has read, Toshack could have been the man to set Michael Keane free. A juvenile specialist. Working where he did, there is a good chance he knew Keane's previous identity, and why he was in a secure home. But unlikely to give that information to Ray sitting opposite in those comfortable chairs. There are other means.

In the bottom two cabinet drawers Ray finds patient records, arranged alphabetically. His heart is tight against his chest, fingers sensitive to everything they touch through the gloves, ears alert for the slightest sound. Ready to react to any disturbance. It feels like he is getting closer.

The patient files start at the back with 'A'. There is no system to Ray's own filing, unless you count throwing everything into a pile in the microwave. Easier to find things that way; the most recent is always on top.

No 'Keane' or 'Duggan'; the last of these would make no sense, but he searches for it anyway. Then he scans through each name tab, looking for something familiar. Nothing jumps out. He goes back over them all again, opening out a couple of pages for every record, wondering if the boy he is looking for is stored under his original name. Still nothing.

Ray swallows to release the pressure in his ears. He might be leaving empty-handed. A familiar feeling in the stomach to when he went through those archives at Murrayfields.

Perhaps Toshack realised he was a chancer, removed the relevant file, knew who Ray was after. But there was no discussion of specifics. He needs to focus. There must be a record somewhere, this is a meticulous man, judging by the filing. Ray checks the dates of the files; nothing seems to go further back than 1996. There must be an archive somewhere.

Flicking his torch around the room at ground level, looking for clues, afraid to turn the lights on, caution is embedded in Ray's movements. Nobody would expect to see any sign of life in a first-floor office at one in the morning. He checks the shelves – nothing but medical documents, magazines, and weighty books. Lever arch files, but no patient records. He focuses in on the space he remembers from earlier, where a batch of storage boxes sit. The light shines on labels facing outwards. The older paper files. As he runs his gloved finger over the spines, a dry smell hits, a reminder of dusty library shelves.

Ray knows he has time on his side. Walks out to check the reception area, knees creaking. He tries the door to the outside hallway from the waiting room. The handle rattles, but remains locked. He is alone, knows there are no cameras, and can picture Doctor Toshack tucked up in bed. But still there is a sense that somebody is watching. Back in the office, he stares at the phone on the doctor's desk, for some reason anticipating it will ring, before going back to his search.

In the cardboard filing boxes arranged against the back wall, he finds more alphabetical ordering, and this time, under 'K', there is 'Keane, Michael'. Ray's shoulders lift, his spine straightens with relief. He is close, can feel the veins in his head throbbing as he carries the box over to the desk.

Ray sits in Toshack's chair, opening the Keane file out. The top half of the inch-high pile of contents are a series of hand-written notes, then part way down typed sheets take over. No photographs. A quick check reveals no other names or admissions records, so Ray goes through the contents in a more orderly fashion. His T-shirt clings to his chest, underneath the regulation burglary black jumper. There is always an adrenaline rush when breaking and entering, but this feels more intense. Perhaps it is just that it has been so long. Ray tries to steady his breathing, calm down. He is safe where he is.

Many of the sheets are on Murrayfields headed paper, showing Toshack as the doctor, and Keane the patient.

The dates move backwards over time. Maybe Toshack is using old material for his research into juvenile psychology. Confidential records, easy enough for a dubious investigator to get their hands on.

The terminology is a struggle to understand, and on some pages, there are records of conversations, Ray assumes between Toshack and Keane, in rooms like this. A report from 1983 confirms the information Dusty provided, recommending the transfer of Michael Keane from Murrayfields Secure Home to Oak Dene Detention Centre. Ray wipes sweat from his brow with the back of his glove, squinting at the words.

The older paperwork in the file has the names of different doctors on it. Ray looks at the clock on the wall and wonders how long it will take to go through everything. He has been there for nearly an hour. Cramp nags at the back of his thighs, perched on the chair. He stretches out, cracking his knuckles, raising his spine. There must be a clue somewhere. He knows there is no record of Keane prior to 1982. Perhaps he should have simply taken the file and read the contents at home.

The reports are repetitive. He searches for information about a crime, a reason for Keane's detention, but finds nothing. Ray sinks deeper into the chair, feels it accept his weight, turns the pages deliberately, reads even slower, starts again, beginning from the back this time.

Then, something jumps out at him, in Toshack's now-familiar handwriting, describing an initial admission to Murrayfields. Two words, bold letters in black on white. He runs a hand across his damp brow, clutches his chest. A name stares back at him. The words shrink, then come back to their original size. They are Michael Keane's previous identity, boldly spelt out in a letter about his new environment.

Martin Sullivan.

A droplet falls onto the desk, a silent splash echoing in his head. Seeing that name again throws him back to their shame, two boys who did nothing when they could have saved a life. You can hide it away, hoping nobody will dig it up again. But deep inside, there will be a reckoning, when you must answer for inaction. Paul is now at peace with himself, where nobody can challenge him. *He couldn't face the fear*, Ray thinks. It still looms over Ray, pinning him to the chair.

Ray stares at the words, then manages to pull his attention away and sees himself reflected in a large circular clock on the wall. The guilty face of an accomplice to a future crime, one he could have prevented.

He grabs the papers and re-arranges them in the file. No time to place everything meticulously back or photograph them. The face from so many years ago returns. The dark eyes and the short hair of the killer across the dual carriageway, so far away from the woods but so close to two boys hiding in fear. A face he saw fleetingly at school months later, before Child X was unmasked.

Toshack's job was to assess that boy, advise whether Sullivan was healed. Ray opens the file again, finds the page that made him freeze. Without knowing it, he has placed it at the back. He reads more slowly, tries, unsuccessfully, to understand the medical phrases. It seems like they covered up the changing of his name from Sullivan to Keane, to protect him in Murrayfields. Had they forgotten what he did? He was a murderer. Only that boy and two guilty onlookers knew this was twice over.

He should replace the file where he found it and leave. If Leckie Harris acts on the information he has no choice but to hand over, discovers his supergrass is also a killer, Ray wouldn't want to be holding on to anything incriminating when the body is found.

The Philip Hughes murder was high profile for a while in Crawley. But afterwards, the fascination in the papers, the chatter at school, faded away. Ray remembers articles about Sullivan's mother, how she was hounded out of town. Perhaps they deliberately forgot about the boy. And, years later, in the eyes of the authorities, he must have been transformed, rehabilitated, thanks to the analysis of Doctor Geoffrey Toshack. Then they helped him change identity, gave him a future. Repeatedly. From Keane to Duggan and now to someone else. Sullivan is out there, one of his remaining three figures, and he has little choice but to lead a gangster to his prey. The connection to Leckie is puzzling. Perhaps he just knows too many bad people. The revelation of who Keane originally was changes little. Morality is so murky now. But Ray will have to reveal the true identity to Leckie. To save his own neck.

Sitting in the chair, Ray ponders a decision. Despite the perilous situation, he must meet this man, the boy who haunted his teenage years, and look him in the eye. Judge for himself, not in the way Toshack did with his fancy words, but to stare into that face that tormented him, and work out if the truth should be told. Leckie is probably going to kill him, whatever he does, whoever he used to be. Sullivan might even tell Ray why the gangster is after him, what he has done to Bad Leckie. Ray should give the killer a chance to explain himself. Then he can work out what to do next.

33

Waterloo Bridge, October 1998

The stranger sits down alongside Carl, offers the bottle of scotch. Carl reaches out for it, clutches at its neck, turns it up and down, measuring the volume. Half full, better than nothing. The liquid swishes, and the figure grabs the bottle back. Places it carefully between them on the flattened cardboard box.

'For later,' the visitor says. 'When we're done.'

'Eh?'

'When we're done,' he repeats, more slowly, with emphasis.

Carl stares at the bottle, transfixed. They both know this is what he wants.

'Not this again,' Carl says, pulling his gloves over his fingers, leaning back against the wall. The cold digs through his coat into his back, settles on his kidneys. He is always cold.

'There's really nobody I can contact? To help you? No family?'

'No.'

In truth, this isn't a stranger; he has visited many times before. Has asked many questions. But Carl has no idea what his name is. He might have mentioned it, but then he struggles to remember most things. Only that he needs a drink, can feel his mouth drying, aches for the burn on his tongue and down his throat. Needs it all the time.

'I'm trying to help you, Carl.' The eyes look across at him, offering hope. But Carl has no need for hope. He is finished with hope.

'Just give me a sip,' he implores, looking at the holes in his shoes. 'Just a little one.'

'When we're done.'

The voice is calm, never angry, always trying to help. The owner looks up and down the alleyway. It has been dark for some time, and the pedestrians who occasionally walk this way, rushing for a late train, taking a shortcut to the tube station, have gone for the night. Just the two of them, under a bridge, hidden from the world. Two men sharing a life, although only one of them is aware of it.

'There's definitely nobody knows you're here?' the visitor asks.

'Nobody cares.' The reply, with a shake of the head.

The new Carl pulls the stopper off the bottle and offers it. Old Carl takes a large pull, then a couple of shorter gulps. Wipes his mouth with the back of his hand. Tips it towards new Carl, who refuses.

The parallel identity is in place. Leading two lives, before dropping one in favour of the other. The way they have trained him. Wiping clean the old monster they said he was. Adopting a new persona. No dead children this time, just a man of about the same age he found here weeks earlier, surrounded by discarded needles and bottles. The perfect person to reconstruct. Carl Marsh, or so he claimed to be. Reborn on the electoral roll, with a new face, driving licence and bank cards. A man he brought back to life, to run alongside himself. This will not be theft; the old Carl has already given up. The imposter has seen it in his eyes. The way there is no challenge when the pain is delivered, the test of whether the subject was ready. A needle to the arm, or the ankle, and no resistance. Old Carl is wasting a life, an identity, and new Carl is taking it.

New Carl walks the length of the passageway a couple of times, to check for stray visitors, finds the area is clear. He watches the tramp drain the bottle, tip it upside down with disdain. Shake it, desperately hoping for more. This will help with the story. Of a down-and-out who has given up on life. Donating an identity to him.

Satisfied nobody will disturb them, new Carl sits down again next to his twin. This is merely a reappropriation of life, nothing more. He senses that although Neil Duggan has fallen off the radar of the authorities, it is best to place an extra level of protection between himself and the vigilantes, the media newshounds, the downright curious. The case of those boys from Liverpool, and how they are being hounded, has accelerated the need to move on. All those eyes that have been staring at him lately, intent on catching him out. Desperately seeking the truth behind his story. He has decided it is best to leap ahead of them.

New Carl is pleased the drunk has closed his eyes. Would have struggled to do this while looking at his desperate face. A face he has studied for weeks, wondering how close to it he would appear. Realising eventually that the looks won't matter, given that he is replacing a person that nobody cares about.

Sitting astride the prone figure, he looks up and down the alleyway one more time. Pins the arms down with his knees, pulls the cushion over the face, ensures the nose and mouth are closed. Drives the material into the man underneath him, unsurprised by the lack of fight. He was right. Old Carl really had given up.

New Carl decides against leaving anything that would identify Neil Duggan at the scene. He had contemplated placing a travelcard in a pocket. But reasoned a man living down here would have nothing to show who he is. Society forgot Carl Marsh a long time ago. They won't miss him. Another faceless statistic among the homeless.

New Carl checks for a pulse. Nothing. He steps away from the body, pulls out a lighter to set fire to the pillow and the man's meagre belongings. Removes the coins from the plastic cup at his feet. Old Carl's first and only direct donation to the future. Bus fare home.

At the end of the alley, he turns the corner towards Waterloo Station, pulling his coat around him against the cold. A rough night to be out in this weather. Heading towards a new address, a meagre flat across the other side of the vast city, procured with a different name. He is ready to disappear into the shadows once more.

34

Milton Keynes, December 1999

The police arrive on a Wednesday morning, tired-looking men in grey suits knocking at the door. Visitors are a rare sight at The Circle. Janice and Carl greet them. The one at the front shows his identity card, then introduces his colleagues. He asks for whoever is in charge, and Carl allows Janice to take over. The names are a blur, but their shapes are familiar. Sweaty bodies, scuffed shoes, impatient to get in out of the cold. Carl wraps his arms around his chest as he follows the men, watching their backs. His stomach lurches. Lydia has brought them here.

On their instructions, Janice asks all the members to gather in the meeting room. Chairs are laid out in two rows, rather than the usual ring, an organic arrangement by the group, Carl believes. Assuming a more conventional position, as if, without knowing it, they are no longer being guided. He sits in the back row, on the edge, trying to control his breathing. He studies Lydia, three chairs to his right, hands tucked under her legs, fidgeting. He focuses on the messages on the walls. Words written by a dead man. Tells himself this is too elaborate a game if they are looking for the demon boy; they would simply march him away if they knew the bigger truth.

Murmurs of uncertainty reverberate. Three suits stand at the front, hands in pockets, before the one who introduced himself at the door moves forward, and his accomplices glide to the sides of the room, stalking their prey.

'Thank you all for gathering together,' he begins. 'I have some unfortunate news for you.'

Carl is aware that the office atmosphere has changed in the few days S has been missing. He watched closely and listened. They believed S was out there growing the business, finding new clients, taking them forward. But at the start of the week, the customer service calls dropped significantly. Longer breaks than normal. Small groups would huddle in the kitchen, where a microphone was hidden within the notice board, talking about what was happening, wondering when their leader would show. Some left early the day before, appeared rudderless. Carl's focus was on Lydia, and how she was reacting. No direct contact between them, as they agreed. Wondering when the body would be found and the knock would come. Time passed at a painful speed. Until now.

Carl scans the whole group. Apprehensive faces as they take in the policeman's words, spoken with the haunted look of a man who has seen what death can bring. Lydia crosses her legs and uncrosses them. 'Sit still,' he wants to scream at her. 'Control your body language.'

These men are outsiders. There were many discussions about how to treat such intruders. S provided the guidance.

Visitors would be curious, perhaps violent, if they see The Circle as a threat. The instructions were to be polite, but say nothing about what the group does, or how it operates. Refer everything to S. He stressed the need to avoid authority, knowing external perceptions, trusting that The Circle would be left alone.

The policeman flexes his leg muscles, rising and falling on the spot. His colleagues watch the group, rather than their superior. Carl catches one of them focusing on him with serious eyes and switches his gaze back to a poster that tells them to 'Think positive, think ahead'. The speaker clears his throat before continuing.

'I am Detective Inspector Greaves, and these are my colleagues, Detective Sergeant Horton and Detective Constable Willis.' He points at them as they are introduced. Their stern faces are unchanged. 'There is no other way to tell you this. Simon Paterson, or the man you knew as Simon Paterson, is dead.'

Gasps, then a couple of stifled sobs, from the group. Lydia shakes her head, holds it in her hands. Carl looks down, to avoid the watching officers. He has been preparing to look shocked since they walked in the front door, trying to erase the memory of the drop, its echoes from the past, the dull thud as the body hit the tarmac. Carl cradles his chin in his fingers, to hide the shaking, breathes as steadily as he can. *Don't overdo it, don't draw attention to yourself.*

'No,' Janice speaks up. Better her the spokesperson than Carl.

'Yes, I'm afraid so,' Greaves replies. His voice is devoid of emotion, a dull newsreader. 'A man's body was found early on Sunday morning on the A5. This is the man you knew to be Simon Paterson.' His eyes droop, and he looks down at a piece of paper in his hand, then back up again. 'At the moment, there does not appear to be anything suspicious about his death, although it is still being investigated by Thames Valley Police.'

Nothing suspicious. Carl tenses his fingers, then relaxes them again. Avoids eye contact with the policemen. Watches the waves crash in on the sand. Breathes. Looks at Lydia. She is still cradling her head in her hands. Covering up.

'What happened to him?' Janice asks. Carl watches her and listens, as he must.

'We suspect it might be suicide.' More gasps in the room. Janice silently shakes her head, stares over at Carl, then back to Greaves. Does she suspect he is involved? Carl wonders what S might have shared with her. But with outsiders here, best to remember the advice about showing a united front.

'Who's in charge here?' Greaves asks. Janice's hand slowly creeps up. 'Thanks. We need to search his office. This whole place. He hasn't left anything behind for you all, has he?'

'No,' Janice replies. Carl is happy for her to take the scrutiny that may follow. There is no longer a record of anybody being in the office at the weekend; he has seen to that. Carl Marsh has no motive for any crime against their leader. Nor does Lydia. Nobody in the room would have one. Carl relaxes a touch, reassured this is not an elaborate trick to flush a boy from the past out of hiding. Has faith in how well they trained him.

Some of the group share anxious looks, others take in the carpet. Lydia appears to wipe away a tear. Does not seek him out in the room. She is playing it well. *Too well*, he suddenly thinks. Has she planned the whole thing? Has he been used? She was scant on the details about the incident, merely that Simon attacked her, and she responded with the swing of an electrical appliance. Carl pictures the newly purchased kettle in his head, sitting on its stand in the kitchen. Replenishing office supplies is a part of his role.

'Now, this is obviously terrible news, a shock for you all. But we are working on a follow-up investigation. That is why we are here.'

Carl tenses, digs his fingernails into his legs, feels a flush to his cheeks. Lydia appears frozen in shock. The way he should be looking. He is conscious of the eyes of the outsiders darting around the room. Pictures two children running along a beach, chasing a soft ball in front of them, splashing along the water's edge. His heartrate slows again, allows him to focus on the man at the front. Surely, they can't make a connection. He steals another glance at Lydia, wondering if she has brought him back into the spotlight.

'We have since discovered more about the man you knew as Simon Paterson.' Greaves lets out a deep sigh, as if he is unburdening a sad truth. 'Something that might come as a surprise to you all.'

Carl places his hands together on his lap, a neutral pose. Another position they taught him when he sat in those rooms with the experts, how to present himself to the parole people. How to look unthreatening.

'It would appear, from what we can tell, that Simon Paterson was not his real name. He had another identity.' Carl studies the inspector's face, a man looking at them with sorrowful eyes. Or is it disdain, for the hapless followers of a deceiver?

'We have discovered that his real name was Steven Harding, although he has used other names in the past.' Carl looks at Lydia again and back at Greaves. They had so much in common.

Nobody in the group has seen this bolt coming, a heart-stopping shock. This man they all unquestioningly followed was central in their thoughts, a constant in their lives. The core that kept them together, dragging everyone up from the gutter. A place Carl had adopted as a starting point for over a year.

Greaves flexes his legs again, like a man trying to raise himself up to a greater height. 'There is more, I'm afraid, and it affects all of you here. It affects this company you work for. There is no easy way to put this.' He pauses, and waves around the piece of paper in his hand as he talks. 'It seems that Mister Paterson, or Harding, was in serious financial difficulty. Your company is in serious difficulty. As far as we can tell, and we have been looking into this closely, Circle Telemarketing has no assets, and is making no money. Your company doesn't really exist.'

'What?' Janice the spokesperson again. More collective intakes of breath.

The inspector suddenly looks like he hasn't slept for days, screws his eyes up. 'I'm afraid it seems to be true. We believe all the money in your company disappeared some time ago, and maybe Mister Harding intended to do the same.'

A few of the group begin whispered conversations. Lydia looks around and catches Carl's eye. He looks away. They cannot show any knowledge about his disappearance, or even a hint of cooperation.

There were no signs of money trouble, even from the

limited information Carl had access to. He processed three supplier invoices the previous week. They were impaled on a spike on S's desk. Carl assumed this meant they had been paid. According to these policemen, this man has betrayed them, taken away what they stood for. Then thrown himself off a bridge, abandoning his flock. A convenient conclusion, if the police draw it.

Maybe Lydia has saved them all from an inevitable crash. Saved Carl from closer scrutiny. Simon's questions had intensified recently, not just the grilling at Truth Time, but around the office, behind the closed door when they discussed security. Testing Carl out. Picking at the corners of his own truth. The one Carl had constructed to keep himself safe. He has become comfortable in his new skin, confidence growing that he is off the radar. No vigilantes banging on his door. Police here in front of him, and none of them marching him away to another interrogation. But caution is still in his bones. He has lived in the shadows for so long it is second nature to avoid the eyes of strangers. Lest they spot the devil child.

Greaves's monotone brings Carl back to the room. 'So, one consequence of this is that your company, this place,' Greaves gesticulates slowly with his arms, 'is going to be closed down while we investigate further. It appears Mister Harding had many debts, and his creditors will be looking to seize assets. I'm afraid your little experiment here is over.'

Carl studies the group again, heads shaking in disbelief, jaws slack. Then he notices that one of the policemen is watching him do this. He returns his focus to Greaves at the front, idly scratching at his face to hide the shaking. He pictures a row of sandcastles leading to a large moat, protecting the subjects inside an imaginary city.

'This can't be true,' Lydia speaks up. She stands and turns to address everyone. 'He would never do this to us. He would never leave us like this.' Her voice is shrill, hopeful. Trying to show she thinks he will walk through the door at any moment and tell them they are all saved. That this is simply a test and that their faith in him will be repaid. Carl wants to applaud her acting. Wonders how much she has been hiding from him. As she sits down, he watches her with a sideways glance. Thinks that now it is he that might need to ask some questions.

'I'm afraid it's true,' Greaves says in a low voice, practised calm. 'Whatever he told you, about his name for instance, that was a lie.'

'It can't be.' Janice this time. They have so much faith.

Greaves looks above all their heads, and Carl follows his gaze to the back of the room, stares at one of the posters, telling them that 'Unity is Strength'. Next to it, another motto. 'Think together. Be together'. A request that is now worth nothing.

'We will have to close this office, pending our investigation, as of now. I want you to give my officers your names and addresses before you leave. You cannot take any equipment with you.'

The faces still show the shock and disbelief. Carl tries to mirror the look, and stays mute, as he must. He then watches Lydia, who appears to have moved on to indignant. Cheated.

'This is now a fraud investigation,' Greaves says coldly. 'I assume none of you object to helping us.' His head inclines slightly, no smile. Like he is still working out how to address a collective force he doesn't understand. 'We will have to interview all of you at some point.' Carl catches the look on one of the policemen's faces again. Bored, annoyed that he needs to talk to a group of cult followers. He should have tried working with them.

The group members slowly file out of the meeting room, and small pockets form in the open-plan area. Carl hangs back, wanting to avoid contact with anyone in view of the police. Particularly Lydia. He needs time to assess her reaction. Wonders if she might have known about the financial angle. Is unsure about what she has been telling him.

The senior officer talks to Janice in hushed tones and leads her into S's office, accompanied by one of his colleagues. The door closes behind them, and the blinds drop. The policeman left behind scans the group, yawns.

Lydia works her away around the edge of the group, stalking her prey, moves in for a hug on Carl. He is forced to play along, squeezes back. Feels her shake. Knows she is acting in front of them all. Perhaps for him too.

'God, I don't believe it. Suicide,' she says, loud enough for everyone to hear. She nestles into his shoulder. Carl wonders how much of a relationship she has declared to the rest of the group. Has picked up nothing in his monitoring.

One of the policemen emerges from the office. There is a folded-up piece of paper in his hand, one Carl placed there a few days earlier.

'Mister Marsh, is it?' Carl digs his fingernails into his palms. The wind drags a kite along the shore.

'Yes.'

'Could you wait here, please? We'd like to talk to you too.'

Carl nods his acceptance. The group start to leave the open-plan for the outside, leaving their details to a bored policeman as they go. Carl watches them gather outside through the front window. There are no smiles, only hushed discussions he cannot hear. There has been no mass hysteria, just disbelief. Surprise that S would abandon them, throw himself onto a busy road. Who would do that to his followers? The police need to carry on believing it.

Janice emerges from the fallen leader's office.

'Carl. Could you join us now?' Greaves asks. 'Actually, could we go to your office?'

'Sure.'

Carl leads them in, holding the door open. He watches Lydia and Janice go, leaving one man standing against the outsiders to the end. Stay calm. Remember they don't know who you are. Do as they tell you, as you always did, and there will be no recriminations. You will keep your privileges.

The strip light flickers above him, demanding a confession. Men in suits again, but this time he is alone, nobody arguing on his side of a table. All those years ago, they talked as if he wasn't in the room. Referring to a boy called Martin, debating what he should answer, whether he was guilty. He would have told them the details, about the fighting, but not in front of his mother. She would think he did it on purpose, always blamed him. They were playing, that was all.

Carl closes the door, avoiding the eyes of the two men for as long as he can. He has gone over his and Lydia's movements and the clearing up several times, confident there will be nothing for them to find. Of course, they have no reason to look for anything.

It is Greaves who leads the interrogation, a new face and voice, over twenty years on. 'Carl, can we just ask you about the computer system?'

'Sure.' Carl moves behind his desk, feels its smooth surface under his fingers.

'We are going to take everything away. But Miss Browning, Janice, told us that you know how it works.'

'A little. Simon set up the system,' he adds.

'Yes, him of course.' Greaves leans over the desk, stares into Carl's soul. 'What was your job here, Carl?'

Carl pauses. Past tense. He must be wary, even though they are still using the correct name.

'I look after the office. You know, ordering stationery, that sort of thing.'

'And the computer system too?'

'Well, not really, no.'

'Hmm.' Greaves shrugs at one of his colleagues. 'What can you tell us about the security system here?'

He is prepared. All the incriminating footage has gone.

'I've only just started in here.' Carl smiles, but the men don't respond in kind. 'We have a swipe system that monitors who comes and goes, and when.' The computer blinks at him in silence as Carl points towards it. 'Shall I show you how it works?'

'No need. We have experts in this sort of thing. They will take it away, take it apart. Just a few questions, that's all.'

'Fine.'

Carl swallows, tries to concentrate on his breathing, imagines the sand under his feet as he jogs along.

'You have a lot of cameras.' Greaves points outside of the room. 'Why so many?'

'Oh, he wanted to protect us.'

'Protect you?' The other policemen snorts.

'Yes.' Stay calm, the way this has been rehearsed. 'He was worried about intruders. People breaking in.'

'And that's why you have them?' Greaves asks.

'Yes. I think, he, Simon, used to change the tapes, every now and again. We only had so much storage space, I think.'

'And Mister Paterson used to do this? Not you?'

'No, him.'

'So, Carl, did you know Simon Paterson wasn't his real name? That it was Steven Harding?' It sounds odd, him being referred to differently. Carl wonders how many similarities they share.

'No.'

'And you had no idea this company was in financial difficulty?'

'Definitely not.' This is true, so he feels he can give a little more. 'I mean, I never got involved in the money side. I used to make sales calls. That's all I've done here until three weeks ago. Until he gave me this new job.'

Why did he say yes to a position of responsibility? Making him visible to Lydia and her cry for help. Lured out of the shadows, into the firing line. Maybe S thought he was a threat, offered him the role to keep a closer eye. But the money thing he doesn't get.

Greaves offers a thin smile. Toying with a child. Some things haven't changed. Carl needs to move himself away from suspicion. He is the innocent one here. All he did was answer Lydia's distress call.

'I would love to help you. But I'm probably not going to be much use. He did a lot of things on his own.' Wanting to slip into the background, walk home alone, lose himself in a board game.

'We will be in touch if we need any more help. Please make sure DS Horton here has your contact details before you go.'

'Write it on here, would you?' Horton asks, handing Carl a notebook with a blank page. 'Don't go leaving the country.' Horton the comedian, the one who was watching him during the meeting earlier. Carl jots his name and address down, remembering the handwriting style he has perfected. All capital letters, nothing identifiable. His mind slips back to another man in an ill-fitting suit taking notes in a similar book, many years ago. And how what they write down doesn't always become the story. Might not be what they read aloud in court.

Lydia's car has gone when he emerges outside. She is playing it as they agreed, staying apart, not arousing any suspicion. Carl cycles home, wondering how long it will be before he can move on. The next identity will need to be arranged.

As he brings out the Monopoly set, preparing a new game with six players, he tries to place himself in Greaves's shoes. Ponders how the police will view the death. A man killing himself to avoid financial embarrassment and betrayed faces.

Carl must look for the next stage. The police are close, and even though they didn't seem to suspect they were looking into the eyes of a forgotten monster, it only takes one stray headline, or photograph, to spark a memory.

Carl takes each piece's turn, beginning with the top hat, throwing three doubles and heading straight for jail. He couldn't make it up. The role playing takes him back to the safety of his room, where he worked out how to preserve the self. Where the door could be closed, and they couldn't touch him; no more sweaty men asking questions. He needs to ensure Lydia gives nothing away, and then let her down gently. She cannot become too reliant on the kindness of a stranger. Then he can drift away, find a new place to hide.

3 5

Crawley, December 1999

'On the line now, we have Joe from Crawley. Good evening, Joe. What do you want to talk about?'

'Hi, Trish. I'm a first-time caller.'

'That's okay, Joe. Just tell us what you want to say.'

Ray is surprised by the difference in her voice through the phone, rather than the radio. It is soft and low, less tinny than when he has heard it over the past year. Normally he is sitting in the cab, listening to the crazy zealots and the semi-drunks as she stirs them into action, while he waits for mysterious men to hand over packages. Tonight, he has the comfort of home, shift over.

'I want to ask if anybody remembers Child X? Martin Sullivan? If anybody knows what happened to him?'

The line goes quiet. It is just after one in the morning, and Ray has bided his time before calling. The radio is turned down low by the bed, as directed by the person who first answered the call. Ray's voice echoes, a few seconds behind real time, in the transmission. He hears the first half of his question, and then the voice of Trish Watney after a short delay.

'I'm sorry, we appear to have lost Joe there. We'll be talking to Brian from Horley after this.'

Silence in his handset, and an advert for a local solicitor is broadcast. She has cut him off. He wonders about redialling, giving another name, and asking the question again. It was easy to get through. There is a loud click in his ear, and the voice of the assistant who initially answered the call returns.

'Joe?'

'Yes.'

'That's not the sort of thing we allow on air. You said you was going to talk about immigration.'

'I know. I was, but this jumped into my head. I wanted to know if anyone remembered it. I wanted to know if Trish remembered.'

The assistant's voice is polite, but insistent. 'That isn't the subject for this evening. It's immigration tonight.'

'I know, sorry.'

Sweat sticks the phone to Ray's ear. There is a pause, and then the voice returns.

'Can you hold the line for a moment?'

'Sure.'

The sound of Simon and Garfunkel in the background brings the phone and the radio into a weird, delayed synchronicity. Ray hears another click, and the music fades in the handset.

'Joe?' It is the unmistakable, rasping voice of Trish Watney, twenty a day deep.

'Trish?'

'Joe, you know that's not allowed. Sorry, but I had to cut you off.' Strange to hear the music from her show, as well as her voice in his ear.

'Why?'

She pauses. There is a sigh. 'I'd like to know why you asked that question. Why you are dredging up old history.'

'I'm looking into the Philip Hughes case. You know, Child X, Sullivan.'

She sighs again. Over the phone he can't tell whether this is exasperation or tiredness. 'That was a long time ago.'

'Yes, it was. I want to know what you remember.'

'Like I said, it was a long time ago.' This is more like the dismissive on-air tone. 'Are you a journalist?'

'No.' He has given up on using that lie. Besides, she would see straight through him. Honesty from now on. Well, mostly.

'Look. Please don't ring up about that again.'

'I won't. Sorry. I really am a genuine listener.'

'Thank you.' More softness in her voice this time.

'I'd like to talk to you about the case.'

'Why?'

'I'm looking into Sullivan. The killer. I know you wrote about him.'

There is a noise like smoke being exhaled, and a pause that makes his heart feel like it has stopped.

'Look, I have to get back to the show. Why don't you come and talk to me tomorrow? At the radio station. Two o'clock?'

Ray needs more information before he surrenders his target to Leckie. Someone he knows has a more infamous past than even Leckie could imagine. In a few days he will have eliminated two innocent men and be ready to give up a liar. But there is a distraction clawing at him from the past, based around the history. Nobody knows Ray saw him in the act, before the child was famous, and he wants to know what made Sullivan kill.

Paul's funeral went unattended earlier that day. Ray parked up outside the crematorium and watched a steady flow of mourners go in through the forgiving doors. Turning over whether it would be right to say goodbye to someone who he pushed to the back of his mind so long ago. Frozen in his seat, fingers gripping the door handle, not enough strength to turn it and walk in. Still a coward.

The famous Hughes murder and the trial of Child X were recorded in the local newspaper. Ray expected the archives of the *Crawley Observer* to be guarded by an obsessive librarian, suspiciously watching over every exploration of their relics on meticulously catalogued shelves. What he found was a box room in their new offices in Three Bridges, piled high with old copies, waiting to be microfiched. He was welcome to have a look, so long as he didn't remove anything.

There was no system, just randomly spread piles of old editions in a room with no natural light. The copies went back to the late sixties. It took him half an hour to find some from the right time period. Little of what he read was familiar, apart from the front-page report of the trial. A photo of the Hughes family on the court steps, and an article written by Trish Watney. The fact that her name has become a constant of his evenings, presiding over the cranks and ragers on the phones at Radio Mercury, gave Ray the feeling that he was not alone. She too has not escaped the clutches of the town.

Looking further back, there were a couple of articles on the death of Philip Hughes, including an appeal for witnesses, again penned by Trish. Two boys knew more about the killer. But they did nothing. If they had spoken up sooner, Sullivan might have been arrested for the death of a kid called John Ellis. And Philip Hughes would have lived. But there is little Ray can do to make up for it now, just try to understand. That child killer is now in Leckie's sights, so justice will be served. Once Ray has found him.

36

she still does that thing where she ask for a drink vodka you now what I mean she ask and if i dont have one she just give me a whack she dont care no more not like she used to she using the stick but she cant do that now i threw it away dumped it in the bins she cant hit me with it no more. she asked me to steal her some fags and i had to she would have hit me if i didnt so i took them and ran from the shop not the local one the one in furnace green with the paki behind the counter he didnt even chase me it was easy.

 i asked for a dog said can we have a dog and she just larfed she say you cant have a dog you cant look after yourself didnt want to say you dont look after me thats your job. so i screwd up the pack of fags and she went mad she used a broom this time cant sit down my legs hurt so much danny did she do this to you danny.

she needs to see what she has made me do. something that makes her stop the drinking stop the men god danny the men are getting worse the last one joined in with the stick he was smiling then they went to the pub probly to celebrate i bet then he came home and they did it over the table he was smiling at me as he did it over her sholder.

theres only one way out of this hell the bitch maybe i should make her suffer instead tie her down or something but bet one of her men will catch me at it and stop me but it might be worth it danny just to see fear on her face and not on mine i bet she dont even see the fear on my face.

how do i escape danny i cant think what am i supposed to do to stop her. she needs to see me suffer but all she care about is her next drink danny was she like this before i think this is different now.

37

Crawley, December 1999

Trish Watney's face is one of ten staring down at Ray from the wall of the Radio Mercury foyer. The station was built a couple of miles from his old house, and on the opposite side of the A23 from where he filmed the councillor and his secretary. A bright new structure pointing to the future. A shiny example of progress. Cigarette butts and litter swirled around the outside entrance when he approached. In her framed photograph, Trish's hands are cupped underneath her chin, smiling in extreme close-up. 'Night Owls', her show, is written on a plaque underneath her name.

She catches him studying it.

'Joe, is it?'

'Yes,' Ray lies, thinking he needs to get inside first.

She shakes his hand. 'Well, hello. I only have half an hour. Do follow me.'

At first glance, she looks older than the picture on the wall, approaching fifty, and the handshake is disappointingly limp, given the on-air persona. Trish Watney stands for righteous indignation, eager to take extreme stances to provoke a reaction from her listeners. They probably suspect it is done for effect, but still pick up the phone and join in. More engaging than the music played on national radio stations at night. When you are waiting for a dirty brown envelope from men in hooded jackets in the freezing cold on the industrial estate, it helps to be kept awake.

Trish leads Ray to a small office inside the station and offers him a seat. She takes her place opposite, behind a desk. Above her is another framed copy of the picture in reception. In here, the focus looks softer to Ray.

'Like I say, I've only got half an hour.' She looks at her watch. 'Well, twenty-five minutes now.'

Ray gets it. He's on the clock.

'Thanks for seeing me, Trish. I really appreciate this.' There must be others who remember the case, but she is the one that told the town about it.

'Not a problem.'

'First off, can I say I really am a listener to the show. I'm often up at night, and I tune in.' He is there as a private investigator, not a hopeless cabbie. She doesn't need to know the reason she is on.

'Thank you, Joe.'

'Ah.' He stares up at her poster, then back at Trish Watney. 'My real name's Ray. Ray Mercer. I'm a private investigator.'

Her eyes bore into him; she shakes her head slowly. 'Well, I…'

'Look, I'm really sorry about that.' It feels like a betrayal, pretending to be someone else. The night before, he didn't want to announce what he was up to with his own name.

Looking back, it was ridiculous to think she would discuss the murder on air. But Ray thought Trish seemed well placed to help. He hasn't had a bet all day, focus shifting to the future rather than the helpless past. He slips a card across her desk. A genuine one.

'So,' she begins, scanning the card, then placing it carefully on a pile of papers on the desk. 'Why are you dredging up old history? The Child X thing, that was a long time ago.'

'What do you remember about the case?'

'What do you want to know?' she rebuffs. Trish stares at him, and dampness forms under Ray's armpits. He has thought of little else since dawn, but now his mind goes blank. This is an opportunity to understand what the adult world of Crawley thought about Sullivan, and he is struggling to come up with a sensible question. Ray reminds himself she used to be a print journalist. She should get the idea of digging into a story.

'I was thirteen when the court case happened. I went to school with Martin Sullivan.'

'Really? Did you know him?' She leans forward, fingers pressed together on the desk. The nails are ragged and short. She studies the detective's card again.

'Oh, no, not really. He was just in my year.'

'So, you went to Thomas Bennett?'

'Yes.' It was a cross so many had to bear.

'I heard some terrible things about it.'

'Mostly untrue.' Anyone who attended the place knew the stories that went around were amazing. So many of them fake, but the gossips spread them, and the journalists wrote them anyway. A smoking student burning down the gym, true. A stabbing behind the bike sheds, false. Kids shot with air rifles, true. Teacher strikes, false. Ray needs to move on.

'What do you remember about the case?' he asks. She won't know he has read every word in the paper years ago, but he wants to find out about what she left out.

'It was terrible, I remember that.' She folds her hands under her chin, mirroring the image behind her on the wall, and looks past Ray, before focusing back in his direction. 'You know, I thought about writing a book about it.' She smiles, probably thinking back to an opportunity wasted, Ray imagines.

Ray nods in reply. 'Really?' *Just talk*, he pleads silently.

'Oh, yes. There was a little bit of national interest, for a short while at least.'

'Did you think he was guilty?' He needs to ask the question.

'Oh, he definitely did it.' She looks across at Ray. 'All the evidence indicated that. He did it all right. A sad business.' She sits back and counts the points off with her fingers. 'An eyewitness saw him kick Philip Hughes off the scaffolding. His footprints and fingerprints were everywhere. He confessed when in custody. The police were delighted with the whole thing.' She clears her throat. 'Well, you know what I mean. Open and shut case.' Her gaze is off to the side, on a small fish tank. Ray watches the green and blue occupants wriggle around in the water. She can't have given up on the story that easily.

'But your article said he pleaded not guilty?'

'You've been reading my articles?' she asks, smiling. Her eyes widen, and her cheeks flush slightly. Trish turns to look at a computer screen, then back at Ray, takes a deep breath. He thinks he might have flattered her.

'Yes. Background, you know.' Ray places his hands on the edge of her desk. There is dirt under his fingernails. He slides them away under his legs.

'Well, he did plead not guilty, to begin with, at the trial.' Her voice has returned to that provocative tone when she is coaxing a reaction out of her callers. She straightens her spine. 'Then he tried to change his plea late on when it was obvious to everyone he was guilty. Claimed he didn't know what he was doing. I imagine his lawyer told him to do that, to reduce the sentence.'

'Did that seem odd to you? That he confessed, then withdrew it, then admitted it again?'

'Not really. Not at the time. It was my first big criminal case. They let me write it because I had the contacts.'

'Contacts?'

'Yes, the coppers at the local nick.' A short-lived smile flickers across her face, then disappears. 'And the mother; in the end, I met her.'

'The mother?'

'Yes.' She examines something on her desk, pokes it into the surface with a finger. 'She died a couple of years after the trial.'

'Oh?'

'Yes. I told you it was a sad case.' Her eyes shift back to the fish tank. Ray compares the face to that behind her again. She suddenly looks tired. Working too many late nights. 'One best left alone now,' she adds.

'So, why didn't you write this book? You sound well placed for it.'

'Too busy,' she replies quickly, shaking her head slightly. 'I suppose I could have pushed it. I started it, but the fuss faded away pretty quickly, especially once the mother died.' She sighs. 'And… it seems the Hughes family weren't whiter than white.'

The skin tightens at the back of Ray's neck. 'How d'you mean?'

She shrugs. 'Just that the truth about them emerged later. Philip Hughes's parents were already separated when he died; they kept that quiet at the trial. Their son was often in trouble. Bullying other kids at school. These days, you'd call him a disturbed child. He had learning difficulties. And the father, Billy Hughes, he was well known down at the nick.' Trish looks to be staring into space again. 'Not that any of that really mattered in the end.'

None of this is particularly helping Ray find out why Sullivan killed. Twice.

'And this wasn't revealed at the trial?'

Trish shakes her head, as if emptying it of an unwanted memory. 'It didn't matter. It was obvious he killed him.'

There is something lurking that Ray needs to ask. 'You knew his name, didn't you, that he was Martin Sullivan, before the trial?'

Trish taps on her keyboard, then looks back at Ray. 'Yes. It was confidential, of course; we couldn't publish it. His real name didn't matter; he was guilty.'

There were two others who knew of his guilt. Before he kicked Philip Hughes off the scaffolding. But they sat on it, lived in silence.

'So, you didn't really pursue the case after the trial? You were a journalist.'

'I still am.' She points at her framed picture on the wall. 'Like I said, I knew the case better than anybody. I started to investigate, but there was no appetite for it. The town moved on very quickly. I guess I moved on. Life moves on.' Ray watches her face tense, the lines on her forehead tighten.

'I'm just trying to get a feeling for how people viewed the killer, this Sullivan, back then. The facts, well, I can't argue those,' Ray says, watching her lean forward, clasp her hands in front.

'No, you can't. I suggest you forget it. Ancient history. That's why I took you off the air. Sorry about that, but Crawley has moved on. You listen to the show; you know we'll talk about pretty much anything.' Ray has heard her give airtime to some extraordinary bigots. Left, right, she doesn't care, just so long as they make you sit up and listen. 'But that case, in this town, it's been buried. The Hughes family moved away years ago. Sullivan's family are all dead. When people found out the truth about the Hughes lot, the sympathy for them sort of fell away.'

'What about the father?' One person Ray didn't see mentioned in print.

She shrugs again. 'The mother, she told Martin Sullivan his father was dead. He is now, but back then he was in prison. And once the kid was locked up as well, the town forgot about him.'

'He was in a children's secure home,' he corrects her. Trish's eyebrows rise, before she recovers.

'Is that what they call them?' she asks. 'You have been digging, then.' She leans forward once more, her eyes widening, untidy mascara distracting Ray. 'You're looking for him now, aren't you? Sullivan. You're trying to find him?'

'Yes.' No point in lying now. She might even help.

'You know he changed identity. He did it at least once.'

Ray thinks through Dusty's printouts and photocopied documents.

Trish continues. 'I assumed he went into some sort of identity protection thing. Like witness protection.'

Ray thinks, but dares not say out loud, *Witnesses are closer than you think.*

'He did,' he agrees. 'But now he's disappeared. Nobody knows where he is.' Not technically true any more. There are three lines of enquiry left. The past has become the temporary focus, with Leckie's change of emphasis.

'Well, I can't help you, I'm afraid. I gave up on it a long time ago. I've got this now,' she says, indicating her office, this station, her shock-jock career. There is no curiosity in her eyes. Just a look of acceptance. A desire to forget, like the whole town.

She stands and offers a handshake. Ray rises to share it.

'Ray, I don't mean to be rude, but I do have a meeting coming up. I wish you well with your search. Although you are probably wasting your time.'

She follows him to the door. He throws in one last thought, the way Columbo traps his killers, just as he is leaving a room.

'What about the mother? You said you met her?' he asks, trying to wring as much information out of her as he can before she kicks him out the door.

Trish straightens herself up. 'Yes, I did. A troubled woman. Unsettling.' She moves a step closer to Ray. 'She killed herself, after moving away.' Trish pauses, then looks reflective. 'A sorry business, the whole thing, don't you think?'

Ray stares at her, wondering why nobody seems to care, even the reporter who got closest to the case back then. The killer has been forgotten, along with his deed. How did this town let it happen? Why didn't he and Paul speak out? Everyone would know the truth, and Sullivan would still be locked up.

'I wish you luck,' she says, opening the door for him.

'If you remember anything that might help me find him, please let me know.'

'Sure.' She shakes his hand again and offers one more piece of advice. 'Please, don't ring into the show again. At least not about this.' She smiles and touches her cheek. 'I like controversial views, but this topic is off limits. Nobody's interested any more.'

'Sorry about the… Joe thing,' he mutters. Treachery from an admirer.

'Forget it,' she replies, as she closes the door.

Ray slips into the corridor, back to the heart of the station. The town has buried its dirty past. The person who got closest to understanding everything gave up. Once he has found the child killer, he might also be able to make a fresh start. After facing the man that Sullivan has become and discovering what he means to Leckie Harris. Ray needs to understand the extent of the betrayal. But more importantly, to look Child X in the eye, to see if he too can be forgiven.

38

Milton Keynes, December 1999

It is an alien feeling, that someone might want to spend time with you. Carl relents, under ceaseless buzzing, and presses the button to let her in, not wanting to draw attention to himself. The neighbours have no idea who he is.

Lydia knows where he lives, that mistake is in the past. Getting this close to a woman is a new experience. Lack of practice has made women impossible to read, so he will need to tread carefully.

A radio phone-in fills the air of the flat as she drops onto the sofa. The millennium is coming, and everything is going to explode because the year ends in three zeros. He cannot ignore these people who are desperate for their voices to be heard. So many believe the end is nigh. Somehow comforting that they also have fears. They cannot see a future beyond a few weeks' time.

'I needed to see you,' she begins, tapping the space next to her. 'We've got to talk about what happened. About what we did.' Tying them both together, complicit in her act. An accident, she said, when she made that distress call. Self-defence.

Carl slides down next to her, the debate tugging at him in the background. A caller claims the presenters will regret not heeding the warnings. That the world will change irreparably. That Russia is to blame. They will destroy all Western computers at the stroke of midnight on millennium's eve. He read about it in a magazine.

'He pinned me down, Carl. I thought he was going to attack me.'

'In the kitchen?' His voice rises as he asks the question, so he brings down the tone to sound more believing. 'I mean right there? Why?'

'I knew too much about him. I knew about his past.'

Everyone has a past, Carl thinks. What matters is how you move on and leave it behind. The silence between them is punctured by a radio advert for a firm of solicitors. Lydia stares up at him, takes his hand. Her fingers are cold, desperately clinging. Don't get too close. Safety can only be guaranteed with distance.

'I told Simon what I knew about him. About his past. That must be why he attacked me.'

'His past? What, this fraud stuff?'

'Not that. He abused my sister, years ago. She killed herself, because of him.' Lydia looks away, to the fading wallpaper Carl has no interest in changing. 'That was when he had another identity. He was running another organisation like ours in Worcester. When Lena killed herself, he closed it down, came here, started again, a new group, our group.'

Carl stares at her, wondering about the echoes of his own life. How, in other circumstances, she might have been a vigilante looking for a child killer. Hunting him down, attacking him with an appliance, throwing his corpse off a bridge.

Lydia sobs gently into his chest, and Carl holds her. Wondering if this is what life is supposed to be like. Trusting in someone with the truth. She is confessing to having a motive for killing, rather than merely defending herself. Perhaps she planned this all along, and he has been duped. But something deep inside him makes Carl squeeze tighter, keep her safe.

'I can trust you, can't I?' she pleads.

'Of course. We share this secret. We're both involved.'

Trust was the one thing it took time to earn, years ago. Privileges could be withdrawn for the smallest of mistakes. Leaving the light on in your room. Stealing food, however small. Ripping pictures out of newspapers or magazines. Bodily fluids on your bedsheets. Anything that was against their rules. All errors took you back to square one on the board, forced you to build up your stock again. Blending into the background was the way to survive. When you became invisible, they left you alone.

She sniffs and looks up. Her eyes are wet, but he suspects hope is there, rather than despair. 'I came here to confront him. And he just went for me. I had to ask him if it was true. To see if he would admit it. What he did to my sister.'

He is holding a broken human being, trying to muster up compassion, feeling her cling to him. Something inside urges Carl to engage, to offer her the love she is reaching out for. But he is poorly placed to do this. The words are difficult to form in reply. No revelations can come in return. With Lydia this close, he can see once again that all they did was hide life from him. Shut him down, extend his imprisonment on the outside.

Carl looks at the top of her head, strokes her hair. He has been taught to separate himself, not get too close. Best to avoid all human contact. It took a couple of beatings in detention to work out that standing up for yourself, engaging with anyone, brought confrontation. And yet here he is, holding on to her, comforting someone when all his training tells him to do the opposite. Is this what life is supposed to be like?

How would she react if she knew the real history? That he is the son of a hopeless mother and absent father, a product of neglect. Entering the system as a killer and leaving as an innocent. Processed and turned into a model citizen. A recluse pushed into hostels, curfews, meaningless jobs, all with the aim of integration. Nobody asked that boy, then young man, what he wanted. Not knowing that he would have begged them to keep him inside, safe in his room, with the games and everything arranged where it should be.

Carl is pulled back into the radio discussion. A shrill woman says that everyone has missed the mathematical point, that the century won't begin for another year, as a hundred years don't end until the last day of December 2000. Carl thinks about the logic, supposes she is right.

Lydia shakes him, moving her head up. 'What would you have done? If you knew he had done something terrible?' she asks.

'Same as you.'

There is no reference point for helping people, but Carl thinks back to his reaction to the phone call that night, her frantic voice. He did not hesitate, sweat dripping in his eyes as he cycled to the office. He did what any decent person would have done. And he wonders if that is what he has become at last. Decent. He has done nothing to encourage her and yet here he is being confided in, trusted.

The end of the century evangelists are replaced by a man with an authoritative air. His tones remind Carl of one of the warders at Murrayfields, issuing unambiguous instructions. Nothing untoward is going to happen on the first of January. Planes are not going to fall out of the sky. Computers will go on working. Terrorists will not mount a coordinated attack. Life will go on as before, except we will be writing something different on our cheques.

Everything will change for the members of the group. Carl should be safer. Their leader was starting to pick at the edges of his story, pushing him to get more defensive. A different style of questioning from the policeman who sat beside him in the cell all those years ago, listening to a young boy. The detective must have worked out his mother was to blame.

'I'm glad you're here, Carl. You listen to me.' She kisses him gently on the lips, then rests her head on his shoulder. 'You believe me.'

And at that moment, he thinks he does. There are others who deceive in this world, on a grander scale than him. Scamming and threatening the innocent, when all he has done is answer their demands, stay in the shadows, and get on quietly with a new life.

The thread of the phone-in has gone. The reception fades out and back in, then the news is being read. He holds on to her, despite the instinct to repel. There is something about Lydia that has taken the fear away. She would not shop him to the press. She has too much to lose.

Several years before, they told him the story was going to break. Of who he used to be. Someone digging into the whereabouts of Child X, and where he was hidden. A consequence of that case where two boys dragged a toddler away and battered him to death on a railway line. Provoking interest in what they felt were similar crimes. He was moved on, reborn as Neil Duggan, in a new town, fresh hostel, fabricated history, more lies to learn. He didn't need much to start again. A process they showed him so well, one he has been able to adapt to stay an additional step ahead, thanks to a homeless man sleeping forever underneath the arches.

He looks down at her, and her trusting face, and for a moment considers telling her the dark truth of the monster they brought out in their sessions, forcing a child to admit the fear, take the blame. As she would have to, if the police dug deeper. She has no idea what she is getting close to. How could she understand what evil really looks like? All she sees is a reformed down-and-out, honourable enough to help her dispose of a body and keep the secret. Carl thinks he deserves his second chance. Helping Lydia proves it. But another confession, to her, would not help.

There was a short stage in his early twenties when he would scream at drunks, asking if they recognised the killer in front of them, looking for somewhere to unburden the truth. In their cluttered and clinical rooms, the analysts called it 'wilful disclosure', directing words at those who he knew would do nothing about it. They were confusing times. That desire to be heard, for the world to know who he was, and how terrible he had been, forced back into the bottle by their careful guidance.

Lydia has enough concerns, does not deserve to have his truth thrust upon her. The decision he has is whether this Carl he represents is the right man to help.

She initiates the sex. Carl resists as much as he should, but it happens there on the sofa. Previously, Lydia has lingered in the aftermath, but she dresses quickly and departs with a cold kiss. The physicality still feels like an out-of-body experience.

Carl turns the radio off; it hasn't been helping him to focus. He has been relieved when they have parted before, knowing that he can return to his own life and the games. But this feels different. He pictures her entering her flat, throwing her keys on the table, collapsing on a chair, pouring a glass of wine. More tears. Wondering what she is doing with the kind and considerate Carl Marsh, whether she deserves anyone after what she has done. Why someone would keep her secret so willingly. Unless they had feelings for her. Carl wipes down the kitchen surfaces in his flat, bringing back the calm and the clarity.

They described it as a significant psychological defect, when he started those sessions many years ago, his inability to empathise. Something he learnt to demonstrate for them on the surface, knowing it was a pathway to release. Sharing this with the analysts, with their eager notebooks and frantic pens. Making his words of admission more believable.

This feels like a connection, something he has not experienced before. The first time he remembers wanting to be inside someone else's head, other than an analyst, attempting to understand him. Is Lydia dragging the humanity out of him? Showing that he needs to live, rather than hide. But then, as Carl lifts the Escape from Colditz board from the drawer, anticipating the chase and the escape, he thinks perhaps he has been over exposed to analysis, is over thinking everything.

Poor Lydia. Falling for this Carl Marsh, a phantom, someone she cannot have. Not knowing that he must leave her, break things as gently as possible. Only not yet. Not this close to a tragedy. He will have to wait to live as others do.

39

Crawley, December 1999

'I'm going to ask you again, for the last time.'

The smoke blown in his face doesn't faze Stefan, or the gun pointed at his head. What worries him more is the sight of Marko writhing in the chair, a gag in his mouth. A severed finger lies on the floor in front of his brother, removed with a pair of bolt cutters. If he were honest, Stefan prefers it this way round; Marko has a higher pain threshold. They have both been tortured before. It was not unknown for Bosnians to twist your arm out of its socket, or put a bullet in your knee, prior to asking questions. This is different – the British way of doing things. Leckie has provided him the opportunity to reveal where the money is, even if Stefan has no intention of telling him. Or the code to the safe.

Marko pants heavily and squirms, throwing out what sound like strangled obscenities in Serbian. Stefan knows what his brother will do to these men if he gets free. They would beg to be killed, rather than go through the torture. He has seen it on the faces of small-town politicians and civil servants. Bosnian and even Serbian petty criminals. British versions would be no different. All men show pain. Eventually.

'Where the fuck is it?' the voice hisses.

One of the three men across the room, kitted out in protective boiler suits, snaps the cutters open and shut in a whipping motion. Gives a throaty chuckle. He won't be laughing if the brothers get them into a torture chamber of their own.

Marko's eyes plead. *Give it up. Let them have the money.* They both know all they need is to escape this place, regroup, and revenge will come. But first they must find a way out. Stefan has more freedom, but the gun at his temple is restrictive. The brothers know to their own past benefit that the back office at the print shop is well soundproofed. None of their men are nearby. Asif's prone body lies by the doorway, a silenced bullet in his head, a needless sacrifice.

But the Mirkovic brothers got where they are today by force of will. By having the desire to impact more pain on their opponent than they could imagine. To torture and kill their families, if need be. Exactly what this old man is threatening them with. And Marko, despite his protestations, must know that Stefan cannot give in. Where do you go from there? Subservience, and that is as good as accepting your own death.

Stefan stays mute, stares at the gun. He can smell cordite.

'Look. I don't want to do this. I don't have to do this,' the voice whispers. 'Just tell me where my money is, and we will go away.' Leckie looks back at Marko. 'And your brother can still play a bit of passable piano.'

Marko rocks in the chair, and one of the men kicks him over. The prone figure snorts and squirms. Stefan watches him, begs Marko to lie still. Be patient. He needs to think. They are businessmen. What might look like a deal can be struck.

'If you take me with you, I can show you where it is.'

'You think I'm an idiot?' The light from the single bulb shines off the top of Leckie's head. 'You think I was born yesterday?'

The face leans in closer, a gloved finger pointing at Stefan's nose. 'You been pissing around with my man. Keeping him busy when he's supposed to be working for me. We been watching. You even did his car in. You can't help yourself, can ya? I asked you nicely to leave him alone. But you didn't listen. So, that makes me think I was wasting my money. Like you took it under false pretences. Like you been dicking me around. So, I come for my money back.'

Stefan keeps his silence. Wonders how long before Viktor or Dragan might stumble on the scene. And how delicious torturing these men will feel. That Marko will remove more than fingers with pleasure; he has seen him bite body parts off his victims before.

'Right. Do another one.'

Marko screams through the gag, as one man holds him down on the floor, and a second snaps at a digit. It takes two attempts to remove the finger, which rolls along the floor towards Stefan's desk, and stops in a bloody puddle.

'And another.'

Stefan looks into Marko's eyes, tears streaming down his brother's face, telling him to be calm, to accept the punishment. Marko shakes his head back and forth, then curls up into a ball, no more shouting, as a third messy piece of tissue is snapped off.

'You're a right cunt, you are,' Leckie announces, matter of fact. 'Putting your brother through this. Just for a few grand. Jesus.'

Stefan's mistake is only fleeting, but Leckie notices. He follows Stefan's eyeline to a wooden casing behind them on a shelf. Pulls it aside, finds the safe. Leckie tests the handle, then bends down to retrieve something from inside his boot.

'No point asking you for the combination, is there?'

'No.' Stefan knows that it comes down to force of will. His brother writhes in front of him.

'We'll get inside it, don't worry.'

The blade rips into Stefan's throat from behind. He gurgles, hands reaching to stop the flow, and falls forward onto his desk, settling into a bloody lake. The last thing he sees, face side on, blurred and twisted, is his brother receiving the same fate.

40

'A MISCARRIAGE OF JUSTICE?'
Concluding chapter from *THE TOWN THAT FORGOT CHILD X*, BY TRISH WATNEY

At the time of the trial, and certainly to those in the public gallery, the evidence presented in the case against Martin Sullivan was clear-cut. He admitted kicking Philip Hughes off the scaffolding on the building site. There was serious intent, with fatal consequences. By not speaking up, Sullivan was unable to prove to the jury that he did not intend to seriously injure or kill. By walking away and not calling for an ambulance, he revealed a callous disregard for human life. There has been no declaration of remorse for his actions.

But the actual burden of proof lies with the prosecution, not the defence. It is their job to convince the jury that Sullivan intended to kill Philip Hughes, beyond a reasonable doubt. From the evidence presented to them, they believed this was the case. It is understandable they felt this way. Yet there are some questions to be asked, including what now appear to be missing pieces of evidence. Particularly in relation to the mental state of Martin Sullivan at the time.

It is difficult to understand why the defence team decided not to let Martin go into the witness box. The jury's conclusion from this must have been that he was guilty. The defence could have done more to help their client in other ways. No questions were asked over what Alan Gregory was doing that day, watching young boys playing. He admitted to being at a local playground earlier, where he had seen the two boys involved. Conveniently, his suspicious background was not brought up.

Martin Sullivan made his statement with no independent witness present, although it was proven that the signature was his. Were these really his words? How tempted might the local CID have been, under pressure to resolve the case, to falsify the statement? Sullivan pleaded 'not guilty' at the start of the trial. Nobody has asked about this change of mind, this denial of his confession.

Indeed, it is this state of mind of the convicted killer that raises the most doubts. Was he abused by his mother? Was he showing off for his older brother, to prove his worth? Was he even legally culpable at the time? None of this was considered. And nobody has read the words the killer wrote in his diary leading up to and after the death of Philip Hughes. Would exposure to this change the opinion of the jury? Or the judge when he came to sentencing? We may never know.

More things to consider:

Where is Martin Sullivan being held now?

Has his identity already been changed?

Would he ever talk about what happened?

Is it possible to track down members of the jury and interview them? Is this allowed?

How to explain that Sullivan's diaries came to be in my possession.

41

Portsmouth, December 1999

The salesman strides out to the line of used cars, adjusts his belt, pulls his suit jacket around him. Ray has been studying him from outside, wondering which of the shysters would emerge first. He was hoping for this one, the man he followed earlier from his home, waiting for the chance to get closer. To look him in the eye.

'Nice runner this one,' the salesman says, showing his teeth, hands on hips.

Ray runs a hand across the bonnet of the VW Golf, wipes dusty fingers on his jacket.

'We will clean it, of course.'

The eyes are dark enough, the hair neatly cropped and gelled. Ray is unsure. The nose might be a little too large. But if you had the money, you could change anything. The voice has a slight south-west twang, more Dorset than Crawley. But that could be put on. Or learnt over the course of many years.

'What are you driving at the moment?' the man who

calls himself Richard Gleeson asks, looking around the car park. Ray's Mondeo is two streets away.

'Vauxhall Vectra.'

'Nice car.'

The model jumped into Ray's head. He pauses, realising it is the same make that is parked outside Steph's house most nights, whenever he passes the place.

'Too expensive,' Ray replies, resting a foot on one of the back tyres, then giving it a nudge. 'Looking for something cheaper to run.'

'I get it,' Gleeson says, a sales glint in his eye.

'How much?' Ray asks.

'You part-exchanging, then?'

'Maybe. Depends on the deal.'

The salesman smiles again, clasps his hands together, as if in prayer. 'We can always come up with a deal. Would you like to look inside it? I'll get the keys.'

'In a minute.'

The man is a few feet away. The lips are too full, and the ears look too big this close up. One question should do it.

'I don't know if I can fit the kids in it,' Ray says offhandedly.

'I know what you mean. I got four. I'm just a taxi driver half the time,' the salesman snorts. Ray ignores the irony, gives the man one of those looks of brotherhood, a 'Yeah, we both know family life is shit,' faces.

'Nice one,' Ray says. 'Mine are teenagers.'

'I've got two teenagers myself, and one grown up and left home.'

'You local?' Ray cannot resist the question.

'Yep. Pompey born and bred. You're not, then?'

Ray doesn't answer, moves around to the other side of the car to examine another tyre. There are paint chips down the offside passenger door.

'We can sort that out for you,' Gleeson adds, noticing where his customer is looking. Ray watches the face in the window reflection.

Ray shakes his head. 'Nah, you're all right. I'll keep looking.'

He certainly will, but not in Portsmouth, the home of the first of his three candidates to be Michael Keane, Martin Sullivan. Richard Gleeson doesn't look right, and his kids are too old, unless he has hitched up with a married mother and is claiming the credit. Nothing fits the story to link him back to Keane. Dusty's information said Gleeson changed his name about the right time, but none of the other pieces in the jigsaw fit. He might have a secret past, but not the deadly one Ray is looking for.

Ray parks outside a bookies' on the edge of Portsmouth at a row of local shops, one he noticed on the way in. Thinking he should celebrate reducing the field by one, knowing the odds of finding his man have improved. It is a local brand, 'Joe Summer', a throwback to the old days before the big companies flooded the high street. Knows he should press on, but there is something irresistible about the traditional betting shops.

The front door shuts with a thump. The walls are covered in racing pages, but the lighting is subdued, harking back to a sepia-tinged age, when the punter pitted his wits against a bookie and all was fair in love and betting. There is still hope before they take your money, but in these places the ratio of paying out and paying in booths is equal. A psychological boost.

Ray settles into a chair and rips up his sheet with 'Richard Gleeson, Portsmouth,' at the top. Pulls out the remaining two. 'Carl Marsh, Milton Keynes,' and 'Jake Seymour, Reading.' Reading will be next; it is closer. Eliminating one suspect gives him the faith to indulge in some sport. He has earnt it, has plenty of time. He folds the two sheets up and sticks them in his jacket pocket. Time to focus on more pressing details.

Ray removes a betting slip from the dispenser. The miniature pens in this shop look ancient, throwbacks to a bygone age. He shakes one that was lying on the table, prepares to face his future. He will be free soon. Free to bet as he pleases, not shackled by debt.

By the time he is down to his last fiver, Ray finds he cannot even spell the racecourse, Wetherby, one he has written countless times before, let alone the name of the horse. The slip is such a scrawled mess, they probably wouldn't pay out if he won. Which he knows for a certainty it won't, even as he slides it under the glass partition to the man at the counter. The face in front of him has been slowly changing with each visit in the past two hours, from suspicion and curiosity to an increasing welcome.

The horse falls at the first fence, and Ray stares at the screen, willing the jockey to remount, drive the nag on to victory, keep him in the shop for another hour, or ten minutes, or just ten seconds. Anything to stay there, alive, blood flowing, clinging to hope. His selection doesn't reappear as the camera follows a close run-in, an outsider winning. *Shoot the jockey and boil that bastard horse down into glue*, he fumes inwardly.

Bright sunshine greets him outside, and Ray squints as he trudges slowly along the pavement to the Mondeo. His arms ache from the effort of shielding his eyes from the light. His head pounds, under the pressure of failure. More courier jobs, then, simply to survive. More eating out of tins and picking through the bins at the Chinese takeaway below his flat. Still shackled to the brothers, despite his debt being elsewhere. He will catch a break. He will be a winner. His luck has to turn.

42

Milton Keynes, December 1999

Detective Inspector Greaves leads his two visitors through the bare office space, into the courtyard at the rear. The printed notices of support inside are gone, save the occasional torn corner on a pinboard and small Blu-Tack circular dots on the walls. The air feels like it has been sucked out of the place. Lydia grasps Carl by the arm as they follow the heavy tread of the policeman who brought the group bad news.

Greaves found them in a churchyard in Oxford, hanging back from the congregation, to wait their turn at the graveside. Steven Harding's funeral, the man who was once meant to be their saviour. Lydia insisted the pair of them went; closure is the word she has heard used before. The eulogy made no mention of the last eight years of his life, of Lena, or The Circle or The Foundation. They were outsiders, ignored. Carl stared at the grave with tears slowly rolling down his cheeks. A sign of vulnerability she has never seen in a man before. Lydia pulled herself into him for support. She still wonders why he helped her. Why he has been so distant since, and whether he thinks she planned the incident. She has run through the scene in the kitchen many times, S's hands on her, the knife on the floor, the kettle in her hand, and how easy it was to kill.

The double doors to the small garden are open. The space is about thirty by fifty feet, half of it paved, the rest grass, with a high wall at the rear, and two wooden benches in the middle. An extension of The Circle fortress. On warm days, this was where people would congregate in small groups to eat, or simply get fresh air on their breaks.

Greaves had emerged from behind a tree, as they were about to leave the funeral, invited them to return to the office. When he appeared, Lydia was glad she was hanging on to another person, could feel Carl shaking too. Wondered what picture the police were piecing together about the body that fell to the tarmac. Whether the two of them were being lured into a trap. Their story was simple: they spent that night together, at Carl's flat. Missing out the part where they threw a corpse off a bridge. The drive back to Milton Keynes from Oxford was quiet, Carl leaning his head against the window. Lost somewhere. As he often appears to be.

She fears the questions, prays Carl will not give anything away. Lydia is prepared to face up to what they did, what she did, because her cause was just. But would prefer to walk away from this dreadful town with its clean concrete approach to rebuilding, return home. But might have to keep an eye on Carl, to ensure he reveals nothing. They are now jointly damned, implicit in her act. His silence has been troubling. Even though they would go down together, she wonders how much he can be trusted.

Greaves beckons them to sit on one of the benches and stands opposite. Runs his hands through his hair and slowly shakes his head. All his movements seem to be measured, calculated to expose her. Lydia looks over the detective's shoulder at two men, dressed in pale blue overalls, standing over a hole in the ground in the corner of the garden. Carl has spotted the same thing, and his grip tightens. She can sense his breathing shorten. The policeman notices what they are focusing on and turns back to them.

'Carl, Lydia. I have to ask you some questions.'

'More questions?' Carl replies.

'Yes, I'm afraid so. Just a few things to clear up. Is that okay?'

Lydia stares at the hole, unable to focus. There is a tightening in her chest. Carl is rigid next to her.

'When was the last time anybody came out here?'

She looks at Carl, dragging her attention away from the overalls, the way the men move slowly, picking at the dirt.

'Well, the smokers would come out sometimes.' Carl's voice cracks a little, and Greaves keeps his focus on him. Where she would like it to remain. She holds on, feeling him shake. *Stay with me, Carl*, she inwardly pleads.

'The smokers?'

'Yeah, they would come out here when it was their break.' Lydia in support.

'I see.' Greaves rubs his eyes vigorously, inspects one of his fingernails. He stares at Lydia this time; she feels like she is shrinking. 'So, it was in regular use?'

'I suppose so. But not so much in bad weather. In the winter.' Carl again.

She would come out occasionally, share a cigarette, to catch the gossip. Searching for clues, gently probing, seeking out snippets of conversation about the leader of the group. Wondering what it was that kept them faithful to Steven Harding, masquerading under a different name. Guessing none of them knew about his past. Even Carl was taken in by his appeal. Although he hasn't seemed shocked by the facts about his past she has revealed. Carl came to her rescue, until they tipped the body over the bridge. That was the point where he seemed to freeze. Suddenly hit by the magnitude of their act.

Greaves looks up at the wall behind them. The place where a camera used to be mounted. An empty bracket is all that remains.

'We took all the cameras away,' Greaves says, pointing at the wall. 'What happened to that one?'

'I don't know. It got taken down before I had the job,' Carl says, eyes fixed on the spot.

Lydia nods. 'Yes, I don't know why.'

Greaves continues to focus on Carl. Lydia breathes more steadily but can feel the tension in Carl's grip. 'We're still looking at all the video tapes,' Greaves says. She can hear the policeman trying to tone down the accusation in his voice. 'It's a bit patchy, isn't it?'

'Is it?' Carl replies.

'Some gaps here and there.' The inquisition is almost light-hearted.

Carl shrugs his shoulders. 'I'm not even sure it recorded half the time. Maybe he was saving money?'

'Possibly.' Greaves looks unconvinced to her. She wonders where the line of questioning is going. Whether Carl has buried some evidence in the garden. Something that might still point the finger at her. She thinks they were together the whole time they cleaned up. Doesn't recall him going outside.

'But you could watch everyone at work?' Greaves asks, pointing up at the mounting on the wall.

Lydia turns to Carl and remembers his role. His grip loosens, fingertips only now. Greaves also notices the change. What has Carl done? She hopes he deleted the video evidence, as promised.

'Potentially, yes, I suppose.' Carl looks at Lydia and back at Greaves. She senses a plea in there. 'But I had many other things to do. I think Simon used to look at the footage, I don't know. Would you stare at people sitting at their desks all day long?' Carl offers a smile.

'Maybe not. But I understand you could spy on your colleagues in other ways. Listening in, reading their emails.'

'I wasn't spying.' For her benefit, she thinks, as much as the policeman. 'Janice, our supervisor, she listened in to calls as well.'

'Sounds a strange job to me,' Greaves remarks, picking at his jacket, then studying the paved floor. 'Why would you need to spy on your work colleagues?'

This stranger wouldn't understand why they were taught to be suspicious of outsiders. Keeping an eye on members of the group would seem even weirder.

'It wasn't spying,' Carl repeats, more firmly, letting Lydia's hand go completely. 'Most of what I did was paperwork. Ordering toilet rolls, that sort of thing.'

Lydia nods in agreement. His role seemed so mundane. She thinks through their conversation in the kitchen area, as they moved the body that night. Did he suspect Simon was in financial trouble?

'We're going to look at everything, Carl. I just wondered why some of it was missing?'

'No idea.' Carl shakes his head. 'I'm sure I couldn't have deleted anything anyway.' Carefully chosen words, Lydia thinks. He is covering for her but has turned his body sideways on. She still struggles to understand the significance of the hole across the yard.

Carl stares at Greaves, giving an explanation. 'He, Simon, had all the passwords for the system. I could only access what he gave me permission to. Which wasn't much.' Carl smiles, giving the impression of a clueless employee, hamstrung by the limits placed on him by an overbearing boss. Lydia knows that to delete the video footage, and the swipe card system history, he would know more than he is letting on.

'No matter. Our people have ways of retrieving things, even things that have been deleted.'

Lydia reaches for Carl, holds him firm. She looks over at the two men pointing at something below them.

'We'll find out what happened,' Greaves says.

'Happened?' Lydia asks, breath short.

'Yes, something happened out here.' Greaves points at the men in the overalls. 'Over there.'

Lydia looks at Carl, sees his eyes wide again, reminding her of that expression just after they let go of the body on the bridge. And a memory returns, a visit to the toilet to compose herself after they bagged up Simon's body. Remembers staring in the mirror at a vengeful killer. Did Carl hide something out here when her back was turned? Has he made a mistake? She squeezes Carl's hand, as if to say, 'We are in this together', hoping he understands the message. Carl lets go again, turns his head towards the back wall.

'I'll come to that in a minute.' Greaves pulls her into the moment, is surely about to reveal why he invited them into the courtyard. 'I need to ask you about someone who used to work here. Tim Durrell?'

The policeman stares intently at Carl as he asks this, and she turns to see the colour fall from Carl's face. He closes his eyes.

'Yes,' Lydia quickly responds, to draw Greaves's attention.

'And judging by the records we have seen, he left the company at the end of October, right?'

'Yes,' Lydia again.

'And when was the last time you saw him? Mister Durrell?'

'It was a Friday, end of October, wasn't it?' Lydia says, imploring Carl to agree, which he does with a nod of the head.

'And he just left, that was it?' Greaves enquires.

'He was here Friday, then gone by Monday,' Lydia adds.

'And where did he go?'

She provides him with an edited version of the story relayed to them by their leader, when he read out an email at the following Monday's Truth Time. Tim was travelling. A last-minute decision. Vietnam, a lifetime ambition.

Greaves points at the hole. 'We found Tim Durrell, buried, there.'

Lydia lets out a small, animal-like cry. Carl brings his hands up to cover his face. She looks at his long fingers and the bitten nails. He has attacked them in the last few days. Greaves is studying Carl, too.

233

'So, neither of you saw him, after he left? After that Friday? The twenty-fifth?' Greaves asks.

'No.' She fills the void.

'And you, Carl, what about you?'

He replies through his fingers, sniffs. 'The same. When he left work that Friday.'

Greaves looks around at the hole, then back at them. Lydia reminds herself to stay calm. She never even spoke to Tim Durrell. Had only known him for three weeks when he disappeared. Her focus was Steven Harding, pretending to be Simon. Tim was just a nobody who upped and left without warning.

'We don't even know for certain that he intended to leave. Seems he went nowhere. Seems he was here all along.'

'Somebody killed him?' Lydia asks. More death surrounding the strange cult. This will draw attention. Something she does not need.

'Yes,' Greaves confirms. She studies the men in protective clothing, poking at the ground. Wants to avoid the inspector's eyes. Concentrate on the overalls opposite.

'And it's definitely Tim?' she asks, quietly.

'His wallet was down there with him. Bit of a giveaway. We're waiting to get confirmation, dental records. But it looks like it was Tim Durrell, yes.'

Tiny Tim, who didn't realise his dream of reliving Apocalypse Now, down the rivers of Vietnam and Cambodia. Lydia turns to look at Carl, imploring him to not appear so suspicious in front of Greaves. She grabs at his hands, which sit in his lap, under his coat. Can still feel him tremble, hoping the policeman doesn't notice.

Greaves folds his arms, faces them. 'The ground was quite freshly dug. Did nobody notice this?'

'Like we said, not many people used to come outside, apart from in the summer,' Lydia replies. Carl nods in agreement, solidarity against the outsider.

'What was the relationship like between Tim and Simon Paterson, our Steven Harding?' Greaves probes, his voice softer now.

The same as it was for everybody, she imagines. Heavy reliance, trust, and hope. All false.

'I can't think of anything special,' Carl says, surprising her with a response, his voice barely above a whisper.

'And, Carl, this Tim did the same security job you do, or did, is that right?'

Carl swallows hard. 'Yeah. Before me.'

Greaves sighs and pulls a packet of cigarettes out of his coat pocket. He shakes them and puts them away again. Like a man realising he has smoked too many today.

'Simon wouldn't kill anybody,' Lydia says, unsure if it is true, but feeling attention needs to be elsewhere. Anywhere but with the two people sitting on their bench. The police are looking at a different death. But a suspicious one.

'Wait. We got an email, from Tim, a week after he left,' Carl says, looking at her, then at Greaves. 'He was in Saigon, in an internet café.'

'Did you see this email?' Greaves asks.

'Well, no, Simon read it out to us.'

'Did he?' Greaves raises his eyebrows, smiles at Lydia. She studies him again. The tired face seems to perk up. Carl is looking at the paving slabs at their feet. 'Well, that must have been a fake. Because Tim Durrell never left.'

'You don't think Simon had something to do with this?' Carl asks, voice cracking. Lydia wonders what other lives this predator might have affected.

Greaves barely flinches. 'Do you?'

'No, he would never,' Lydia replies for them both. She smiles, a true believer standing up for the man who led the group so selflessly, the icon they followed. 'Would he?' she asks, hoping to show a realisation that this man may have been a false prophet. Who then took his own life, jumping off a bridge.

'Miss Arnott, I'm just asking questions. This started off as a fraud investigation, remember. And now, this.' Greaves points behind him at the men in overalls. 'We don't know anything for certain. I'm trying to establish the relationship between the two men.'

'Tim was just one of us,' Carl interjects.

'I'm sure we'll find evidence in there, or on the body.'

Greaves leaves them and walks towards the men leaning over the hole. Lydia resists the temptation to follow and look, watching the side of Carl's face flinch. Squeezes his hand, as if to silently tell him to control his nerves.

The policeman returns and tells them there are no more questions for now, thanks them for their time, asks if they can see their own way out. A reminder not to touch anything inside. He has the eyes of a man who has seen this before, but still cannot shake the sadness of death.

'We have to look more closely at the evidence. But it doesn't look good for Steven Harding. All your colleagues will need to attend a local police station in the next two days. We are re-contacting everyone.'

'Why?' Carl asks, his face darkening, pulling his arms

around himself. Lydia feels strangely calmer, relieved the spotlight might move away from the apparent suicide.

'Fingerprinting. It's just to eliminate everyone from our enquiries.'

It is an old phrase, could mean anything. They cannot raise an objection.

It looks to Lydia that Greaves has made some assumptions that might send them in a different direction. The detective knows Steven Harding was a fraud, believes him to be a coward who took his own life instead of facing his followers over the financial mess he created. Who also might have eliminated a man who got too close to his truth. Greaves might then reason that suicide became an honourable option, protecting the group. A convenient conclusion, if he is heading that way.

Lydia and Carl leave The Circle for the last time, a place where people came to terms with themselves and their pasts, to quietly reassemble the pieces of their lives. The others were duped, but she knew the truth behind the Simon smile. All that remains are the shattered memories of a liar, and the buried body of someone she reasons knew too much. Like her. Except Lydia reacted quickly and had Carl at her side to help.

When they reach her car, Carl keeps walking, away from the industrial units, towards a tunnel that runs under the railway line. Lydia hurries after him, catches up, tugs at his sleeve.

'What's up? You can trust me. I had nothing to do with what happened to Tim.'

'I know,' he mutters.

'Well, what's the problem?'

Carl turns but avoids her gaze. Probes gently at stones with his foot.

'I… I can't tell you. You don't need to know.'

'What is it? Carl?'

He shakes his head, leans against a dividing wall that separates the units from the railway. 'It's best that we… that I stop here. Stop all of this.'

'You can't,' she begins, touching his cheek. Carl pulls away. 'You can't abandon me, after what we did. After what we went through,' she pleads.

'It's for the best,' he mumbles, finally looking up. 'It's better for you, for me, that we stop it right here. This, today… they're asking too many questions. It's too close, too much.'

Carl turns and walks through the tunnel. Lydia watches him leave her, then studies the chipped writing on the sign pointing towards the city centre, thinking about Lena, and how she has done what she set out to do. How it might be too dangerous to be carrying a weak passenger, who appears nervous under police scrutiny. By the time she turns her head back to look, Carl has disappeared on the other side of the tunnel.

43

Crawley, December 1999

Ray drives straight to his first job of the evening, a regular starting point, one of the faceless trading units on the industrial estate. The site used to house the Mother's Pride factory, a company that has now fled the town that once helped it to prosper. There used to be less than one per cent unemployment in Crawley, even under Thatcher. Gatwick Airport provided everyone with a lifeline. Freddie Laker was a saviour. As Ray waits in the parking space outside the unit, crunching a stale packet of crisps, he contemplates the forgotten new town dream in front of him. Wonders who lied to them, and whether they were all fools to believe it.

There will be a package to deliver back to base, where his next set of instructions will come. The digital clock counts down the minutes. When the numbers click over to zero, he locks the Mondeo and approaches the metal doors. There are no other vehicles in the damp early evening, just shadows cast by vast, lit pylons and tired, fabricated units. Despite the decay, there is a vibrant world rumbling underneath the surface, powered by the Serbs, the Deshis, the Moldovans, where anybody can make a living if they aren't too fussy about how they make money.

Ray thumps on the door. Bolts slip, and a heavily bearded man puts his head around the entrance, frantically searching left and right. Ray follows his gaze, then looks back at him. This is a new go-between. There are large circles under his eyes that almost reach the hair on his cheeks, as he pulls a grubby baseball cap tight on his head. Silence, no sense of recognition.

'Collection?' Ray asks. This is already one word more than he is supposed to use, but he is anxious to return to base, build up the cash again.

'Wait.' The door slides heavily across, closes.

Ray knows he is in the right place, at the right time. Metal groans and the door opens again.

'Here.'

The fierce beard hands over an envelope, then closes the door with a clang, echoing around the car park. Ray stares at the door, then the package in his hand. They never tell him what he is transporting in advance. This is not drugs, or girls, or boxes that he thinks might contain weapons. He guesses this is cash, probably a substantial amount. Destined for Stefan's pocket.

He knows he is trusted, not being Turkish, or Bosnian, or Greek. Ray is always the man they use for metal-grey places like this. For the dubious work. He thinks of Leckie Harris, and the money he must pay back, as well as delivering his target. Ray is confident he will turn two faces into the one he needs to find. But he is less sure about the debt. Weighs the package in his hand and wonders if he is brave enough to take the chance.

The Glory casino lurks at the end of a row of offices, near the train station. The car park is half-full, mostly upmarket motors. Ray places his deathtrap carefully between a couple of Audis. Suddenly wonders if someone like Leckie Harris might be a customer of the establishment. Logic kicks in and he breathes more easily. The Glory is a stronghold of the Chinese. Local villains, even those of an ancient vintage, would not be welcome. It is early in the evening, but casinos run full time.

Ray used to be a member of the place but is proud of the fact that he has stayed away for four months. Sticking to what he knows, the horses, the dogs, sometimes the football. Sport is easier to forecast. Cards and the roulette wheel are something else, a place where debt can be racked up too quickly. At least in the bookies' you bet what you have in your hand. Casinos love to offer you credit. And the Chinese have their own peculiar way of reclaiming debts. He has seen the broken limbs and bruises on others.

It is decision time.

Red or black.

The murky light inside is familiar. Barely enough to see the shade of your chips or the colour of the money you are handing over. Or the amount you tap into the machine, taking your credit. Ray knows there are two things habitually missing from these places. Clocks and windows. Designed to keep you there and throwing your money away. You don't see the time passing, or realise it is morning until you have done your bollocks on the wheel again.

Red or black.

A simple question. Ray's hand goes to the small bulge in his jacket pocket, feels the weight. Hasn't even checked how much is in there yet. If he acts, he could wash the money clean, do the brothers a service. Double the amount inside, hand the original back, walk away with the same for himself, have plenty left over after paying Leckie's expenses. The alternative is to go slowly, using a betting shop, take the fiver he gets for every courier job, drop each one on a favourite, watch it grow. Except that hasn't been working well lately. If he goes all in, one bold act, he only needs to be right once.

Red or black.

Ray closes the cubicle door in the toilets. Examines the envelope under the strip light. Nothing is written on the outside. It looks like he could reseal it, but he can't be sure. There is an all-night store not far away, where he might be able to buy a new envelope, exchange them. Provided he hasn't lost all the money of course.

He shakes the contents, still sealed, drops it on the closed loo seat. The corner is damp, and he dries it the best he can with toilet paper. Thinks how easy it would be to simply rip it open, grab the cash, throw it on one spin of the wheel.

Red, then.

Ray teases open the envelope and peers inside. A considerable number of notes, kept together with an elastic band. He has gone this far, no point in turning back now. He tips the money into his hand.

Fucking euros.

****

Ray is late returning to base for his next package. Three hours late. There is no reply on the radio from Asif, so no rush, he feels. He tried Ladbrokes on the high street, and they refused to take foreign currency. One of the regulars behind the counter laughed in his face. He eventually hit upon the exchange booth at the airport. Turned the notes into pounds, returned to the casino, sat bravely on his stool and doubled it twice, lost half of it again before ending back where he started. Then decided to have one game of blackjack, turned a twenty-one. Paying five to one on his stake. For once, Ray knew it was time to stop. Gordon from GA would have been proud.

Another trip to the airport, and a stern-faced teller turns his pounds back into euros. He reseals the envelope, fills it with the original amount.

Ray parks up a couple of streets away from Tilgate parade on Scott Road. Distance providing necessary caution. Needing to think through his response, if challenged about the state of the package. This was what they gave him, he will say, try to avoid eye contact with Stefan as he does so.

He passes the Grasshopper pub and makes the turn towards the shop fronts, practising the look of innocence on his face, ready for the cheery antagonism that will come from Asif in the taxi office. Knows as it is late in the evening, he will have plenty of work to catch up on.

Ray approaches the office. The lights are off where Asif is normally sat, badgering drivers into breaking their necks to make appointments. No signs of life as he edges slowly forward, half expecting Marko Mirkovic will jump out. All that greets him is an eerie silence. The print shop next door is also quiet. Ray looks around the parade, watches a group of young men come out of the pub and walk towards the bus stop. Feels like he is the only one aware that something is amiss.

Retreating to the back of the parade, Ray makes his way to the spot where he last saw Marko, pointing at his broken brake light. There is no door in the wall where the rear entry to the print shop used to be.

He creeps inside into darkness, touching the envelope inside his jacket, reassured he has something to offer the brothers if they appear. Flicks a switch. Nothing. Enters the room where he received the warnings about being robbed for a second time. They still trusted him, but this was his last chance.

Here the light does work, a single bulb hanging from the ceiling. The space is empty, save for a few fragments of broken chair in a corner and torn clothing crumpled on the floor. Moving closer, Ray finds a shoe, a brown brogue, sticking out from the pile. He thinks Stefan might wear something similar but can't be certain. The brothers have gone.

Ray pulls the envelope out, as if to hand it over to an invisible Mirkovic, an unseen ghost haunting the room. Replaces it in his jacket, hands shaking, wondering what this means. And who might have done it. The Turks, he supposes. Always at war with the brothers, with anyone from the Balkans. Best for him to stay out of the battle. Retreat to a hiding place, a sanctuary where nobody knows he exists. And pay another visit to the android teller at the airport exchange booth. No need for euros any more.

44

Worth Church, near Crawley, December 1999

The engine cools as he peers through the drizzle at the gravestones. Two hours to get there, having taken Lydia's car without asking. Another reason for her to give up on him. The rain slants diagonally onto the windscreen, then starts to ease, removing the excuse to stay inside and avoid confrontation.

The church sits on the northern edge of Crawley. Martin Sullivan is banned from there, by ancient order. But he doesn't exist any more. Crawley is a stranger, just like all the other places he has lived. The childish memories of the town, of playgrounds and harmless fun, have faded. There is just one windswept afternoon associated with this spot, when a metal box transported him there and back. This is where they come to bury their dead, where they came to bury her. That last visit was nearly twenty years ago, a compulsory journey, to mourn something he never had.

Stones of the past stretch out in front of him. That bitch is in there somewhere. Easing the door open, he steps out towards the lines of dead, shielding his face from the wind. She must be faced one last time.

He finds her meagre tribute after five minutes of searching. God knows who paid for it. She lies at the end of a row in the corner of the graveyard, flowers marking the other names nearby, the well-remembered, the loved. The dead living on in the hearts of their family and friends. Sharon Sullivan's plot is forgotten, a miserable weed, representing thirty-nine years of wasted life. There is comfort in the fact nobody appreciates her, the modern indifference of a community.

There are signs of faded assault scrawled across the marker of the woman that thrust verbal and physical abuse on her sons. She drove Danny away to take up the flag, eventually to an honourable border patrol death. Martin was jealous of his escape, responded in a different way. Desperately sought the attention of the woman who should have been protecting him. Forced to strike out, until he was noticed. She has paid for her wilful ignorance. Those sessions in the calming rooms explained everything to him.

He is comforted by the faint comments, that she was ultimately neglected, and that he lives on. They warned him about coming here, many years ago, to avoid being recognised, or dragged into his past. Advised to look to the future and not backwards. He has returned to check that she really is dead, so that boy can be cast aside. This woman has haunted the other men he has become. Forced them to give up on life. There has been no knock on the door after the fingerprints were provided, but the need for a new existence, and to move on again, is pressing. The next identity is ready, for when the investigation is over. This time it will be different. He is going to live from now on.

Looking at her name, etched so carefully and vandalised in the distant past so effortlessly, he wonders what might have become of him if he had met someone like Lydia when he was younger. Someone who could have shown him where his future lay. And how other people have fears too. That he isn't a monster.

He sits down on the damp grass above his mother, legs crossed, surprising himself, sobbing tears of pity. Confused as to why she still provokes a reaction. Pulls a hand up to his chest, to ease the sharp pain, consumed by the fear, the regret, the anger. The outburst feels like it has been short. He wipes his face on a sleeve, looking around to check if anybody has seen him, but there is no sign of life. He pulls himself back up and walks to the car. The cold feeling of the penknife in his trouser pocket is there, but he resists the temptation to add abuse to the slab. He has brought the means for greater damage.

In his early sessions they shared the hell she went through in Crawley, he assumed to draw the guilt out of him, but he wished it all upon her. Assaults in the street. Shit literally posted through her letterbox, before she moved away. He guesses the clippings could have been deliberately selected. Now he is rehabilitated, a model citizen. No mother to hold him back.

He could escape to his room and the games, while she was persecuted. Responsible for the demon that knew no better. Her death freed him, helped him to reflect. That day they lowered her into the ground, it became clear what he had to do to be released. If he followed their process, demonstrated a sense of rehabilitation, and blamed himself rather than her, there was a way ahead. Self-awareness was one of the words they used in those rooms to describe it. He listened more than they gave him credit.

Soon after her demise, while the tape recorders ran, with new faces but the same angles of questioning, he carefully changed the answers. They said they could help him if they understood what drove him to kill. It was impossible to show them what it felt like to be ignored, simply because he couldn't buy her a drink. The final expert, the one who fought for his release, got the ultimate version of the truth. Toshack had the patience to look deeper. He was rewarded with what they needed to hear, the good side of the mother, the happy memories. The day three of them went to Margate, just after his father left. A tale of ice cream, sand in his hair and mouth, wet clothes on the long journey back. Toshack needed to see a balance, an explanation for the anger.

Explaining the death of Philip Hughes became easier. All they did was fight. And who wants to lose one of those? You try to win. That kid shouldn't have been up there on the scaffolding with him, had plagued him all day. Shouldn't have called him an 'arse bandit', should have let him be Obi-Wan Kenobi, shouldn't have boasted that he could take him out with one hand tied behind his back. Standing up there on the building site, the challenge was made, and he shut him up. The boy back then had no choice.

The sledgehammer echoes around the graveyard. The side of the monument crumbles first, then after the third blow a large piece drops away. He finds that aiming close to the edge is more effective, where the stone seems weakest. The slab is almost gone after another half a dozen swings. She will feel his presence. One final crack reduces it into a crumbled pile, spreading out debris around his feet. The remains are kicked around, ensuring the pieces are arranged on top of her body. She festers underneath, devoured by creatures with no idea who or what she was, or what she bred. Removing any acknowledgment of her presence on earth.

He should have done this years ago. Realised that he can live, rather than hide. Somebody out there has grown to like him. Trusted him. Relied on him when in trouble. But Lydia can't hear the truth behind the practised lies.

He wipes his shoes on the broken stone, not wanting to bring back any traces of her. It would upset the way of things. Order will be restored. Nobody steps out of the shadows to challenge him as he returns to the borrowed car, sledgehammer over his shoulder, to carefully place it in the boot. He is still alone, mission complete. Needs to return to being invisible. It is time to look forward and find a new life for Carl Marsh.

4 5

Milton Keynes, December 1999

And the winner of the prize of being handed over to Leckie Harris is… Carl Marsh of Milton Keynes.

The M1 junction numbers crawl their way upwards as Ray heads north. The Mondeo struggles to leave the inside lane, buffeted by lorries, as he keeps an eye on the traffic, checking to see if he is being followed. Realises he hasn't considered this since he started on his quest. Thinks back to the cab attack, the empty scene at the print shop, the missing Mirkovic brothers, all his misfortune lately. Wonders whether someone has been nobbling his horses. He grips the steering wheel tightly. Ray is down to one name now and hopes this is his man. Dusty has never made a mistake before, but if he has, Ray will run. All his possessions, packed in a battered suitcase, are in the boot.

Jake Seymour from Reading might have been closer to Crawley, but thirty minutes parked outside a respectable semi-detached front door that morning, watching a wife and two kids leave, eliminated the secondary school teacher. Jake's thin face greeted him at the door and told him immediately this wasn't Sullivan. The eyes avoided directly looking at Ray, a man hiding from something, but not Leckie Harris. Not Child X, unless he had a brilliant plastic surgeon. Ray pretended to be searching for a different street and left. He should have gone through the face-to-face formalities sooner.

Ray looks across at the shoulder bag in the passenger seat. Filled up when he cleared out the office that morning, grabbing his post, forlornly hoping for a payment from Councillor Bevan. All he found on the floor, where the mail drops, was a Radio Mercury padded envelope, hand addressed, presumably from Trish Watney. The Bogart poster is rolled up in there for company.

He has no choice but to condemn someone, to clear the debts. The killer he knew as a boy has been on the run from a dangerous man. Must have wronged Leckie somehow. Ray knows the consequences of inaction, has lived with that for years. And there is a small, weighty prompt with a lit-up screen and a nagging typeface in his pocket, a reminder of someone who will not tolerate failure. One face for Leckie's target is probably as good as any other. He could just hand over the details and cross his fingers, but the hacker only narrowed down the chase. Ray must get up close to this Carl Marsh, look him in the eye, form a judgement of his own.

Heaven knows Ray is a different person from who he was at the age of twelve, so has to wonder if that kid he briefly knew from school has changed. If he is going to sign a death warrant, he needs to confront him, the way he should have done years ago. Ray could have saved Philip Hughes, by talking to someone, anyone. He is certain now, after the failure of two close encounters, that he will recognise him.

As the road signs start to include Milton Keynes, Ray pictures Martin Sullivan again, the boy who fleetingly attended his school. The face was in the local newspaper briefly after the trial. Ray followed him once, just after the first sighting at Thomas Bennett. It struck him dumb, watching that kid jump on his friend Marty Breaker's back in the queue to go into the science block. Knowing instantly that was the boy he and Paul saw in the summer. At that moment, wishing Paul was by his side.

Ray tracked Sullivan that same day to Tilgate shops, watched him go in and out of the newsagent's, stopping to talk to Cathy Miller from his class. He wanted to scream at her to keep away; didn't she know what this boy had done? Sullivan's non-attendance from October was glossed over by the teachers. The following year, after the trial, all of Crawley knew the identity of the monster in its midst.

The mobile phone rings in his pocket, but Ray ignores it, despite the fact only one man knows his number. Concentrates on the turning off the motorway, needs to focus. The debt to Leckie is under control. He has just enough money to pay back the five hundred loan. Ray celebrated narrowing down the field to one man in Reading earlier, dropping into a Corals by the local bus station. Knowing the time was right, the mood was with him, and he was invincible. As it proved to be. Following an hour of near misses, scrawling losers on betting slips, his final note went on an outsider called Pirate Bonanza at Haydock Park. As it crossed the line, he felt lighter, taller, superhuman. Able to see into the future. One where he will be free, when he hands this man over. There should have been more on it, nothing worse than the winning bet you didn't put enough on, but your last tenner is your last tenner.

Off the motorway, the Milton Keynes grid system is baffling, labelled with both street names and letter/number combinations. Ray imagines taxi driving must be a nightmare here. Sometimes the roads simply lead to nowhere. You know where you are in Crawley; the neighbourhoods are colour-coded and the place is laid out in sensible districts. He heads first for the home address Dusty has provided, searching for a place called Fishermead, and drives through the centre of Milton Keynes twice before realising his mistake. He pulls in at a petrol station and buys a local map.

Studying the pages, Ray has already passed close by. Perran Avenue does not look as grand as it sounds, a mixture of randomly arranged three-story blocks and terraces. The cars parked along it are far from new, so his Mondeo fits in. Tatty, overgrown gardens sit in front of the buildings. No rubbish, though, which is something. If Martin Sullivan is building himself a new life here, it is with low aspirations.

Ray drives slowly enough to study the flat numbers, and parks across the street from the address. An unremarkable block, peeling paintwork on the window frames, shabby brickwork. Two women walk past, laden with shopping bags, and he slinks down a little in his seat. They ignore him. He watches their wide frames pitch from side to side, wobbling like pins resisting the drop in a bowling alley. The wind bullies empty trees. The pattern of the bricks takes him back home, to a place where a young boy trailed his hands over similar ones at the end of Iona Close. He is standing behind a wall again, listening to celebrations on the other side. Frozen with fear.

Ray turns up the heater to full blast, closes his eyes. Reminds himself of his mission. Wonders how come he ended up here, doing the bidding of Leckie Harris, the chattel of a different beast. No more Mirkovic brothers, as far as he can tell. But the debt is no longer theirs. If Leckie hadn't bought it out, and he could have held on until those Turks took revenge on their rivals, there would be no debt to pay back. He would have no source of income, but also no five-figure noose round his neck. And no requirement to sit there, contemplating sending a man to a murky end.

He looks across at the block of flats. Nobody comes in or leaves. Ray still can't think what this Sullivan has done to Bad Leckie, other than owe him a massive sum of money. The history, the truth about the target being the infamous Child X, that might not need to be told. Leckie wants him regardless of who he was. The guilt of two cowardly witnesses will mean nothing to a man like him.

After over an hour of no movement from the block where Marsh lives, impatience takes over, and Ray crawls around the neighbourhood a little, then gives up and heads for the work address instead.

The map steers him to an industrial unit in an area called Stacey Bushes. At least in Crawley place names make sense. The shutters are down, so Ray knocks on the glass front of the unit next door, where the receptionist fills him in on the local story. Her eyes light up and she leans provocatively across her desk, taking him through the sordid details. That their former neighbours, 'Circle Telemarketing Services' no longer exist. That the boss of the company committed suicide, and they found a dead body in the garden. Ray must hand somebody over to Leckie Harris. A corpse won't cancel the debt. She tells him that neither of the dead men was called Carl Marsh, as far as she can remember. A Simon, she thinks.

Returning to Fishermead via a confused, different route, he discovers the local centre has a Ladbrokes, the red livery pulling him in, the familiar clawing in the guts winning. Sometimes you just get a good feeling about the day. The image of a jockey from earlier returns to Ray, raising his fist in triumph, viewed on a screen in a bookies' a hundred miles away. When you are on a roll, make the most of it.

Under the bright neon of what must be a newly fitted out shop, he raises himself up on a high-backed chair, unfamiliar, but comforting. He starts by following trap six at Hackney dogs, knowing that with the recent wet weather an outside start away from the inner scramble will provide an advantage on that track. There are wins on the first two races, and the invincibility returns. The world smiles at him again. A sign that Carl Marsh, Martin Sullivan, is within reach, unaware of his fate.

The strength of Ray's conviction continues, a third win. He feels the bulge of notes in his back pocket, delights in the adrenalin flowing through him. This is living. This is how betting is supposed to be. He ponders the next race, knows he needs to change trap at Hackney, and considers the horse racing venues. When things are going well, widen the scope. Ray processes the bewildering number of opportunities to gamble, ignores the colourful pleas of the gaming machines, hits upon Sedgefield, a track he has a good record with.

A jockey and trainer combination catches his eye. A pairing from Hampshire, travelling all the way north for a meaningless meeting. Something is up. Ray follows the hunch, a bold twenty at five to one, and another comfortable winner. He strides to the payout counter, smirking at the woman who hands out the purple notes. She gives him a knowing look that he misses, caught up in the joy. Life doesn't get better than this.

Ray returns to the same seat, eyes up another dog meeting at Walthamstow. He could stay here all day, raise enough money to start his life again. Begin anew, the same way this Sullivan has done repeatedly.

As he picks up the stubby pen, ready to write out another winner, the phone rings in his pocket. He stares at the screen, knows it will be Leckie Harris, prods the red button to refuse the call. Returns his attention to the list of runners. The phone bleeps as a message pops up on the screen.

'Call me. I want an update.'

Ray carefully replaces the phone in his jacket pocket, pulls out another betting slip.

Thirty minutes later, after several losses, desperately following the previous winning trap at the dogs and two fallers on the horses, Ray puts his last tenner on a hurdle at Wincanton, praying for the same result as earlier in the day. Hoping that history will repeat itself in his favour. The nag tails off early. 'Send the bastard to the knacker's yard', Ray wants to shout, but holds it in. Nobody screams in the shops, they just shuffle off to the cold outside and contemplate their failure. All Leckie's advance, the currency he exchanged for the euros, including the winnings from the morning, gone.

Ray stumbles out to his car, slumps in the driver's seat, head resting against the steering wheel. He should throw himself under a train, or at least break something in anger, but there is no energy to react. Ray sits there, smelling the damp interior of the Mondeo, watching the trees bend in the wind. He stares at the glowing red shopfront of the bookies' that provided him short-lived joy, followed by the familiar continuation of agony.

'Why do I do this?' he whispers to himself. He has no answer, never has.

His thoughts turn to how quickly fortune can change. The run of form at Hackney and the other tracks. How the life of this boy he encountered years ago, and who has lived in secret for so long, is about to be altered. How he needs to stop hiding, has no choice but to face up to Child X.

Leckie will expect action. He is probably halfway to Milton Keynes with his men, tracking Ray down through his mobile phone, spotters in all the betting shops looking for him. A group of three black men pass on the pavement, babbling words he can't make out, voices rising and falling, hand gestures frequent and violent. Reminiscent of late-night Langley Green streets back home. Alien, yet strangely familiar.

The buzzer for number eight has a tinny sound, makes Ray wonder if it can be heard inside. There is no answer. Maybe his quarry has already been tipped off by the woman who worked for the company next door, that teller behind the counter in the betting shop, or the guy in the petrol station where he bought the local map. He tries each of the other buttons for the block in turn. No replies.

An old man comes out of the flats and tips his hat at Ray as he passes. Ray catches the entrance door, nodding, trying to act as if he belongs there. Inside there are nine pigeonholes for post. The slot for number eight has some junk mail, in the name of Carl Marsh. Ray looks across at the door for number two and guesses he should be thinking about the flat a couple of floors above. As if compelled by his staring at it, the door opens. Two large men stand at its threshold, glaring at him, and before they can object, Ray slips out through the main entrance, the door closing with a soft thump.

Ray returns to the stillness of the car and settles in to watch. The heater refuses to blow. He wriggles his toes and stamps his feet for warmth. Carl Marsh must return home sometime. Ray pulls his coat further around him and opens the shoulder bag, looking for something to eat. The envelope from Radio Mercury slips out. Tearing it open, a note falls to the floor in the seat well. Ray retrieves it, shaking the crumbs of a forgotten scotch egg from his fingers. Inside the package he finds a flimsy, old-fashioned school exercise book and a batch of yellowing typed A4 sheets, kept together by a bulldog clip.

The note is from Trish Watney. In a tidy, sloping hand, it reads, 'I gave up on this years ago. Thought you might find it useful.'

The bundle of pages read like an investigation into the case of Child X. Must be the unpublished book she mentioned. The title suggests Trish thought Crawley forgot about that boy. There are notes from what look like interviews, articles he recognises from the local paper stuck onto sheets, thoughts on the case. Tightly spaced typing, pages turned in at the corners, a heavy, ancient read.

In contrast, the notebook feels flimsy in Ray's hands. He flicks through the pages to start with, wondering at its relevance, then slows down, remembering how it took patience to unearth the name of Martin Sullivan in Doctor Toshack's notes. The cover says 'Daniel Sullivan, Wallis House, Form 4B'. There are two different handwriting styles inside.

Ray begins to read, then looks up to see a woman standing at the entrance door to the block. He has missed her approach. A small shopping bag is slung over her shoulder. Perhaps she is an accomplice, has brought supplies, helping Marsh to hide out from the world. To hide from hapless private investigators, desperately seeking a way out.

Her blonde hair swirls in the wind, and she pulls it back behind her ears. There is no smile as she surveys the empty street. Ray sinks in his seat. She looks up at the windows. Following her line of sight, Ray knows from his earlier trip inside that she is searching out number eight, and Carl Marsh. A curtain twitches, a shape moves. His prey, Marsh, Duggan, Keane, Sullivan, all these men, is up there, watching. The woman pushes hard at the buzzer. The communal door opens, and she steps inside. She must know him. A light goes on in the flat, confirming that someone has been there all along. Ray huddles deeper into his coat and tries the heater again.

He goes back to reading, breaking off occasionally to glance up at the curtain. His attention is drawn back to the words of teenage angst and filthy drawings. It reads like a form of diary, written in a schoolbook. But towards the back, with the second writer, it becomes less legible. Some of the text is written at odd angles, filling in spaces. The grammar and spelling are appalling. The handwriting becomes more erratic as it goes on. The word 'invisibal' catches Ray's eye, the 'i's dotted with circles rather than points. A mind empties itself out, regularly referring to someone as 'bitch'. But the author becomes clear. Ray is reading the words of a child killer, of Martin Sullivan, writing in his brother's book. Hatred and frustration spilling out, angrily drawn across the pages.

How did Trish Watney get her hands on it? Did she steal it? Or pay the mother? And why did she do nothing about it? Ray thinks back to the calm reflection of a journalist he met a few days before, giving nothing away about this item. Wonders how come she decided to pass it on. Surely, she could have provided inside knowledge of a murderer's mind years ago. Made a fortune with it. Ray remembers the ancient articles in the *Crawley Observer*, her clipped words across the desk in her office, how she mentioned that the boy never testified, or revealed why he killed. And in his hands is some sort of explanation. Ray can imagine someone like Doctor Toshack drawing conclusions that would help. For twenty years, Trish Watney has been hiding a deeper truth. It is easily done.

The writing ends abruptly. No mention of the young detective Ray, pretending he was Jim Rockford, on his trail outside a newsagent's. Ray can picture a twelve-year-old boy, crying out for attention, desperate for his mother to care for him. Unnoticed until he kicks Philip Hughes off the scaffolding. Striking out before that above the underpass brought no response, so maybe he went further. Trish mentioned how the town has moved on. They wanted the facts, not the reason why. This was a child killer, all that mattered. Perhaps nobody would have believed two boys with another tale to tell.

Reading the scrawled words, Ray wonders whether Sullivan deserves a warning. He rests his hands on the steering wheel, contemplates driving off, simply passing on the name and address. Leckie has plenty of men to chase him down. Men with dirty hands, mud-stained boots and no scruples. He is about to turn someone's life upside down, throw that boy to a wolf. Ray will be a killer now. He looks up at the curtain, still drawn at number eight. Doesn't everyone deserve the chance to correct their mistakes? This Carl Marsh might be nothing like that little kid, desperately seeking attention on the pages. What must it be like to look over your shoulder all your life? Waiting for some fool like Ray to knock on your door and give you away.

Ray jumps as two kids smack his wing mirror, sprinting past. They scamper off in the direction of a hedgerow, laughing at a high pitch. His old man would have chased them, given them a good hiding. Ray's feet are rooted to the floor.

He rolls up the exercise book and slips it inside his coat pocket, adding the mobile phone, and hides Trish's words under the seat. He needs to concentrate on the target, not why a town didn't care about injustice. Facts are all anybody wants; they bring certainty. Thinking too much can get you lost, just like with betting. Over-analyse, and you will miss the horse that gut feeling is telling you will romp home.

'Make sure,' Ray mutters to himself, looking in the driver's mirror.

The mobile phone vibrates in his pocket.

'I need an update,' demands the text.

Ray grips the wheel again, sees his knuckles turn white. Leans into the leather in front of him with his forehead. The only time he is decisive is sitting in front of a betting slip. Things must change. If a woman gets involved, that is her problem.

Unpeeling his fingers, groaning as he lifts himself out of the car, Ray slowly follows the path towards the block. Towards a place he could easily have broken into. He needs to stop the procrastination, looks again at the curtain; no movement.

Ray pauses at the buzzer, still handcuffed by hesitation. Should he tell this man that a dangerous criminal is looking for him? Does he need rescuing? Ray leans against the wall by the entrance, tracing the chipped wood trim of the front door with a shaking finger.

The woman springs out of the entrance, sweeping past him, and he catches the door before it closes. The bag has gone from her shoulder, and she stares straight ahead, down the path. From behind it looks like she wipes something away from her face. Ray wonders what Sullivan has said or done to her. He stands on the threshold of the block for a second time. He can't tell if his quarry is watching her from above; nothing moves up there. The opportunity has come. Just an internal door on the second floor to get through. Time to undertake a moral judgement of his own. To decide if this man should be told about the fate that awaits him. If, of course, he is the right man.

Marsh's previous visitor climbs into a small Nissan parked about three cars down from Ray's Mondeo and drives off. The main entrance door clicks closed behind him. No going back now. He creeps his way up the concrete stairs to the second floor. A bold eight announces this is Carl Marsh. Ray takes a deep breath. Time to face up to his past failings and confront the fear.

46

Milton Keynes, December 1999

Lydia's message, posted through Carl's entrance door and presumably placed in his pigeonhole by a neighbour, asks him to call. Asks why he is hiding from her, forgetting he has no phone. She says they need to talk about what happened. There is no experience for him to fall back on, no rulebook that explains how to withdraw from a relationship, the 'r' word she used. He had hoped she would simply give up on him, if he ignored her, let him fade into the background. A plausible story, given she has killed someone.

A visit to the local dole office confirmed that nobody is hiring men with no work history other than call handling in a failed marketing company, branded in the local newspapers as a cult. Not that Carl was looking seriously; it was for show, for the police in case they enquired. There are no money worries; he has lived frugally, always set cash aside out of necessity, in case he needs to move on quickly. And the early work has been done for the new identity. He is ready, will wait for the new millennium. Not raise suspicion with the police before the next phase.

An inquest is scheduled for early in the new year, for Tiny Tim. Reading the local papers and judging by Greaves's reaction to the body in the office back yard, it seems the police investigation is favouring a cult leader murdering one of his group, then committing suicide. He no longer needs the relationship with Lydia to maintain the appearance of normality. He will be able to fall back into the shadows, make Carl Marsh disappear.

Lydia's story is too toxic to get close to. Whatever her motive, they both need to move away. Separately. She deserves more than this. More than him.

A couple of days to navigate alone, before Christmas Day. It has never been a time for celebration. There would be a meal in the secure home, the warders who drew that year's short straw joining them, offering a begrudging glimpse of humanity. The inmates wore hats, pulled crackers, read out jokes, but it was an illusion. Many of the kids were short term, or on remand, had real families elsewhere. You could see they were thinking of their relatives' faces, rather than those gathered around. Carl was always happy to get the meal over with and return to the order of his room. Keeping a sense of it being like any other day. When you had nobody, Christmas served as a bleak reminder.

The only present he ever got for the bitch was a box of Matchmakers, using money stolen from her purse, which she ate for breakfast on Christmas Day, not offering him any. All she ever gave him were second-hand toys, or Daniel's hand-me-downs. No skateboard, or train set, the things he asked Santa for. Her money went on booze and cigarettes.

Spending Christmas with Lydia would only complicate things, make eventual separation more difficult. Better to cut the cord now, with no ceremony. He can look forward to an all-day game of Risk, his preferred way of tackling the festivities.

His buzzer goes and Carl peers at the entrance to his block from behind the protection of the curtain. She is down there, a plastic bag in her hands. Her car sits across the street.

'Let me in, Carl. I have something for you,' over the crackling intercom.

He can't imagine what she could possibly give, but her pressing is persistent. He needs to avoid undue attention.

The heavy outer door clicks and her heels echo up the stairs. He has relented. There will have to be one final meeting, to conclude things, or she will not let go. He thinks of the tears she has shed, pouring out her past, her desire to expose the leader they all followed. The mission that led her to Milton Keynes and The Circle.

When he opens the door to her, he backs away inside. She follows and drops a plastic bag on the wooden chair.

'Here you go. Just the joggers and the T-shirt you lent me.' A delayed exchange of clothes, after Carl dropped off her blood-speckled items the week before, the excuse to borrow her car keys.

Her voice is calm, but there is alcohol on her breath. Lydia pulls her hair back behind her ear, the way she does when she has something important to say. But silence hangs between them, as she looks around the living room. Carl wonders if she is searching for signs of another woman, a reason for ignoring her. For no longer providing the support she needs from another human being. He is worthless.

She nestles on the arm of the sofa. A determined-looking woman studies him, probably infuriated once again by how tidy the place is.

'Thanks for that,' he mutters, pointing at the bag. He can live without the contents.

'I just wanted, you know, to make sure you had them back.' Still calm.

What more can he say to her? He is hurting her, walking away, or more precisely standing still, with no explanation. She cannot become involved with a monster. Her deadly act was a reminder of his own past. And that he is compelled to push people away. But he finds the words hard to find, now she is there. Surprised by the hold she seems to have on him. Her interrogation begins.

'Where have you been? In my car. I've been around here a couple of times.'

He pulls his arms around him, picturing the pile of rubble down south. He needs to shut down her questions. 'I had to do something.'

'What?'

'Nothing.' *Just walk away*, he silently pleads. *Don't get involved.* Maybe if he behaves like a shit, this will be easier. For him.

'Where did you go, Carl? Just tell me.'

'To visit my mum.'

'I thought you said all your family were dead.'

'They are.' Her eyebrows rise, puzzled. 'I went to see her grave,' he adds.

'Ah.' She nods. 'I could have come with you.'

Not a good idea. 'I had to go alone.'

Lydia rocks on the sofa arm, clears her throat. 'Tell me

about your mum. You never talk about her.'

Carl shivers. What could he possibly tell her? She has come from a household that refused to see the truth in front of them. One that created a vengeful killer. He has come from nothing.

'She died years ago, when I was a kid.'

Would she leave him alone if he told her the truth? That he was Child X, that devil from twenty years ago. That being with him would be dangerous. She cannot come with him to the next identity. The money is in place. The current rental agreement ends on the last day of the millennium.

'But you know so much about me now. So much about what I did. We are linked, aren't we?' Her voice rises, the eyes moisten.

'We have to stay apart. The police will suspect. They might think we were involved,' Carl pleads.

'In what, Simon? Or Tim?'

'Both.'

She pauses, rubs her temples. 'What did I do wrong?' she asks.

He studies her, wonders what it might be like to have a relationship with another human being. Other than one where they sit opposite you in a chair with a clipboard in their hand, and a tape recorder running, thrusting out questions, listening for the right response. Maybe those analysts still think of him, the infamous case they had, the boy they manipulated into a respectable member of society. A subject accepting the role they gave him, facing his demons.

Even Carl can't let her think this is her fault. 'Nothing.'

'So, why are you ignoring me?'

'I'm not…' He pauses, thinks about how to phrase it carefully. How to let her down, without raising suspicion.

'You think I'm bad, don't you? You helped me, and now you regret it.' Lydia sobs as the words come out.

There is a sadness in her eyes, one that almost makes him want to reach out and hold her. Hold someone. But he must resist, has been taught to go through life alone.

'I don't think that. You had your reasons.'

Lydia frowns, tucks the hair behind her ear again. 'Jesus, Carl, you're such a coward.'

He shrugs, wishes she would just leave. She is perched on the arm of his most comfortable chair, where she has sat before, watching him tidy his flat, judging.

'I killed someone, and you're scared,' she says. He looks into her eyes; she inclines her head slightly. 'Scared of life.'

Carl looks across the room at the table. A Monopoly game is half-hidden underneath the box lid. The pieces are poised, need his guidance to move on. He wants her to go so he can roll the dice. She cannot see the truth. One she might stumble upon if she hangs around.

That truth is more complicated than a cult leader taking his own life, overcome by the guilt of financial collapse and the murder of Tim Durrell. Tiny Tim knew too much about a man called Carl Marsh, and who he used to be, and had to be silenced. Faking an overseas trip was easy, as was sending emails from his account. When Carl buried his predecessor in the courtyard, he planted enough of a trail that would lead to S being the assumed culprit, in case the body was found. He had not anticipated Lydia giving a helping hand to this narrative.

So, Lydia must leave, for her own safety. They have a bond, but this was built on her mistake, not his. He had no choice but to help her. Dragged into a relationship he didn't need. He will always have to stand alone, drop back into the shadows. Lydia must stay away, because if she asks too many questions as others have done before, she might face the same fate. And he doesn't want that to happen. He didn't want any of this to happen.

When he looks up, she is standing close, hands outstretched. 'Carl?'

Carl shakes his head slowly. 'Just go,' he pleads.

Lydia backs away, steady, silent steps taking her to the door. 'There's something about you, Carl. Something I don't understand. I don't know what it is.' She pauses. 'But maybe you're just like the others, like Simon, whatever his name was.' The eyes narrow, darker. 'Maybe you're no different.'

She must believe this, Carl decides, has to leave, forget that he ever existed, stay away from monsters. He says nothing, watches her pause, hopefully for the last time.

Lydia closes the door quietly. Carl sighs, thinking at first this is relief, but then wonders if it might be something else. He has no idea what it is to care about another person. To love. He knows he is throwing away an opportunity. To live life with someone else. But he has no choice. He will never escape his past.

'You have to forget me, Lydia,' he whispers to himself, 'I'm not worth it.'

He searches the wall to the right of his door, scanning for the panic button that is now a distant memory. A necessity when they started moving him around after his release. In case his identity was discovered, and revenge came upon that little boy. Bloodlust for the monster they called Child X. He became invisible in the shadowy world of those tenement flats, surrounded by the other forgotten elements of society, people who were unaware of what lurked among them. But they still offered him the plastic box to press, as a precaution. They knew he could be a target. That kid is gone now, and there is nothing to scramble a concerned probation officer. Fear of reprisal has become a thing of the past. Now he only fears himself.

The sound of her shoes clipping on the concrete stairs fades, prompting him to lift the lid off the Monopoly board, the pieces reminding him of the need for self-preservation. A clean break, confirmed by the forgotten contents of a plastic bag, which he tips into the kitchen bin. He can revert to his protective shell and restore order. They taught him well. If he keeps the world out, nobody can become infected.

As Carl picks up the dice to throw on behalf of the dog, there is a knock. He wonders what she wants. The parting seemed so final. He opens the door without hesitation, taking in a sharp breath, prepared for a final volley of assassination.

A stranger stands there, about his age, in jeans and waterproof coat, blinking at him. Poorly dressed for a salesman. He wonders which neighbour has let him inside the block. Maybe he slipped in when Lydia left. A salesman with nothing in his hands.

'Yes?' Carl asks, closing the door so there is only a small gap. His hand shakes as he scans for threats in the corridor behind the figure.

'I'm looking for Carl Marsh. Are you Carl Marsh?' the man asks.

47

Milton Keynes, December 1999

Carl has been careless in opening the door, needs to turn the defences back on. At least this man is using the correct name. The stranger's eyes flit past Carl, as if checking for somebody else, then back down to the owner's own scuffed shoes. He looks up again, leans against the door frame, makes no attempt to barge in.

'Look, sorry, we don't buy things door-to-door.'

'Oh, no, it's not that. I'm looking for Carl Marsh.' The visitor hesitates. 'I have some urgent news for him. Is it you?'

'Who wants to know?'

Carl could close the door in his face. Perhaps this is a journalist, following up on the demise of the murderous cult leader, seeking out his followers, hunting for gossip. The figure squints, as if studying an exhibit, and shifts his hand on the doorframe. Carl studies him back. The fingernails are bitten. There are a few days of stubble, deep circles under the eyes. The man looks pale, sweat on his brow shining under the artificial light of the landing.

'I need to talk to Carl. It's really important.'

There is a steady blink, followed by a slight nod of the head. No smile, but probably no threat either. If Carl shuts the door on him, he might draw attention. There is nothing to fear. The past is invisible.

'Look, can I come in?' Still no attempt to enter. 'My name is Ray Mercer. If you are Carl, I have to tell you something important.' The visitor steps back, raises his hands. 'There is something you need to know.' His voice echoes around the landing. This man seems to think he has found someone. 'It's about the past. Your past.'

The last two words a stage whisper. The idea that he is sniffing around for more gossip on the dodgy cult goes out the window. Carl Marsh is of greater interest.

'What's your name again?'

'Ray Mercer.'

The figure pulls a card out of his back pocket and gives it to Carl, one hand holding the other steady. It says he is a private investigator. Carl takes another look around the landing. No vigilantes are waiting to jump him, but a neighbour might emerge from a door, stick their nose in, drag him into the crosshairs. Carl shivers. Looks across again at the empty space where there is no panic button.

Nobody has examined Carl this closely since Lydia, that night in the bar, on his first anniversary. She had this knack of holding your gaze, making you think she could see straight through you. The visitor stays back, rests on his heels. He thinks he has found Carl. That could be fine. But Carl needs to find out what else he knows.

'Come in.'

Carl steps aside to let his visitor pass into his living room.

Ray scrapes his shoes quickly on the mat and walks towards the table. His attention seems to be drawn to the Monopoly game laid out, and he turns and gives a strange smile. Like he understands, but of course there is no way that he could. Carl leans back against the door, the escape route.

'Thanks for letting me in.'

Carl must behave like a normal person, say normal things. Yet this man knows where he is. There isn't supposed to be a trail.

'You think I'm Carl Marsh?'

'You as good as told me, just now.'

'How did you find me?'

'Oh, it wasn't difficult,' Ray says, arms hitched in his pockets. 'I need to tell you something.' He reaches inside his coat and pulls out a flimsy, rolled-up book. Holds it one hand, then puts it away again. There could be a threat with the visitor, but he shuffles from foot to foot, muttering to himself.

Carl feels like a stranger. Struggles to remember the details of his backstory. Where Carl came from. Why he is in Milton Keynes. Where he is heading. This Ray is disturbing the equilibrium.

'You want a tea? Or a coffee?' A normal thing to ask.

'No, I'm fine, thanks. I just need to talk to you.'

Carl slips into the armchair and points at the small sofa. 'Sit down, please.' No harm in being polite. Ray's coat rustles as he sinks down onto the tatty furniture. 'What is it?' Carl asks.

'You, Carl.'

Ray leans forward, hands on his knees, about ten feet away, pulls out a folded piece of paper, and studies it. Carl feels the scrutiny. He is sitting in the court again, all those eyes on him, feet dangling and not reaching the floor, people whispering to each other, scribbling notes, labelling the kid. One woman in the front row of the jury staring him down every day, wanting him to burn in hell. Nobody cared about that boy they put in the dock. Nobody cares now. Carl leans back in the chair, folds his arms, ready to defend himself.

This Ray is focused intently on his face, inclines his head again, and nods once more, puts the paper away. 'It is you, Carl. I've found you.'

The words swim around Carl's head. 'Found me?' He hopes there are no more questions.

'Look, I know who you were. About the changes of identity. About moving around. I know who you were many years ago.' Ray's gaze is firmly fixed on him. 'I know about Martin Sullivan. That you are Martin Sullivan.' Martin pictures two children paddling along the shore, splashing in and out of the waves.

They told him this moment might come. That some journalist or vigilante would come after him. Drag him out into the street and shout. Exact retribution. This man knows who he was, is. Martin's arms are heavy, sunk into the chair, there is no resistance this time. He has reacted swiftly before, when provoked. When Tiny Tim started asking questions about his past. Maybe he is ready to surrender.

'Martin?' Ray leans further forward in the chair, unzipping his coat. No beating or snapping on of handcuffs. Simply sitting, watching. 'Martin, I went to school with you. I'm from the same town. I'm a Crawley boy too.'

Martin winces at the sound of the place name.

'Someone asked me to track you down. Well, not you, but another name, Michael Keane. And I found out who you were, and who you are now.' Ray rubs his eyes, sighs deeply. 'Now I'm here, I know it's you. Thing is, Martin, I don't know what to do.'

Ray shuffles forward, appears to be close to toppling over. They could have been best friends at school, but Martin wouldn't recognise him.

'Who are you again?'

'I'm Ray Mercer. I've not changed my name, Martin,' he adds.

The name they kept repeating at the police station the first time he was taken there. Martin sees the reddening face of the detective, as he paces up and down in the cell. Pushing Martin to tell the truth, face up to what he has done. Promising he won't tell his mother. Guaranteeing that this is for the best.

Martin stands, ready to reach out and silence the truth. He hasn't heard his original name spoken in over twenty years. That boy no longer exists. Ray rises too, groans a little as he pulls himself up, but retreats to the table. Martin doesn't have the energy to make up the distance between them.

Ray takes a mobile phone out of his pocket, stares at the screen, pushes a button firmly, then puts it back in his pocket. What looks like indecision on his face. There is no threat. He simply knows who Martin is.

Martin staggers back and drops into the chair. A child again. They cured him, showed him how to handle the anger, the hatred of women, the rejection of love, all those descriptions for his mental state. The words stuck, sank into his consciousness. They explained him away. The devil child.

'I just don't know what to do. I know who you were. We both went to Bennett. You less time than me.' Ray folds his arms, the coat rustling again. Does Martin have any fight left? Does he deserve to keep on running?

'It's not just the identity changes. I know what you did. About them letting you out eventually, about that telemarketing company now as well. But I'm not the one you need to worry about.' Ray rubs his eyes vigorously, looking like he is trying to erase something. At the doorstep he appeared calm, if unsure of himself. Now he rocks from foot to foot, agitated.

'What do you want?' Martin asks, clearing his throat. 'You want money?'

Ray shakes his head, leans back against the table, nudging the Monopoly board. One of the dice drops silently to the floor. Martin watches it lie there, face up, showing a 'one'. The die has been everywhere with him for over fifteen years. Makes him wonder what he has done with the opportunity he was given. A second chance, a new life, and all he chose was to cower in the shadows, step back from everything. Hide his troubles away, like that battered suitcase. Meeting Lydia provided a glimpse of what he could have done with freedom. Showed how he has neglected himself. But then she had her own agenda. He was just a gateway to remove one of her own demons.

Ray starts to laugh, then frowns. 'Money's always useful, but no, not money.' He shakes his head, seems fixated on his shoes. 'I don't know what I want. But you need to know why I tracked you down.'

Martin feels his body shrinking. He is in that police interview room now, the detective badgering him for a confession, walking up and down, that bitch on one side sitting stone-faced, smoking and staring at the wall, the solicitor barking complaints, the social worker avoiding his gaze, looking at her notes. The detective's questions, over and over. How it happened. Why he didn't call for an ambulance. Why he ran. How could any of them know what it was like?

'I thought nobody cared any more?' Despite the warnings to be on his guard, and his own careful movements, Martin had hoped he was invisible. But deep down was prepared for a visit like this, when it inevitably came.

The private investigator exhales deeply. 'I shouldn't be telling you this...' He breaks off, examines his watch carefully. Pulls the mobile out of his pocket again. Martin senses his visitor needs to tell someone where they are. The phone is his way of doing this. But still he hesitates.

'Have you heard of a man called Leckie Harris?' Ray asks.

'No.'

'You sure? Leckie Harris?'

Still it means nothing. Martin shakes his head.

'Shit.' Ray covers his face with his hands, leans back against the table. 'Shit. I shouldn't have come here. Should have...'

The sentence is left hanging. More hesitation. Martin wonders why this man is so paralysed, given what he knows.

'Who's this Leckie Harris? What's he got to do with me?'

'He forced me to look for you. I had no choice.' Ray pulls his hands down. 'Well, he made me look for a man called Michael Keane. I didn't know it was you.' He sighs again. 'It's a long story.' There is what looks like pity in his

277

eyes. A look that was so rare years ago.

Keane. That old, forgotten name, chosen by them. Someone they educated, turned into their model citizen. He grew up into a nobody, meaningless jobs, hiding in the shadows, nothing to provoke being tracked down. Maybe this Leckie just read the papers years ago, is hunting every bad child, pricked into action by those Bulger killers. And Martin is just another faceless name.

'You're in danger, because of me. We're both in danger.' Ray puts the phone away.

'Danger? Why?'

Martin stands, leaning on the arm of the chair for leverage. His bones ache, and suddenly he longs for sleep.

'They call him Bad Leckie. That's all you need to know.'

'Never heard of him.'

Ray's face twists a little, puzzled. 'I don't know why he wants me to find you.'

'How did you find me?'

'It's my job,' Ray says, half a smile on his face. His eyes drop again. 'Wasn't difficult. I tracked you back, and then forwards, from Keane. Remember, I'm local. Was local. You were notorious, once. I've read a lot about your case. Newspapers from back then. Books that didn't get published. Other stuff. A lot about the truth.'

'The truth,' Martin mutters, and wonders what it really is. He is not in immediate danger, or there would be men racing up the stairs. But he needs to be decisive.

He studies his visitor. Similar build, if a little thin in the cheekbones. Both with a full head of hair. Same age. He knows mannerisms can be copied.

'I need you to tell me why you did it. Why you killed Philip Hughes,' the figure demands.

'I don't know. I can't tell you.'

****

'Tell me.' Ray's voice rises for the first time. His cheeks feel like they are on fire, eyes misting over.

'I don't remember.'

'This might help you.' Ray pulls out the first item he took from his coat and throws it at Martin. 'It's all there.'

The old exercise book hits Martin in the chest and drops to the floor. He bends down to pick it up and runs his fingers underneath the name on the cover. Ray knows this says Danny Sullivan. He guesses an older brother, judging by the two styles of handwriting inside. Martin leans against the arm of the chair, shaking. Starts to read, from the back of the book. Pinches his eyes, the top of his nose.

'Where'd you get this?' The voice cracks.

Ray stares into the face of this enigma. A child they talked about when he was a kid, the killer, the one your parents threatened you with if you misbehaved. And yet, reading the words, and Trish's abandoned investigation, he knows there was pain. That the case would probably be treated differently now.

'I've read it all, what you wrote there, the journalists, other people. About how desperate the police were to find a killer. About how they didn't care why you did it. Nobody cared. But I do. I want you to tell me.'

'It was years ago. I was a kid. I was twelve.' Martin holds up the exercise book, scrunches it up into a ball. 'You read

279

this.' Ray nods. 'You read the state I was in. What that b…
my mother thought of me. How she never helped me.' The
fugitive has appeared so calm until now. The whites of his
eyes shine, wide open. He continues, lowering his voice.
'You were twelve, once. We went to the same school, you
said.'

'Yeah, I was twelve, once.'

'Well, that boy's gone. I'm a new man. I'm rehabilitated.
They said I was. I am.'

'The reports said so, yeah.'

'You read their reports?'

'Some. The doctor who signed you off, approved your
release. I even met him.'

The approval of society. Ray could just take the word
of the experts. But he is implicated too. If Paul and he
had acted, when they saw what was believed to be a tragic
accident, Philip Hughes would still be alive. That boy whose
words he has read, who was struggling for recognition,
might have been pulled back from the edge.

'I still don't know what to do,' Ray repeats.

'Do?'

'Yeah. One text message.' Ray holds the mobile phone
out in front of him again, 'and Leckie knows where you are.'
His hand trembles like a drunk.

'I'm innocent,' Martin declares, sat in the chair.

'I know you're guilty.' Ray sighs. 'I have no choice. Can't
you tell me why you did it?'

The sound of the ticking clock echoes.

'You read those words. I was lost. I was just a kid.'

Ray thinks of the desperate scrawl in the exercise
book. Remembers what it was like being twelve, and to be

forgotten. Is drawn back to the reality. The violent reality, if he cannot deliver what Leckie needs.

'He's got to have somebody. He's got me by the balls. It's you or me,' Ray says.

'Give him someone else.'

Ray studies the man he has been pursuing to pay off his debts. No apparent threat from across the room, despite the fact he has him cornered. He had expected more of a reaction, although his hammer is still under the driver's seat. The man opposite is his means of escape, yet he is unsure what to do. Throwing a bogus identity at Leckie Harris wouldn't work. There would be comeback, eventually. Leckie employs men who bury bodies in the woods for fun.

'Can't do that. I can't pass on a death sentence. It's you or me.'

'Doesn't have to be you or me.' Martin's face is still, serious. 'There's a way out of this.'

'How d'you mean?'

'This Leckie bloke, he wants an identity for Keane, right?'

'Yeah.'

'Does he know it's Carl? Or even Martin?'

'Well, no.' Ray pauses, then adds, 'but he knows it's someone from Milton Keynes. I told him that.' He looks at the mobile phone, recalls Dusty's words about surveillance, and still can't escape the fact that Leckie's men could be there any minute.

'That might not be a problem. When you hand me over, do you think this Leckie will ever let you go?'

Ray replaces the mobile in his pocket, runs his hand over the shape. Coughs. He just wants to sleep, forget the whole thing. Wake up in a warm, friendly bookies' and write out some slips. Start afresh.

'Will you ever be free of him?'

'If I find you, my debts are wiped.' But Ray knows creditors never give you up.

'Thing is, how would he know for certain who was who? That who you give him is the right man?'

'It matters to me. I'm dead if I don't hand you over.'

Ray stares at the man who has occupied his mind for the previous six weeks. The expression betrays no panic, the forehead lines crease. He is struggling to get across how serious the situation is.

'You don't know why Leckie wants to find you?' Ray asks.

'No. He sent you looking for someone called Keane. Remember?'

Ray can hardly forget. And Leckie has claws.

'I still owe Leckie money. I thought finding you would square the debt, but…' Ray sniffs and pushes out one deep breath. 'I will still owe him, even when he has you.'

Ray sighs, slumps onto a wooden chair by the table. If only he could stay out of the betting shops, the casinos, then he would have a chance. If only he could find that big winner he needs.

'I have money. How much do you owe him?'

Ray shakes his head. 'Five hundred. He's called in the debt. Wants it tomorrow.' He empties out his trouser pockets, revealing nothing. 'I just can't…' He stops, and tears slide down his cheeks.

'You're screwed, whatever happens, aren't you, Ray?'

Ray looks at his shoes. He can't remember the last time

he bought a new item of clothing. The last time he spent any money on anything other than food or gambling.

'There is a way out of this, Ray. You can start again, we both can. We give him a Michael Keane. Just not me.'

Ray pulls himself up to his feet, his entire body aching, and leans against the table for support, disturbing some counters on a board game. Picks up a red hotel, drops it back on the 'Chance' square. Martin glares at him momentarily, then breaks into a brief smile.

'I have just the person in mind,' Martin says. 'He can be your Michael Keane. There is a way out of this for both of us.'

Ray stares across the room. Struggles to match the figure, and his scheming, with the child in the exercise book.

'You know I've changed identity before?' Martin begins. Ray nods in reply. 'I have a new one ready. You use that. There is somewhere new to live, available now. You can escape this Leckie bloke; he won't know where you are.' Ray wonders how he can think so clearly. 'I stayed hidden for years. So can you.'

'Ha.' Ray folds his arms, touches his coat again where the mobile phone is. 'A new identity? What about the money?'

'I have money. Look, I worked for someone who just died. About the right age. He changed his identity too. He was a crook, a fraud. The police think he killed someone. It even made the papers. They cremated him last week. Give that man to this Leckie. Tell him this is your Keane.'

Ray stares open-mouthed. Wonders whether the child killer had something to do with another, recent death. Tries to fit the pieces of the puzzle together. Working out the form in a maiden hurdle on a wet Wednesday at Chepstow is easier than this. Martin presses on.

'We give him a dead man. One who has changed who he is. A killer. There's a sort of justice in it. Your Leckie gets what he wants. You go free, take on a new identity.'

'But what about you?'

'I can take care of myself. He doesn't know about Carl Marsh, remember?'

'No, he doesn't. Shit.' Ray looks down at his shambling coat, feeling half-dead, mulls it over. A new life. No debts. The potential for new credit.

'This way, we both get away.'

'You can pay him what I owe?' Ray asks.

'Sure.'

'He needs it dropped off tomorrow, it was going to be Boxing Day, but…'

The face of the historical killer in front of him relaxes, smiles. Ray had a decision to make today. About whether a boy from his distant past deserved the chance to stay in hiding. It was all going to depend on how honest he was about why he killed. And whether he would admit to the previous murder, the one above the underpass. Neither of these has been answered. Ray now faces a different decision. Whether to seize an opportunity for himself. To start again, free of the shackles.

'I'll sort it,' Martin announces.

Martin reaches under the armchair and pulls a bundle of papers out from underneath. Hands over a roll of twenty-pound notes. Then passes Ray a large envelope.

'Meet Robert Walker. I was going to switch on January the first, you know, make the most of this new millennium thing, a good chance to be someone new. We don't look the same, but photos are easily changed. Be him. Be Robert Walker.'

Ray pulls out the documents of his possible future.

'You need to give me the details of this dead man,' Ray says. He will be taking a risk, deceiving someone like Leckie Harris. But he has been taking risks for years, every time he enters a bookies'. 'I need to tell Leckie. It needs to be believable.'

'Look.'

Martin hands over a recent newspaper article. 'Local man was fraud and murderer. Local cult exposed,' the headline screams. Ray reads the first paragraph. Realises what Martin is suggesting. Studies a picture of Steven Harding, aka Michael Keane, as far as Leckie Harris might be concerned.

Martin's voice pulls Ray's attention back to the man opposite. 'Give me your mobile. I assume this is what you use to contact him?'

Ray mumbles agreement and tosses it to Martin.

'I'm gonna give him a dead man. We pay him what you owe. Then you're free. Free to be Robert Walker. We can go to this flat tonight, in Northampton.'

'I…' Ray stares at the contents of the envelope. This person he has been searching for is buying him a new life. What difference would it make? Leckie can have a dead man.

'He definitely doesn't know it's Carl Marsh?' Martin asks.

'No, just that you're in Milton Keynes.'

Martin flicks through the history in the mobile, manipulating the buttons with more dexterity than Ray could ever muster. Ray knows he will only find incoming calls, from one number. A handful of texts going both ways. No specific details sent to Leckie Harris. This could work. Ray looks over Martin's shoulder as he types out the message, the name, address and date of death of a stranger, a different Michael Keane. Ray tries to breathe steadily, fight the pain in his chest that moves down his arms and legs. To focus on what might happen next. Claiming a life that he is overdue to live. Somewhere nobody can find him. Remembers a packed suitcase in the boot of a car outside.

Martin looks up from the screen and slips the mobile in his own pocket. 'Tell me where you're supposed to be handing over the money. We need your car.'

48

Beachy Head, New Year's Eve 1999

The back of his head bounces off something cold and solid. Arms pinned behind, he raises his knees slowly, finds that his ankles are bound together. Cramp claws down the backs of his legs. Nausea rises, steady movement in the dark transporting him to those journeys to and from court. There was more room inside the van for those trips, and he could see his captors, hear the shouts, the swearing, the banging on the outside. All preferable to the sounds of the vast court, under the harsh lighting, not understanding what they were saying.

He is alone now, rolling and lurching on the floor of a vehicle. Searching for a reference point, a memory of how he ended up there. He thinks he woke up to a noise, but then, nothing. Tries to shift his weight, turn sideways, but can only wriggle a small amount. Blinded by something cutting into his eyes, darkness crushing him. Like that first night when they slammed the door, a guilty boy lost. He tries to shout out, but there is a gag pulled across his mouth, making him retch, bringing up burning liquid, spilling onto his neck.

Rolling with a thump, he hits metal again, breath rushing out, choking. A rustling when he moves, and a strangely familiar smell. Covered in what sounds and feels like plastic. A sarcophagus in a bin bag in a car boot.

It feels like everything stops, and he kicks out, to make some noise, but the cramp grabs again, pain shooting through his legs. Then there is movement again, gently rolling, like being rocked to sleep, but he cannot surrender to that. The speed increases.

There is no point in tracking changes of direction, or time. He has no idea how long he has been like this. Nobody is coming to rescue him. The vigilantes have found the young killer. Despite all the careful planning, and the fact that he is several times removed from that boy, they have tracked him down. He can picture Ray Mercer, the man who knocked on his door, catching him unprepared. Cautiously telling him who he really was, uncertain what to do next, an agent who ultimately thought he deserved a chance to run. He stole that man's life to preserve his own. Reasoning Ray's fate was not as deadly as his.

The vehicle takes a turn, driving him into metal once more, crushing the breath out of him. Travelling starts to get bumpier, as if they are off-road, and he bounces on his back, the movement shunting his body along towards his feet, concertinaing his legs. The gag makes him choke and cough again. He tries to roll onto his front. The plastic bag sticks to his lips, forcing air out of his nose. He is going to suffocate. Maybe that is what they want. He has been so careful for so long. But Ray managed to find him.

The vehicle lurches, then stops, his head banging again. His bones ache. Shouting is futile. Over a ringing in his ears, he hears what must be a boot opening, although there is no additional light. Voices mumble above. Then there is a sensation of floating, before he realises he is being lifted, raised for a sacrifice. The drop to the ground comes as a shock, and he gasps as contact is made on his left side, trying to curl up into a ball, but unable to bring his legs up to his chest. None of his muscles will do what he asks of them.

The impact must have cleared his head a little, because he hears what sounds like another car draw up, doors opening and closing. Footsteps approach.

'What a fucking stink. Fuck me.' The words seem to echo, like they are in a chamber. Cold rushes through him.

'Yeah.' What sounds like a second voice.

'You sure it's him?'

'We watched the place for two days. Only one in there. He had ID.'

One of the voices moves closer. Something prods at his legs. 'Why's he in that thing?'

'Just being careful. We didn't want anyone to see him.'

'What, and putting him in a black bag doesn't look suspicious, does it?'

'Nobody saw us.'

Neither voice sounds familiar, but they wouldn't. The faceless mob have found their prey. He wriggles on the ground, which feels damp through the bag, trying to get some movement into his muscles.

'Take it easy, sunshine.' The tone of the voice changes, more relaxed, addressing him for the first time.

'D'you want me to get him out?'

'He can fucking suffocate, for all I care.' The speaker sounds calm, rather than angry. 'Go on, cut it open.'

The new Ray freezes, wondering if they mean the bag or him, and he is turned over again, onto his back, an exhibit ready to be exposed. There is a squeaking sound, the bag stretches, and cold air breaks in. His eyes are still covered, but it feels like there is more light. He tries to roll onto his front as the retching returns, gasping for air, snot and blood forcing him to choke. Arms still pinned behind.

'Shut up and lie still,' the voice says slowly, friendly advice from a counsellor. 'I just want a chat with you.'

The accent sounds like London, and the threat is clear. He thinks back to how the original Ray tracked him down, unearthed the truth, and held those painful written words in his hands. He thought taking over the life of a private investigator with no debts, no work, and no contacts would give him somewhere to lie low for a while. Ray seemed to like the idea of starting afresh with a bag full of money and only a vague idea of how to stay hidden. Maybe he has been double-crossed, against the hasty deal.

An attempt at swallowing catches in his throat. Cramp grabs along the backs of his legs once more. He will just lie still. It sounds like the figure is behind him.

'Fuck, did you do him over?'

'He resisted arrest,' the other man chuckles.

'State of him.' The voice gets closer, in his ear. 'Now, you won't be able to move much, not for a while anyway. Not with what they've given you.' He breaks off to ask a question of his accomplice. 'You didn't overdo it? He's a fucking mess.'

'Nah.' A faint reply. He strains to listen; ears start to ring again.

'What you've been given, you're not gonna run off, I know that. So, don't try.'

There is another muffled exchange, before the commanding voice comes close. 'I want to tell you a story. You should recognise it. Because you were there.'

He knew this day might come, and what would happen if somebody worked out who he was. Relationships, helping others, carelessness, all things to be avoided, all his potential undoing. Memories of their instructions to stay hidden. Maybe deep down he wanted there to be justice at last.

'You probably been wondering why I gave you the job. Least, you should have been. And you should have worked out why, by now. When you found him. Least you said you found him.'

The speaker pauses, then delivers a blow to the ribs. The prone figure groans, breath forced out like a squashed cushion. 'John Ellis. You remember him, don't you?'

The name cuts through him. It feels like ancient history. He lies motionless, face down. Thinks he can hear seagulls above. The voice has moved slightly further away, like he is standing immediately above.

'You were as guilty as that scumbag mate of yours. They thought John Ellis killed himself, or had an accident, didn't they? We know better, don't we? You saw it.'

From Ray's description, he can make an educated guess who it is. Silence might be the best option. He tries to make himself as small a target as possible. To become invisible again.

'You saw it, you and your queer mate. Was he playing with you while you watched?'

Another blow to the back, just above where his hands are tied. Breath escapes, agony crashes in. Something pushes his head into the ground, dirt on his face. Leckie is going to kick him to death. Kick both the wrong and the right man to death. His head is still fuzzy. Some of what Leckie says makes sense, but pain interferes.

'You two, you both saw that little shit killing John Ellis.'

The pressure is lifted from his head, there is a short rush of air in his ears, then a crunching sound, a boot stamping down. He wants to pass out, to save himself. Thoughts drift in and out of focus. Nobody would hear him scream, even if he could make a noise. This beating has been coming for many years. All he can do is gag and whimper, surrender to the confusion.

'I killed the fucker, you know. Your queer mate. To put him out of his misery.' The voice sounds light-hearted for a moment. 'He was sorry for what he did, unlike you. Sorry for what he didn't do. He fucking begged me, pleaded for his life. Waste of breath, but there you go.' The voice gets closer again, and an ear is tugged sharply. 'You did fuck all, both of you. Fuck all.'

Blurred images haunt the prone figure. He is at the scene, but actively taking part, not watching like this man says. He just wants this to end, to surrender. Knows this is the Leckie Harris Ray spoke about, but this is a strange case of mistaken identity. Nothing ironic about it.

Leckie lets go and pulls away. 'See, I don't give a fuck about John Ellis. It's not about him, you bent scumbag.'

Trying to piece the fragments together. A distant past is fighting to come into focus. He holds his breath, waiting for the next blow. The storyteller continues.

'Let me tell you about Philip Hughes. Just a kid. Same thing happens to him. He gets killed. Another tragedy, in the same town. Fucking tragedy it was.' A weight pushes down through his chest. 'Murdered by the same boy who killed John Ellis. Do you see what the problem is?' A foot rolls him over. 'State of it, Jesus. Philip Hughes would be alive today if you two had the decency to tell somebody what you saw. If you hadn't been busy fiddling with each other in the woods. Philip Hughes was family, you scumbag.'

He tries to raise himself up, shakes his head furiously, but the torturer pushes him back face down.

'Listen, your bent mate told me the truth, before he died.'

He tucks himself up as small as possible.

'Confessed it to someone inside, about how he witnessed a murder. His guilt got the better of him. Told some lover of his. How you both did nothing. Stories about the old town always get back to me. I know plenty of people. He did nothing, just like you.' He pauses, then leans in and hisses. 'You fucking bent coward.'

The downward force goes through his back into his chest, probably a boot again. Feels like his heart is being squashed flat. Anger driven through him into the earth. He shakes his head, tries to yell out, struggles to move, pinned down in the mud.

'So,' the voice continues, not relinquishing the pressure. 'It didn't take me long to put it together. But I'm a patient man. I like to do things properly. Your queer mate gets out, I pay him a visit. He's dead sorry, he says, tells me everything, including about you. You can make anything look like suicide.'

Martin freezes. The owner of the voice is dangerous, according to Ray. Holds a life in his hands, not knowing who he really is. In a way, he has the wrong man. Part of him wants to scream he is mistaken; he wasn't gay, he didn't have a lover in the woods, he wasn't the one who did nothing. But the truth won't help.

'And because of you two selfish fuckers, that bastard is still walking around. And you made up some bollocks about some dead bloke. You think I wouldn't know? He won't get far; I'm gonna find him. He's gonna wish he weren't born. He'll plead with me to kill him quickly. But I wanted to sort you out first.'

Another blow to the side of the head, and things turn blacker behind the binding. He can't move. The anger seems to be growing. Both possible identities are dangerous. He tries to shout, but the gag cuts into his mouth. He chokes once more.

'That's why I sent you off looking for him, whatever the fuck he kept changing his name to. We have a mutual friend, you see. Good with computers. Everyone has a weakness, and he did as I asked.' There is a brief chuckle, then a rasping cough. Even if he could ask what Leckie is on about, it would be pointless.

'I wanted to see if you had the bottle to do the right thing, when you found out who he was. You had chances to tell me about your dirty little secret. Well you didn't, did you, Raymond? You... did... fuck... all.' The last four words punctuated with kicks to his sides.

He chokes again, more forcefully this time, lies still, a defeated punchbag. There is more muttering, too far away for him to hear. Two sets of hands pull him up to a sitting position, and the gag in his mouth pulls tight. It moves slowly back and forth, and then is released. Vomit erupts on the ground and into his lap. A hand grabs him by the hair, and he prepares for a final attack. Bright light invades instead. The binding has been released around his eyes, and he blinks hard, peeking out, expecting more pain. Blood dried on his lips, over his cheeks. Hands still trussed behind. No chance of fighting back.

'Fucking state of it.' This is another voice, not the storyteller.

The binding on his wrists is untied, and he shakes his hands. There is no feeling. Two strong grips pull his arms above his head. Pain shoots into his shoulders. The scene comes into focus. Night, in a field. Three men, all dressed from head to foot in orange overalls, wearing gloves, and plastic covers on their shoes. They look like slaughterhouse workers. One of them on his left leans in and stares, blinks, then puts his hands on his hips. A sneer on his face. His eyes tighten, and he twists his head slightly, to get a better look.

'Who the fuck is this?'

He is not Ray Mercer, but there is no way he can reveal his identity. So, this is what Leckie Harris looks like. What he is. The man who was searching for Michael Keane, but not necessarily Martin Sullivan. Or so he thought. His only chance is to talk.

'You made a mistake. I'm…'

The fist strikes him on the cheek, stopping the protest. He slumps to the floor and realises both sets of hands have let go.

'Who the fuck is this?' the storyteller repeats.

'It's him. No mistake.'

'It's not him. Fuck's sake.' There is still venom in the voice. From the ground he looks up to see a finger being pointed at one of the overall-clad men. 'Are you fucking blind?' A shake of the head, a stab of the digit. 'Can't trust you... fuck. I should have asked Bernie, he knows him.'

The punch catches the culprit on the jaw, and the man doesn't even flinch. There is no retaliation.

'Look...' Martin begins, trying to wriggle into a sitting position.

'Shut the fuck up, you.' A fist is waved in his face. He swallows something hard. 'Gag him. Fuck's sake.' Leckie shakes his head, spits on the ground.

Martin tries to stand, but they are on top of him, and the rag is replaced. The taste makes him choke again. They continue their argument, ignoring him.

'He was where you told us. We watched the place for two days. Nobody else went in or out. It's him. All his ID was there.'

'Where's the ID?'

The two helpers stare at each other. One volunteers an answer.

'We chucked it. We didn't want it to be traced.'

'Well, it isn't him, is it? It's some other fucker. You muppet.' Leckie bends down and points at the bound figure. 'Who the fuck are you?' Rotten tobacco, booze and violence on his breath.

Martin squirms, unable to answer. Cowering, as he did before, hoping for someone just to hold him and tell him everything is going to be all right. Praying that they would stop asking so many questions, always the questions, and leave him alone.

Despite the throbbing in his head, something becomes clear. They thought he was Ray, but don't know who he is. That private investigator who came to save him, who provided the chance to escape and make another switch, rather than turn him over to this man. This Leckie who has been searching for him, unaware of the irony of his mistake.

Ray said they went to the same school, wanted to know why he killed. There was no explanation to give, other than the words he wrote years ago. Ray made no mention about being a witness to what happened with John Ellis. The first time. The one Martin thought nobody knew about.

All Ray confessed to was that he had instructions to find him, tell his client where he was hiding. He moved on, making Martin think an identity swap would be a safe one. The bitterness in the voice of the storyteller is clear. Martin needs them to think he is an innocent bystander.

'C'mon, who are you? You're not Ray, I know that.' Leckie grimaces and pulls the gag down.

'Tim,' he squeaks.

'Who?' A shouted reply.

'Tim Durrell.' His ears have cleared, the seagulls calling to him to run. His legs are still tied.

'Fuck off. What? Who are you?'

'I'm nobody.' Just what he has always wanted to be.

'Well now, suppose it don't matter who you are.'

The storyteller delivers a swift kick in the balls, catching him by surprise. Martin's eyes close, his only way of coping with the pain, and he keels over in the grass, somewhere he wants to stay. Dry retches.

'Fuck's sake,' Leckie shouts, then walks away, muttering to himself. Martin lies motionless, hoping they will just leave him alone. It seems an age before the figure returns. Martin's tears taste of guilt. He is doomed either way.

'Right, here's what's going to happen,' Leckie announces, staring at the prone figure. His two accomplices lift Martin up to his feet, so he and Leckie are eye to eye. 'I'm going. I'm not going to see you again. Nobody's going to see you again. I've got somebody else to go and find. To cut into fucking bits. Barry, sort this one out.'

'You mean?' Barry looks at his boss and Leckie nods, a death sentence. Trying to shout for help, all that comes out is a low grunt. As he opens his mouth again, pain crashes through his ankles, sending him to the floor. The one called Barry looms overhead, holding a baseball bat.

'Don't bother. Nobody can hear you out here,' Leckie hisses. 'You're wasting your breath.'

The agony is intense, ankle bones shattered. From the floor Martin watches Leckie walk away towards a car, taking off his protective clothing. Another man appears, to open the back door for him, then drives them away. Martin is already forgotten, the concern of only two remaining men in orange overalls.

He notices the horizon is endless, twisted, as he is, in a different direction. The noise of the sea beckons. They are less than thirty feet from the edge of a cliff, oblivion stretching out in front of him. Should he take control of his fate, and simply crawl over there, rather than be pushed? The option is removed as two sets of feet start rolling him towards the edge.

Martin offers no resistance. He thinks of Lydia, of her mission to rid the world of a deceiver, that ended up with her becoming a killer, like him. She is free now. And so is Ray. Child X has inadvertently done something honourable at last.

Ray didn't have to share those angry scrawled words in that flimsy book from the past, from a time when he needed someone to notice, to listen. As they drove over to Northampton, Ray spoke of a moral duty to return the material. Now Martin understands where that sense of duty came from, thanks to the storyteller. They switched futures, sending Ray on the run. Not knowing exactly why they were both targets. And Martin thought he was picking the smart identity to hide with.

An angry thug, distinctly unhappy that he is not a private investigator, snaps him out of the life swap.

'You made me look a right twat.'

The colleague alongside him chuckles, amused by Barry's predicament. They roll their target closer to the precipice. Martin needs to persuade them he is an irrelevance.

'Help me, please.' A last plea for life, somebody else's, but a life all the same. 'I'm not who you think I am. I know nothing.'

'Don't care who you are. You got in the way, that's it.'

Sussex mud tastes of dark chocolate. Breathing is still difficult, with clotted blood up his nose. He tumbles towards the edge, not enough strength to resist their intent.

'Fucking bastard,' Barry shouts, giving him another kick in the back.

The panic rises, and he starts to wriggle, tries to stand, but his ankles betray him. Barry's mate laughs again. Does he deserve to escape? The system thought it had cured him. They labelled him a monster, and they were right. When he was about to be exposed, he fought back, removed Tiny Tim. Helped Lydia cover up a killing. And then there was the original Carl Marsh, suffocated and abandoned under a bridge in London, swapping identity with Neil Duggan, enabling him to stay hidden. The appearance of Ray at his door was his chance to make amends.

He is kicked closer. Only a few feet to go.

'Fucking move.' Barry is anxious to get this over with.

The coaching on how to change and stay hidden fooled him into living a continual lie. It was too easy to follow their instructions. That young boy was manipulated in those sessions, turned into the person they wanted. Forced to live as a nobody for so long, and now he is tired of it.

The blackness of the sea beckons, roaring its claim, bringing back the dark isolation of that first night they locked him away. Surrounded by their furnished truth. Labelled, then reformed to order. Maybe you cannot change your darkest inner core. Switching identities and direction each time was pointless. No matter what name they gave him, or how they pretended it was a new beginning, the face behind it remained the same. He failed them.

As he looks out across the clifftop, he thinks of the man he pretended to be for a few days. Martin was doomed regardless of whether Ray turned him in or not. And now he has Ray's fate. He whispers a 'good luck' to the new Robert Walker.

'Right, you bastard.'

The boots propel him to the edge. The image of the private investigator, gratefully waving at him from behind the window of a cramped flat, with a fake new life, lingers as he closes his eyes. He did the right thing.

His muscles tense, waiting for the final kick from behind.

ACKNOWLEDGEMENTS

Enormous thanks are owed to the following who have been invaluable in bringing this story to the page:

Jackie and Peggy for their patience as this has come together. Gretchen Smith again for her inspiration and support. Russel McLean and David Smith provided guidance early in the crafting of this story, and Sharon Boyle gave generous input and advice in the later days. All at Troubador for their support in bringing this to life. Stony Stratford Library for providing a peaceful haven to write early drafts. Martin Stephenson and Eddie Reader for the soundtrack. And finally, to the town of Crawley which has been an inspiration in so many ways.

For more information on Mick Lee, go to
www.micklee-author.com